TURQUOISE and TERRORISTS

TURQUOISE and TERRORISTS

a novel

Lynn Gardner

Covenant Communications, Inc.

Published by Covenant Communications, Inc.
American Fork, Utah

Printed in the United States of America
First Printing: March 1998

 14 13 12 11 10   10 9 8 7 6 5

ISBN-13 978-1-57734-245-8
ISBN-10 1-57734-245-3

To Beverly, Bill, Deborah, Dorothy, Mark, Tanya, and Vern, who have listened, questioned, polished, and probed through *Pearls, Diamonds,* and now *Turquoise.* Every writer needs the kind of critique and support you give. And to Glenn, who so patiently and lovingly supports me through it all.

Prologue

In the two months since they foiled a major diamond theft at the Museum of Modern Art in San Francisco, newlyweds Bart and Allison Allan have been separated by their jobs: Bart in Europe recruiting additional agents for Anastasia, the anti-terrorist branch of Interpol, and Allison winding up her job as an interpreter at the United Nations in New York City.

Because Allison nearly lost her life on more than one occasion in San Francisco, and was lucky to escape with only a serious compound fracture of her arm, Bart is adamant that she'll have no part in Anastasia's dangerous business of stopping terrorists before they strike. Allison, on the other hand, is determined to work alongside her agent husband—just as her mother has worked side by side with her father in the elite organization.

Who could have foreseen, when this war of wills began, the unbelievable outcome of one woman's determination?

Chapter One

"Bart! Look out!"

My husband twisted the wheel of our rental car sharply to the right to avoid a collision as a large, white van nearly sideswiped us. We veered off the road, heading straight for a steep embankment.

Hitting the gas pedal, Bart spun the wheel back to the left. Momentum carried the right front wheel across the gap in the pavement of the shoulder. A truck roared by, barely missing us, its horn blaring as we careened back onto the highway. As I caught my breath, the white van raced down the road and out of sight over a hill.

I sank back in my seat, hand over my pounding heart to keep it from leaping out of my terrified body. "Nice driving, Andretti," I said when I could breathe normally again.

Bart glanced in the rearview mirror, then at me. "Are you okay, Princess? How's your arm?" The loving concern in his tone conflicted with the anger in his eyes and the grim line of his lips.

"Thanks to your superior driving skills, I'm fine. And the arm will be much better when I get this cast off." I leaned my head against the headrest, closed my eyes, and took a deep breath. "When we headed off the road, I figured this pretty little blue convertible was history, and so were we." I sat up abruptly and looked at Bart. "That was an accident, wasn't it?"

"I'd like to think so," Bart said, speeding past the truck that almost hit us. His expression told me he didn't think so. As we topped a hill, the only thing in sight was a road sign informing us that Santa Fe was twenty miles ahead. The white van had disappeared.

Interstate 25 stretched out before us, solitary gray ribbons undulating through delicately colored desert in sun-bleached brown, mauve, and green tones. There was no turnoff into the sagebrush, juniper, scrub oak, and small, scrubby pinon pine trees that spread out on either side of the highway.

"Where did the van go?" I asked. "How could it just disappear like that?"

"Good question, Princess. I haven't a clue."

As Bart barreled down the highway, we scanned the sides of the road for a turnoff or exit. There simply was no place it could have exited.

"Does Interpol have special dispensation with the New Mexico Highway Patrol?" I inquired casually. "I hate to be a backseat driver, but in case you haven't noticed, we're doing ninety."

Bart slacked off the accelerator and punched the cruise-control to a sedate seventy-five miles per hour.

"I can't believe I've been with you a whole fifteen minutes and already somebody's trying to kill us," I teased. "Maybe it's a good thing we were on separate flights. They probably would have tried to blow up the airplane."

My blond, azure-eyed husband relaxed a bit and stretched his six-foot, four-inch length as much as he could in the confines of the compact convertible. He turned to me with a smile. "What can I say? You're trouble with a capital T."

"Sorry, Charlie. You can't blame that on me. I've been alone in New York for two months and no one has taken a shot at me, tried to run me down in the street, or forced me off the road into the river. *You're* the magnet for all the trouble when we're together. But since I've quit my job at the UN and plan on being by your side for the next few eternities, it looks like you're going to have to educate me on staying alive."

He just looked at me, then reached out to touch my cheek briefly before his eyes returned to the road. "I forgot how beautiful you are. I thought I'd memorized every freckle, every feature of your face, the way your gypsy hair falls across your shoulders, your eyes the color of emeralds. But it was so long . . ."

Bart leaned across the console and pulled me toward him. He kissed my forehead, my nose, then my lips.

"I hope you've got at least one eye on the highway," I murmured breathlessly. "I'd hate to end up back in the hospital with another cast before I get this one off."

"When did you get rid of the big cast?" Bart asked, resuming a more normal driving position with his eyes on the road and one hand on the wheel, the other holding mine.

"This morning before my flight. It was supposed to be on for another week, but Dr. Cooper took pity on me when I told him I was joining you for the first time in two months and substituted this small, more manageable one. The bone's healing well; scars will be minimal, and I only have to wear it for another week or so."

"No more diving headfirst through elevator hatches for you. Next time, think about protecting yourself first, and the bad guy second, and keeping that neat little body in one piece for me."

Abruptly he changed the subject, conveniently sidestepping my comment on educating me, which I'm sure he recognized as a left-handed request for training as an Interpol agent. "Have you been to Santa Fe before?"

"Once as a child, when Mom came to chronicle the stories and music of the Navajo nation. I remember an old grandmother who took an interest in me. She had a granddaughter about my age, but I don't remember their names."

I looked at Bart, trying to read his mood. "Ready to tell me what's going on? What's Anastasia doing in Santa Fe? Are my folks there yet? Are we actually going to see the Three Tenors' concert?"

Bart kissed my hand and laughed. "I'm glad you're here, Princess. I've missed you, and your incessant questions—and I can use your talents."

"I'm totally at your disposal. Fill me in."

"Word's out terrorists plan to kidnap the world's most famous tenors and their entourage at their highly publicized benefit concert. As Interpol's anti-terrorist specialists, Anastasia got the job of preventing anything from happening to Jose Carreras, Placido Domingo, and Luciano Pavarotti, and the celebrities joining them. We'll be at Rancho Encantado with the Tenors and their group, providing protection. Since your forte' is people, your assignment is to get to know everyone at the Ranch. I want to know their backgrounds, their jobs, their families, anything you can find out."

"Do I look like a snoop?"

"No, Princess. But your friendly-as-a-puppy nature enables you to get close to people. They confide in you. We want to know if someone on the Ranch could be a plant, or could be bought. The compound needs to be traitor-proofed and our security in place before the celebrities arrive."

"Where are Mom and Dad now?" I asked, my excitement at the assignment Bart was giving me only slightly tempered by our close call with the white van. Did he realize he was doing the very thing I'd quit my job at the United Nations to do—the very thing he vowed when we were married would never happen?

I shivered, not sure whether it was with exhilaration at the thought of getting to work as a special Interpol agent with Bart, or the memory of our close calls thus far in the three months of our marriage.

"At La Fonda Hotel in Santa Fe," he replied. "They should be finishing up their interviews with potential Anastasia replacements this afternoon, choosing about six from the dozen I culled in Europe. I suspect they'll try out all of them on this job, and the ones that work best with our group, they'll keep permanently."

"Only six?" I asked. "I'd think you'd need all the help you could get. With less than a dozen agents in Anastasia, how can you expect to keep tabs on all the world's new terrorist groups, much less the established ones?"

"Jack's decision. As head of Anastasia, your father doesn't need the moles and traitors in Anastasia that are tearing the FBI and CIA apart. Our lives depend on trusting the members of our team. So he likes to keep the organization intimate, like family."

"Is that why he brought Mom into it?" I asked.

"I think he had some of the same problems I have. All my instincts tell me I shouldn't involve you in this business, but I miss you so desperately, I'll have to take my chances that you'll be okay. I think that was probably how Margaret began—doing little things for your dad that gave them an excuse to be together. Finally, he sent her to take the training and made a great agent out of her."

I looked at Bart. He turned his face toward me and just shook his head.

"Why not?" I asked. "It only makes sense. You said in San Francisco you couldn't possibly do your job and worry about me at the same time. If I was a trained agent, I could be with you, help you, and you wouldn't have to worry. You could concentrate on the bad guys."

"No way, Allison. Don't ask—don't even *think* about it. Even if I knew you were as good as your mom or your dad, I'd still worry about you. Your propensity for getting into trouble—right into the thick of things—would make me crazy."

"But . . ."

Bart held up his hand. "No."

"Think how much more help I could be on this job if I were trained to ask the right questions—if I knew what to look for instead of having to be directed all the time."

"No."

"I could go over your head, to the big boss." I reached across the console and ran my fingers up the back of Bart's neck and through his short, blond hair.

He pulled my hand to his lips and kissed it. "No."

"No, I can't go over your head, or no, it wouldn't do any good?"

"I'd hope your father would have better sense than to let his only daughter get involved in the business."

"He let Mom."

"Her life was already in jeopardy, and Anastasia needed her help. Different story."

"But you don't know that he'd say no."

"Don't ask." Bart was not smiling. "Promise me you won't ask."

"Why would I promise anything like that?" I said, not enjoying the turn this conversation had taken. I turned to the window as we passed another new gambling casino being built on the reservation we were driving through.

"To make your husband happy. To please the man who loves you more than anything in the world." Bart took my hand and put my fingers to his lips. I turned back to him. "To give him a little peace of mind," he said, his voice plaintive and his look pleading.

I relented. "Okay. I promise I won't ask Dad to send me for training."

Bart turned his piercing gaze on me. "I know that tone in your voice. You found a way to get around your promise before you made it."

"You asked for a promise," I smiled. "I gave it. What more do you want?"

"Your assurance that you aren't going to pursue this with Jack. He's a professional to the core, but he's also a doting father. I'm sure you could wheedle your way into getting whatever you wanted from him. Promise me you won't approach him in any way about becoming an agent, or taking the training—or any other facet I may have overlooked."

Leaning back, I stared at the Sandia Mountains we were leaving behind and the blue sky that stretched endlessly beyond. It looked as though we were driving on top of the world. I'd felt on top of the world until two minutes ago.

Bart was waiting for an answer.

"Yes," I said. "I promise you I will never speak to Dad about any of this."

Bart looked suspicious. "Alli, that was too easy. What have you got up your sleeve?"

All innocence, I turned to my handsome husband. "You asked me to promise something that you said would make you happy. Dear fellow, I aim to please. Whatever your heart desires, I will attempt to provide."

"Now that's a promise I'll hold you to," he said, reaching across to kiss me. "What I desire most of all right now is . . ."

"I know what you desire right now," I laughed, "but short of pulling off the road in some secluded spot, which is non-existent on an interstate highway, you're going to have to wait a while. So educate me. The more I know, the more help I can be."

I was safe. Bart only made me promise not to *talk* to Dad. I wouldn't break my promise to my husband. But I hadn't quit an exciting and fulfilling career as an interpreter at the UN to sit at home waiting for my husband to have time for me. I planned to be an active and contributing partner, working at my husband's side wherever, and at whatever, his job with Anastasia took him.

Before we finished this assignment, I'd have my wish.

Chapter Two

"You're right," Bart admitted as we passed a sign informing us we were ten miles from Santa Fe. "There are some basics you should know, especially about protecting that great little body of yours." With a suggestive smile, he put my hand to his lips, then turned it over and tickled my palm with his tongue. "I want you just like you are, and I want you all to myself. I figure once Jack and Margaret know we're in town, we won't be alone again till this is over. I'm going to enjoy every minute of this afternoon before that happens."

"You won't get any argument from me," I said. "I spent the entire flight from New York to Albuquerque planning your seduction, since I know once you're involved in a case, I come in a far second."

Bart faked a pained look. "Never."

"You talk a good line, Romeo, but when you're on the job, all else pales, even when I haven't seen you for a month."

"I'm totally penitent, and I'll make sure it doesn't happen again—if it ever really did," he added with a roguish smile that melted me inside. He was quiet for a minute, and then Interpol took over. "What I need you to do when we get to the Ranch is get close enough to stable hands, cooks, gardeners, the concierge, even the delivery people who come regularly, to know who's supposed to be on duty and when. If a regular doesn't show up, find out why, and get to know their replacement immediately."

I laughed. Bart couldn't help himself; he wasn't even aware when he kicked into special agent mode. But this was what I'd wanted, so I certainly wouldn't complain.

"You don't think they'll be suspicious of me?" I asked. "Surely they'll know what we're there for."

"In a day or two, word'll get around. Everyone on the Ranch and around the opera will know who we are and what we're doing. But you're there recovering from a broken arm. You aren't part of the security or Anastasia. You're on vacation, just come to lend a little physical support to your lonesome husband."

"Yes, sir, boss."

With the fright of the attempted hit and run behind me, I relaxed and enjoyed the unique southwestern scenery. As we approached Santa Fe, homes styled like Indian pueblos dotted the rolling, scrub- and pinon-covered hills. Except along waterways in this semi-arid climate, trees never reached more than ten or twenty feet high. Pinons ending up looking like sprawling shrubs, and the dark green juniper stretched prickly arms at interesting, twisted angles.

Bart exited I-25 at St. Francis Drive, heading north through the city. The architecture was intriguing. Houses, gas stations, motels, restaurants, businesses, everything in the city was of the same unique pueblo style: rose-beige or ochre-colored rectangular, adobe buildings with rounded corners, flat roofs, and small windows. I liked it. It felt comfortable. Not to mention picturesque.

Suddenly we were out of town.

"Where are we going? We just left Santa Fe behind," I said, puzzled.

"Rancho Encantado and the Santa Fe Opera are about five miles north of town, a couple of miles apart. The Ranch is sprawling, a hundred and forty-eight acres, so in some ways it will be a little more difficult to secure than a hotel in the city, but hopefully easier in others," Bart explained.

St. Francis Drive became Highway 84-285, the Taos Highway, a modern four-lane road that offered great vistas of the Rio Grande Valley framed by the Jemez and Sangre de Cristo Mountains on either side. Open blue sky stretched endlessly above gently rolling mountain peaks, augmenting the perception that we were driving on top of the world.

Lenticular white clouds iced the purple and blue of the mountains to our right. Sangre de Cristo. Blood of Christ. The name intrigued me.

Bart pointed out the distinctive Santa Fe Opera on the left side of the highway, all but hidden in the piñons and juniper. The only thing visible from the highway was the famous soaring, half-circle roof that covered the stage, leaving patrons seated under the stars and open sky.

"We'll crawl all over the place in a day or two and get the security set up. First, we need to secure the Ranch. We've got three days, four at the most, before everyone arrives. When they descend upon Rancho Encantado, they have every right to expect to be safe and secure."

Suddenly a white van shot onto the highway in front of us from a dirt side road, skidding across both lanes. A cloud of dust obscured the road as bullets pinged off the frame of our windshield.

"Get down!" Bart shouted, slamming on the brakes. The car behind us squealed tires as it braked to avoid hitting us.

When the dust cleared, the white van was far down the road.

"They've got a souped-up engine on that thing," he muttered. "Won't do us any good to try to catch them. No wonder they disappeared so fast the first time."

Bart exited the main highway onto a narrow, two-lane country road while I gripped the armrest, still holding my breath, unable to even speak. Huge trees on either side, their branches reaching across to each other, created the illusion of a shady green tunnel ahead. Tunnels I didn't need. White vans I didn't need. People shooting at me I didn't need.

But before we entered the green bower, Bart turned left onto an even smaller road.

"Is this the way to Rancho Encantado, or are we making a detour to catch our breath?" I asked, finally able to find my voice.

Bart laughed. "This is the way. Didn't you see the sign?"

"Too shaken by the attack, I guess." I flexed my shoulders and rubbed the tension out of my neck. "Glad my guardian angels were on duty so the shots missed the windshield—and us. I'm also glad the gunmen hit and ran. I'd hate to have them stick around to try and finish the job."

Bart turned to me, his expression full of concern. "How're you doing?"

"I'm okay," I smiled. "I just can't figure out how you can come through something like that without even skipping a heartbeat."

"It's all in the set of the jaw," he said, his blue eyes twinkling mischievously. "I have my teeth re-capped every three months to repair the damage I do grinding them when I'm attacked."

The road wound in and out and up and over rolling, red-earth hills covered with deep green pinon pines. But there was no sign of Rancho Encantado. Simply endless hills rolling right up to the foot of the Sangre de Cristos.

Then a rail fence materialized. A large adobe sign behind it proclaimed "Rancho Encantado." Even when Bart turned onto the dirt road, there wasn't a building in sight.

"I keep waiting for this wonderful hotel to appear on the horizon. Where is it? Are you sure there really is such a place?"

"Maybe it's enchanted, like the name suggests, and only appears for believers," Bart said. "If you don't believe it's out here, you'll never find it."

"Actually," I explained, "'encantado' means rambling when referring to a *casa* or house. If you're speaking of a person, they'd be absent-minded or distracted. 'Encantador' is charming or enchanting. 'Encanto' is the charm, spell, or enchantment placed by the 'Encantadora'."

"Which must mean enchantress," Bart said.

"Right. You'll be speaking Spanish before you know it."

"There's the Ranch."

I'd been expecting something big, grand and luxurious. What appeared was a modest two-story adobe ranch house that didn't seem sprawling at all. It was certainly nothing I could picture accommodating the famous Three Tenors, who had popularized opera and were known all over the world.

"I'll dump the bags at the front door and park the car. Will you check in—and make sure your folks haven't arrived yet?" Bart whipped the sky-blue convertible into the half-circle drive in front of the entry and hopped out. Before I'd recovered from my surprise at the appearance of the place, Bart had deposited the bags on the front steps and was back in the car. "I'll park. You go register. They're expecting us."

When I didn't move, Bart reached over and opened my door, unbuckled my seat belt, and, with a little shove, said, "Time's awastin'."

In a daze, I walked up the steps, passed a propped-open screen and pushed open the weathered wooden door that led into the foyer. I absolutely could not imagine Luciano Pavarotti here. I wasn't sure *I* even wanted to stay.

Then I stepped inside. A streak of sunlight pierced the cool, dark interior, highlighting dancing sunbeams. It was as if I'd been met by the *Encantadora* and sprinkled with magical dust that attuned my soul to the enchantment. Rustic, unsophisticated, casual, comfortable, and inviting were adjectives that immediately came to mind. I was instantly overcome by the charm and ambiance of the place.

"Hello."

Startled, I turned, expecting to see a fairy godmother, or the Good Witch of the East, or, this being New Mexico, a Native American medicine woman bedecked in buckskin and turquoise.

Instead, the friendly voice belonged to a young woman with thick, long, auburn hair and wonderfully warm, smiling, hazel eyes.

"Hello," was all I could muster.

"Can I help you?"

I shook off the sensation of the mystical and turned to the registration desk tucked in a small alcove.

"I'm Allison Allan. My husband and I have a reservation."

A smile animated her oval face. "Yes, Mrs. Allan. We've been expecting you. I'm Molly." She hit a couple of computer keys and looked up at me. There was a flicker of hesitation, a hint of consternation, then another smile.

"You're in room 109. If you'll fill this out, please, I'll get your keys." She pushed a registration form and pen toward me.

"Have my parents arrived yet? Jack and Margaret Alexander?"

"Not yet. They called from town, asking if you'd checked in, and said to tell you they'd be another couple of hours."

Bart made his entrance at that minute. "When they come, don't tell them we're here. It was a long night, we've both had long flights, and we're going to crash for the rest of the afternoon. Unless it's a dire emergency, we don't want to be disturbed by anyone."

Molly nodded. "Yes, sir."

A blond young man in chinos and a pastel plaid cotton shirt appeared out of nowhere. Molly handed him our key. "Mr. and Mrs. Allan are upstairs."

"Hi. I'm Brian." He popped the key in his pocket and grabbed my luggage. With a happy "This way—follow me, please" flung over his shoulder, he took off across the well-worn, dark red tile floor. Bart was right on my heels with his bags, neither of them giving me the opportunity to examine the place.

Straight ahead, I caught a glimpse of heavy wooden beams, a white adobe corner fireplace surrounded by homey chairs, and French doors dazzling with sunlight before Brian turned a corner and Bart pressed me to follow him. The impression of an old Spanish *casa* formed as we hurried through a cool, shadowy sitting room furnished with heavy, carved wooden furniture. It was warm, comfortable, and inviting.

Abruptly, we turned and headed up a blue and white Spanish tiled staircase.

"The Ranch house doesn't have an elevator," Brian offered brightly. "You get your exercise around here when you stay in the main lodge."

"There's more than this?" I asked.

"Oh, yes. We've got cottages, *casitas*, the Casa Piñon and the Betty Egan House on this side. On the other side of the road are the Pueblo Encantado Villas. We've put up Prince Rainier's entire entourage, the Dalai Lama and his party, and Princess Anne from England with all her people. All sorts of movie stars stay here. This week, Bryan Adams and Barbra Streisand are coming, and those three opera guys who sang at Dodger Stadium. Boy, will this place be hoppin' with all the people they're bringing!"

As we reached the door to the first room, Brian paused in his enthusiastic narration and dropped my bags to dig out our key and check the room number. His perpetual motion machine came to an abrupt stop.

Brian looked at the key, then at me. Then his questioning blue eyes scrutinized Bart: muscular, and head and shoulders taller than either of us. With a seemingly satisfied nod, he grabbed the bags again, and, continuing down the carpeted corridor, made a right turn, stepped up one stair, and stopped at the end of the short hall. "Here you are," he said with a cheery smile, unlocking the door and preceding us inside room 109. He put the suitcases on the floor, turned on his heel and stepped briskly out into the hall, allowing us to enter the room.

"If you folks need anything, just call downstairs and we'll do our best to keep you happy. You know about the pool and tennis courts. The stables are just beyond them. The food here is wonderful. Enjoy your stay."

Bart held out a tip, but Brian stayed where he was, outside the door, and held out his hand. Bart had to take it to him.

"Thank you, sir." He clicked the heels of his tennis shoes together and did a mock bow from the waist, then disappeared down the hall with a happy smile.

"Strange kid," Bart said as he locked the door and turned to me. Then he looked perplexed. "I was going to suggest a hot shower so I could give you one of my specialty back scrubs, but how do you shower with a cast on?"

"Very carefully. With the cast wrapped in plastic. And I will take you up on the back scrub." I turned to unpack my suitcases. A huge bouquet of exquisite, long-stemmed peach roses caught my eye.

"Oh, Bart! They're beautiful. Thank you." I threw my arms around my thoughtful husband and kissed him.

"Did you count them?" he asked, pulling me close. "There's one for every day we've been together."

"I thought I was the only one who counted those wonderful days. You're really a soft sentimentalist at heart, aren't you? Not the tough, macho agent you pretend to be."

"Just a man smitten by love. Out of ninety-two days since you came back into my life in June, I've only seen you nineteen—and eight of those nineteen days were before we were married. Not nearly enough. I've about been out of my mind with loneliness with you in New York for the last two months."

"Well, I'm here now," I assured him, "and you're going to have to beat me away with a stick, because I'll never voluntarily leave you again. On the other hand, I'm not naive enough to believe that you won't leave me while you run off trying to make the world a safer place."

"Why would I leave a body like this?" Bart murmured, holding me close and nibbling my neck. "Do I remember a promise of seduction?"

"To seduce is to draw away from duty," I laughed. "You're too willing. But I'll be glad to show you how I'd planned to get your attention." I slipped out of his arms and reached for my suitcase, examining our rooms for the first time.

Etched glass French doors separated the bedroom from the sitting room. Big pink checks on the sofa and pink striped overstuffed chairs didn't seem overly feminine when balanced with antique spindle chairs, an x-based table, tin-punched light covers, and a lounge covered in honey-colored ribbed corduroy.

Bart took my suitcase from me and set it down. "That can wait. I can't." He pulled me into his arms again. "Being without you has been worse torture than my six months in that Tibetan prison."

His mouth was hot and hungry on mine. I pressed my body close to his, clinging to him, loving the feel of him next to me, not wanting to ever let go again.

Bart sank to the lounge, reclining against the curved end, and pulled me down next to him. I kissed him softly again and again, feeling a desire I'd tried to put from my mind for two months.

Suddenly a chill shivered through me. Bart felt it, too. He rolled into a sitting position with me on his lap. "I'm cold," he said. "Must be too much air-conditioning. How about that hot shower now? Then we can snuggle into that inviting-looking bed and keep each other warm."

"I like your agenda," I replied, looking for an air-conditioning vent I could close.

There was none.

I shivered again, my psychic senses quivering like a divining rod.

Chapter Three

Voices from the hallway outside our door penetrated my sleep. I looked at the clock on the nightstand. Five-thirty p.m. Mom and Dad were either staying in the room across the hall, or they'd come to rouse us. A door closed. The voices subsided. They must have room 108.

Bart pulled me close against him and buried his nose in my hair, kissing my neck.

"You *are* awake," I said, turning in the circle of his arms to face him. "Did you hear them? I think my folks have the room across the hall."

Bart groaned and pulled the covers over our heads. "Be very quiet, and maybe we can extend this a little longer."

"Dreamer. If you have fifteen minutes before Dad pounds on the door, you'll be lucky. In fact, I'll give him five minutes before he's out of their room, and another five to get the information out of Molly that we're here, and our room number. We might as well get up and dressed so we'll be presentable when he comes calling."

Bart mumbled something unintelligible and pulled me closer, stroking my back.

The door across the hall opened, then slammed shut. Footsteps padded down the carpeted hall. Throwing the covers off, I slipped reluctantly out of Bart's arms. "I'm going to be properly attired when Dad comes back to start planning your strategy. You can do business wrapped in a sheet if you like."

I grabbed a pair of jeans and a sweatshirt from my suitcase, then changed my mind and shrugged into a denim shirt instead. The room certainly wasn't cold now. I was just transferring clothes from my bags to the chest of drawers when someone came back up the corridor.

Pulling the pillow off Bart's head, I tossed him a pair of pants as Dad pounded on the door.

"Wake up, you two. We've got work to do." Another door opened in the hall.

"Coming, Dad," I called, smoothing the comforter back on the bed as Bart deserted it for the bathroom, clutching his clothes.

I opened the door, and Dad swept me into his arms. "Bunny, it's good to see you."

Mom was right on his heels and pecked a kiss on my cheek. "Hi, hon. How's your arm? When did you get the new cast?"

"Healing well, and this morning, before I left New York," I answered, motioning them onto the pink-checked sofa. I plopped into the pink-striped chair to put on my tennis shoes.

"Did you get your people chosen?" I asked, struggling to tie my shoes because of the cumbersome cast. Dad came to my rescue and did it for me.

"It's been a long time since I've had to tie your tennies," he teased. "Yes, we got the job done. Looks like a pretty good group. I just hope they all work out."

Dad settled back into the sofa and put his arm around Mom. I thought he had a few more lines around his steel-gray eyes, and probably a few more gray hairs since I'd seen him in San Francisco two months earlier. He was average height, average weight . . . so average-looking, in fact, that he could become any man, anywhere, with little by way of disguise—a perfect Interpol agent.

"Your friend, Oz, had a lot of nice things to say about you," Mom said with a wink and a smile. "If I didn't know better, I'd say he'd been smitten."

Mom was an older version of me, with the same compact, petite build, except her eyes were dark and mysterious while my green ones revealed every emotion. Her dark hair constantly escaped in wispy tendrils from the classic bun she fashioned it into.

Bart came out of the bathroom stuffing his shirttails into his jeans. "Won't do him any good. She's spoken for already." He perched on the arm of my chair, kissed the top of my head, and rested his hand possessively on my shoulder. "So, who did you pick?"

"We asked them all to work with us on this case, since I have a feeling we'll need all the help we can get. We'll tell them after this is over who made the cut. That'll give us a chance to see everyone in action and how we mesh. To become a permanent part of Anastasia, we agreed on Elsa . . . ," Dad began.

Mom interrupted him. "That one took debate and compromise. You'll notice she was the first one he mentioned. She's Norwegian, tall, blonde, thirty, and drop-dead gorgeous."

"But super-qualified," Bart added. "Actually, she seemed too good to be true."

"And you're the one who originally interviewed and selected her." I turned to look up at Bart, trying to swallow the bitter taste of jealousy that overcame me when my husband and beautiful women were involved.

"Your lovely emerald eyes have deepened several shades of green," Bart laughed, tipping my chin up so he could kiss me. "You know I only have eyes for you." He settled on the floor at my feet, his arm across my knees.

"Besides Oswald Barlow, whom you'd already worked with in San Francisco, we picked Else Elbert, David Chen, Lionel Brandt, Rip Schyler, Dominic Vicente, and Xavier," Dad reported.

"Interesting that he only goes by one name," Mom said.

"Well, you certainly went international," I said. "If they're true to their names and my language training serves me correctly, let's see if I can tell you a little about them. You said Else is from Norway; her name means of nobility and one who's brilliant."

"I'd have to agree with that," Bart nodded.

"David, beloved or important one." I thought for a minute. "Chen: one Chinese meaning is mountain peak, or isolated and solitary—lonely."

"Pretty close," Dad nodded. "He's extremely personable, but has a detachment that gives you the feeling he's sort of standing back, observing, not participating. Came with amazing recommendations."

"Lionel Brandt. French, meaning youthful lion, golden-haired; one of fire," I continued.

"Incredible," Mom exclaimed. "He's twenty-eight with a mane of tousled blond hair, and is so full of energy, he nearly bounces off the wall."

"Rip Schyler. He should be Dutch. The name means mature, ripe, a scholarly, wise man. A protector."

Bart stared at me open-mouthed. "Are you sure you haven't seen the dossiers of these guys? Rip is sixty, gray-haired, horn-rimmed glasses, has a doctorate in criminology and another in abnormal behavior."

"People have a tendency to grow into their names; it's sort of a self-fulfilling prophecy thing," I said. "If the patterns I studied continue to be true, Xavier is Arabic and both brilliant and splendid."

"He's definitely Arabic, and brilliant. The splendid hasn't yet manifested itself," Mom said.

"Okay, *Encantadora,* let's hear about Dominic Vicente," Bart said.

"Both are Latin names. Dominic is 'child born on the Lord's day,' and Vicente is 'conqueror.' I'd guess he was Spanish."

"You'd guess right. Pretty good, Bunny. All that money for college was worth it." Dad beamed with parental pride. "We've got a great team member right here."

"Allison's talents will be invaluable in planning councils and collecting information. I don't want her in the field." Bart spoke softly, but his tone was firm and unyielding.

Silence fell heavy with that critical announcement.

"Trouble will find her anyway, Bart," Mom laughed. "That's one of her other talents. Now, I don't know about the rest of you, but I'm starving. Is there any reason why this conversation can't be continued downstairs in the dining room?" Mom had just demonstrated one of *her* special talents: unsticking sticky situations.

The view across the Rio Grande Valley from the dining room was a study in desert pastels. It was already apparent that we were in for one of Santa Fe's spectacular sunsets and had perfect seats to view it. The popular dining room filled as Maria, our waitress, took our order.

The sunset reminded me of one I'd experienced in New York as I finished my last discussion taught by two missionaries from The Church of Jesus Christ of Latter-day Saints. It had appeared as a benediction to a deeply spiritual experience—one that I couldn't wait to share with Bart. But the moment had to be just right—and this wasn't it.

"What's Else's assignment?" I asked, curious to know what her special abilities were and why everyone was so awed by them. Our dinner arrived, and the question went unanswered as we sampled the visual and olfactory pleasures put before us. The chef had either outdone himself tonight or we were in for some marvelous meals during our stay.

"Encounter any problems getting here?" Dad asked Bart.

Bart nodded, his mouth full, and glanced at me. I caught the signal and answered Dad.

"We were forced off the road by a van between here and Albuquerque. The van disappeared before we could catch it. Then it repeated the stunt near the Opera, with added fireworks."

"Any idea who it was?" Dad asked Bart, his fork halfway to his mouth. Bart shook his head.

"No. It was a commuter van apparently filled with businessmen, innocent-looking enough, but I'd been watching them in the rearview mirror. They sped up to every car, pulled alongside as if to examine the occupants, then sped on to the next one. When they got to us, the driver hung back in the blind spot of my mirror for several miles, then suddenly came alongside and turned the wheel into the right lane as if we weren't even there. If I hadn't been watching him, he'd have probably hit us and knocked us into the deep arroyo that just 'happened' to be there instead of a shoulder wide enough to recover."

"And you couldn't catch them?" Dad asked.

"No. They've got a hot engine. By the time we reached the top of the hill the first time and could see down the road, there was no van in sight. The second time, they were waiting for us. Luckily, they kicked up a cloud of dust leaving the dirt road, or they might have been able to see what they were shooting at."

"Okay. They know we're here, and what we're here for. No honeymoon this time to get ready for them," Dad said, consuming the formerly abandoned bite. "We'll have to be on our toes."

"Did you figure out who we're dealing with?" I asked.

"It's Hamas or one of their radical branches," Dad said. "We couldn't pin it any closer than that."

"Interpol's still checking," Mom added. "They'll let us know if they find out who's leading this group, but it probably wouldn't make any difference. Our plan would be about the same. Unless, of course, they bring in professionals."

"What would you do differently?" I asked. Initial hunger satisfied, I abandoned my dinner to pursue my goal of learning the business of Anastasia—stopping terrorists and preventing terrorism. Every aspect of it fascinated me.

Mom explained the more intricate problems of dealing with known professional assassins as opposed to ordinary terrorists.

"Bart," Dad said, "you'll need to go to Los Alamos tomorrow."

"Can I go, too?" I asked.

"Well," Dad said, "I was going to send . . ."

"She can go," Bart interjected, reaching for my hand. "You can switch assignments tomorrow."

"Who were you going to send?" I asked.

"Else," Dad said.

At that moment, a vision of blonde loveliness stepped into the dining room. Conversation in the room ceased. Every eye was on this exquisite creature, who came straight to our table. Spun gold, chin-length hair fell in soft parentheses around her pale, patrician face. She moved with the grace of a dancer and the confidence of a model, aware of the appreciative glances and seemingly amused by them.

Dad and Bart stood. I did, too. Directly between Bart and the goddess.

"You're Else," I guessed, extending my hand with a smile. "I'm Allison, Bart's wife. Welcome to our group."

Else's grip was firm, with incredible strength in those slender, delicate-looking fingers. She smiled down from her elegant, almost six-foot height with penetrating gray-green eyes. "Allison, you're even prettier than Bart described," she said in a low, intriguing voice with no noticeable accent. "I'm happy to meet you. I'll enjoy working with you as much as I have with Bart."

She turned to Mom. "Margaret, your daughter is lovely." Then to Dad and Bart, "Please, don't let me interrupt your dinner. I'm meeting Sky and Xavier. Oh, here they are now."

She turned and swept away, leaving us standing in her wake. I sat down, outwardly calm, but my emotions were taking a wild roller-coaster ride. I turned to Bart. "You've worked with her before?"

"Briefly, just before I went to Tibet. She's very professional," he said.

"She's very beautiful," I said, trying to keep my voice light and impersonal. "Actually, beautiful doesn't come near describing her. She's also absolutely brilliant. I'll bet one of her majors was psychology."

Mom laughed. "Apparently you were paying attention in your psych classes, too."

I leaned across the table toward Mom. "Probably more woman's intuition than psychology. My danger antennae quivered when she came in the room—one of those 'protect your husband and your marriage' reflexes."

Incredulous, I turned to Dad. "You were going to send Else instead of me with Bart tomorrow?" My astute husband knew what my reaction would be when I met the exquisite Else. He'd done his footwork ahead of time. My supposedly wise and intelligent father hadn't a clue what he'd been about to do.

"I'll educate your father first thing," Mom promised.

Dad brought his radio to his mouth and spoke quietly into it. "Yes?"

"I didn't hear anything," I said to Bart, puzzled.

"It doesn't ring or beep. It vibrates so it doesn't disturb anyone, and only he knows he's being called," Bart explained.

"*We're* being called," Dad corrected, pushing his chair from the table. "It's begun."

Chapter Four

"David Chen, our silent sentinel, was riding the perimeter of the Ranch and spotted a white van parked in an arroyo a mile or so from here," Dad reported. "He watched them load a bunch of boxes into the van from a secluded cave. When they left, he checked the cave."

"What did he find?" I asked, leaning across the table.

"Arms and ammunition."

"Did he see what they took out of the cave?" Bart asked.

"He thought more of the same."

"Moving it because they know we're here and they're afraid we'll find it, or moving it because they're getting ready to use it?" Mom said.

"Anybody's guess, at this point," Dad said.

"What about the van?" Bart asked.

"He got the plate number. But all that will tell us is that it's stolen or a rental, and whoever rented it has some supposedly legitimate cover."

"What now?" I asked. "If the van's gone and no one followed it, what can you do?"

"Get Lionel, Dominic, and Xavier down to examine the cave and make sure they're on top of the perimeter defense."

Dad stood up.

"Where do you want me?" Bart asked, pushing away from the table.

Dad looked from Bart to me. "Go ahead and finish your dinner. If I need you, I'll call." He nodded to Mom. "You, too, honey. There's no need for everyone's dinner to be spoiled."

He strode toward the table where Else, Sky, and Xavier were just ordering dinner, signaled to Xavier, then left the dining room. The tall, slender, dark-eyed Arab with an intriguing jagged scar down the side of his neck immediately rose and joined his boss.

Bart pulled his chair back to the table and picked up his fork, but didn't eat. He gazed out the window at the spectacular sunset streaking the evening sky with incredible shades of gold, orange, and red.

"Nice sky," I said, hoping to pull him back from whatever far plane he was on. I had to repeat it.

"Huh?" My husband finally turned to focus on me.

"Breathtaking view of the sunset," Mom said. "Too bad you're missing it."

"And letting your dinner get cold," I laughed. "If you want to be with them so much, go, for heaven's sake. Mom and I can certainly take care of ourselves."

"Why on earth would I want to be with a bunch of guys crawling around a dirty cave when I can enjoy the company of two beautiful women, watch an incredible sunset, and finish a great dinner?"

"Fancy footwork," Mom said. "You're good, Bart. Jack's never learned to cover himself that fast, or as convincingly."

Bart started to protest. I reached for his hand and squeezed it. I knew he'd rather be in the middle of the action than sitting here wondering what was going on.

We were interrupted by Else asking what was up. Mom explained all we knew, and the beautiful blonde returned to their table to report to Sky.

"What are we doing tomorrow, that you'd rather be with me than Else?" I asked Bart.

"Whatever we do, I'd rather be with you than Else," Bart assured me, slipping his arm around my shoulder and pulling me close to him.

"Nice touch, Romeo," I laughed. "Your dancing's getting better and better. What did you say we were doing?"

"We need to meet a man in Los Alamos. And I do need you to start getting acquainted with the help here at the Ranch."

"Will do."

Maria, our waitress, convinced us dinner wasn't complete at Rancho Encantado without savoring one of the chef's delicious desserts, so we all ordered something different and sampled each of them. They were all wonderful.

Mom pushed back her chair. "I'm going to walk around and check the place out."

"How about if we come along?" Bart said. "We haven't seen the layout yet either."

As the sun dipped below the horizon, we wandered under an ivy-covered trellis toward the pool and the stables. A cluster of long-armed slender cactus shared a small garden spot with a dalliance of white daisies and bright red poppies bending in the cool evening breeze. Twilight brought a chill to the air, and I snuggled close to Bart.

Suddenly, hoofbeats pounded through the small grove of trees ahead. A huge black horse, running at full gallop, thundered straight for us, its rider crouched low over the horse's streaming mane. Mom jumped one way and Bart shoved me the other. It raced between us, grazing Bart's shoulder as it passed, knocking him off balance, then disappeared into the dusky night.

"Are you okay?" I asked as he got up off the dusty road.

"Fine," he said, brushing himself off. "How's your arm?"

"The cast saved me from the cactus. I'm not as scratched as I would have been. Mom?"

"All right, but I'd sure like to give the careless rider on that horse a piece of my mind. We could have been seriously hurt." She stopped. "Unless that's what he had in mind in the first place."

"You think he did that on purpose?" I asked, my heart thumping wildly.

"Like Jack said, 'It's begun'," she said quietly.

I wasn't ready to be plunged back into the world of danger in every shadow, of person or persons unknown trying to kill me for reasons I wasn't sure were valid, even in their twisted minds.

We walked silently past the tennis courts, the basketball and horseshoe areas, to the pool and cantina. Just beyond, the stables seemed deserted. The corral was empty. A black and white dog kept vigil beside a door under a light on the outside of a small building that may have been the tack room.

As we headed for the door, it opened, throwing a beam of light across the corral, spotlighting hoofprints in the soft dirt. A lean figure with cowboy hat and bowed legs was silhouetted briefly in the doorway before the man shut the door and strode toward us, the dog following at his heels.

"Hello," Bart said as the man approached under the lighted corral gate.

"Stables are closed," the man said, not breaking his stride as he reached us. It was apparent he wasn't interested in stopping for conversation.

"Who just rode out of here on that big black horse?" Mom asked, stepping directly in front of him so he had to stop for, or sidestep, her petite, determined presence.

"Nobody rode out of here tonight," he said, pulling his hat lower on his forehead, a gesture that could have signaled either respect or dismissal. He stepped around Mom and opened the white iron gate with the "E" inside a cowboy hat silhouette, holding it just long enough for the dog to follow.

"Excuse me, sir," Bart said, grabbing the gate before it clicked shut. "Someone just about ran us over, riding from this direction."

"Nobody rode from here tonight." He turned and faced Bart, hands on his hips, face hidden under the shadow of the hat brim. "We don't have any black horses in our stables. Good night."

The dog led the way, anticipating his master's departure. In three long strides, the man caught up, and man and dog were quickly lost in the shadows.

"Gabby, amiable soul, wasn't he?" I said, linking my arm through Bart's.

"Allison, it's time you got to know the help," Mom said. "Find out who he is, and who rides a big black horse. I'm not mistaken about the color. It was still light enough to see, and the silver mane and tail were certainly distinctive. Someone should recognize the description. Unfortunately, I didn't see the rider well enough to describe."

"I'll walk you back," Bart offered. "Are you coming, Margaret?"

"Shortly. I'm going to nose around a bit. You two go on."

Mom headed into the stables as Bart slipped his arm around my waist and steered me back to the casa. He stopped at the front door.

"Where are you going?" I asked, surprised at being left on the doorstep.

"I'm going to scout around a little, too. You'll find out more alone. We want people to see that you aren't here on business like the rest of us. You're recovering from a broken arm, remember? Now go do your thing."

He kissed my forehead, opened the door, then turned and strode down the half-circle driveway into the darkness beyond.

In the sitting room, few people occupied the comfortable chairs around the big white adobe fireplace, which tonight contained a cheerfully blazing fire. I thought about joining them, but decided to find Maria, our waitress. She was a friendly soul and might know something about the big black horse with the distinctive silver mane and tail and the reckless rider.

The pretty, dark-haired, dark-eyed girl of about seventeen was clearing the last table in the now empty dining room.

"Maria, I wanted to thank you for convincing me to try dessert. It was absolutely delicious. Does the chef do that every night, or was tonight something special?"

"Oh, no, Señora. Nothing special. He cooks like that all the time. We are all busting our buttons since he came to la casa." She laughed and patted her stomach. "I have gained twelve pounds, and I think it's all right here."

A devastatingly handsome, dark-haired, muscular fellow entered the dining room to bus the dishes as Maria spoke. "Are you sure that's Enrique's cooking and not something else?" he said. His tone was grating. The innuendo was suggestive and degrading. Maria's face flushed and her dark eyes flashed with anger, but she bit her lip and said nothing.

I watched him load the tray, his eyes never leaving Maria's scoop-neck blouse, watching as she leaned over to wipe the table. A current of emotion arced between the two. He laughed at Maria as he picked up the heavy tray.

"Who was that?" I asked, watching the swinging door between the kitchen and dining room close behind him.

"Jaqueez. He think's he's God's gift to women."

"His good looks are eclipsed by his egotism. That was an ugly thing to say."

"He's full of pretty words as long as you keep saying yes to him, but once you draw the line and say no, he becomes hateful." Maria looked up, her dark eyes brimming with tears. "I let him sweep me off my feet. I was flattered that he would pay attention to a plain nobody like me. He brought me presents and flowers. For one week he made me feel like the most beautiful person in the whole world. Then he took me for a drive, to a secret place he had found in an old turquoise mine."

Maria stopped to wipe her eyes on her apron. "'Something very special,' he said to me. He spread out a blanket just inside the mine, poured wine into beautiful glasses, gave me a turquoise ring. It has the power to make one be loved, and he said he would love me forever. Then he tried to undress me. When I wouldn't let him, he said I didn't love him, that I had led him on to get the presents. Then he tried to . . ."

At that point Maria dissolved into tears. I put my arms around her and held her while she cried on my shoulder.

"I'm sorry, Señora," she said between sniffles. "I don't even know you, and here I am telling you my life story. I should not bother you with my problems."

"It's perfectly all right, Maria. What happened then?"

"He called me bad names and tore at my clothes, but I ran away before he could disgrace me. Now he tells everyone he slept with me, that he was not the first. Señora, it's not true. I have never been with a man." Maria's big black eyes pleaded with me to believe her.

"I believe you, Maria, and please call me Allison. I'm going to be hanging about while my family's doing their thing. Maybe you can show me around when you're not busy, and tell me about your family. I think they must be very special people to have a daughter like you."

"Yes, I could do that. Thank you, Señora Allison." She drew in a deep breath and straightened her back, as if preparing for an ordeal. "Now I must get back to work."

"Oh, Maria, before you go, can you tell me who rides that big black horse?"

"I've never seen a black horse here," she said, her forehead wrinkling in a thoughtful frown. "Did you see it on the Ranch?"

"Yes. Someone almost ran us over a little while ago. There isn't a black horse in the stables? One with a silver mane and tail?"

Maria's eyes grew wide. "Black, with a silver mane and tail?"

"Yes. Do you know who rides it?"

"No one rides it." Maria's voice fell to a soft whisper. "It's the ghost horse. It comes to warn you when something bad is going to happen." She bit her lip, as if sorry she had said anything.

"This horse nearly trampled us. It was real. And who's the tall, rather curt man at the stables?"

"That would be Jake. He runs the stables. He's rusty steel on the outside and marshmallow inside. My brother works for him after school. Juan says Jake wants everyone to think he's tough and mean, but he's really not."

"Thanks, Maria. You've been very helpful. I'll see you around."

Maria walked toward the kitchen with her back stiff and her head held high. She was an authentically nice girl. A pox on Jaqueez!

The chairs around the fireplace were empty now, so I wandered back to the front desk to talk to the night clerk. Eric was on duty, a red-headed, freckle-faced, jolly type of about twenty-five. "Good evening, Mrs. Allan," he said. "Are you enjoying your stay at the Ranch?"

The switchboard jangled before I could answer. I waited while he answered it.

"No one's there again." Then Eric looked at me. "You're staying in room 109, aren't you?"

"Yes, why?"

"Three times someone has called the desk from that room, but when I answer, no one's on the line."

"Must be my husband. I'll go see what he wants." I turned to go when the front door opened. Bart walked in.

"Bart! I thought you were in our room."

"No, Princess. I told you I was going to look around outside."

"You haven't been back upstairs?"

"No."

"Then who's making phone calls from our room?"

Chapter Five

Bart took the tiled staircase three steps at a time, drawing his gun as he went. I was right behind him. "Stay back," he ordered as we rounded the short hall to room 109.

He keyed the lock and burst in—to an empty room. We searched the closet, bathroom, behind the sofa, under the bed. No one was there.

"There wasn't time for anyone to leave," I said. "It had been less than a minute since the phone rang. I was standing there when the switchboard buzzed, and you came in right after."

"Unless someone slipped out of here into another room."

Bart stepped into the hall and motioned for me to follow. He pointed at room 108, my parents' room, and I listened at the door while he moved silently down the hall and around the corner, listening at each door as he went. I joined him at the top of the stairs.

"Get someone with keys to these rooms. I'll stay here and make sure no one leaves this floor. We'll search them all."

I hurried downstairs and asked Eric for keys. That required the manager, who had gone home already. I pressed for the night assistant manager, or even Eric himself, to come with keys so we could check the other rooms.

Beth Halgood, assistant night manager, was summoned from some far corner of Rancho Encantado and took her sweet time getting there. While I waited anxiously, Eric checked the room registrations. Rooms 108 and 109 were the only ones occupied tonight.

Eric was in grad school and had been working night shift at the Ranch for nearly six months, studying on duty while it was quiet. I kept him chatting about the Ranch and how it was run and the people who worked there.

When Beth Halgood finally arrived, a little out of breath from her exertion, I explained what happened and asked her to please let us into the rooms to see if anyone was hiding there.

"Is that what you brought me here for?" she said, hands on her ample hips. "I could have saved myself a trip. Eric, weren't you told about the phone in room 109? There's a short somewhere in the system. We've had the phone company here a couple of times trying to find the problem, but they didn't fix it. That phone just rings all by itself every once in a while, and there's no one on the other end."

Beth turned to me with a satisfied smile, as if she had, all by herself, solved the world's major problem.

"Only in our room, or does it happen with other phones, too?" I asked.

"No. Just in room 109, and only occasionally," she said in a tone that clearly indicated the issue had been dismissed. "Anything else I can do for you?"

"My husband's expecting me to bring keys to those rooms. I don't think he's going to accept that answer, especially when he's responsible for the security at Rancho Encantado. Since the rooms aren't occupied, you could just give me the keys and you wouldn't have to bother."

Climbing the stairs could have been one reason for her reluctance to pursue the matter. Beth didn't look like climbing stairs was something she did very often. She looked like she did more sitting and eating than anything else.

A pouty expression crossed her round, plump face, then disappeared. "Eric can go with you . . . Mrs. Allan, is it? I'll cover the desk. We want to cooperate fully with you people."

"Thanks so much, Beth, but I'm not a part of Interpol. I'm just enjoying a short vacation with my husband and letting my arm heal. I know they appreciate your help."

I gave her a wide smile and hurried Eric up the stairs to find Bart sitting in the middle of the hall, his back against the wall, talking on his radio.

Eric anxiously opened each door, watched Bart do a cursory examination of each room, then locked the empty rooms again, shaking his head, puzzled.

"Thanks, Eric. Tell Beth we appreciate her help—and yours," I said, walking him to the top of the stairs and subtly encouraging him to leave us.

"Okay, Sherlock. What's the smirk for?" I asked Bart as Eric descended the stairs.

"I decided a little 'breaking and entering' was in order. If these rooms had an outside entry, our telephoner could be long gone by the time you got back here."

"So you'd already been inside when I finally finagled keys?" I laughed. "Did you catch the assistant manager's explanation of the telephone calls?"

"No. Enlighten me."

"It's a short in the system—only in our room—and it happens 'occasionally.' And this is the first time in the six months Eric's been here that it's happened on his shift. Also, room 109 is usually the last room they let, for whatever reason. Eric didn't know why, but his instructions were to always fill everything else up first. Could be that malfunctioning heating-cooling system, I guess."

"A tidy bit of information gathering, Watson. I may keep you around," Bart said, wrapping his arms around me, kissing me, and then quickly turning me toward the stairs. "Now, let's go see what Margaret found that's keeping her out so long. I thought she'd be back before now."

We hurried downstairs, checking out the main house. Not finding her, we reluctantly left the warm, inviting fire blazing in the fireplace and hurried into the dark, chilly New Mexico night.

"How on earth are you going to secure this whole place?" I asked on the way. "There's just too much area to keep an eye on all the time."

"That's what Lionel's here for; he's our expert on protective measures. With Xavier and Dom's help, I expect a snake couldn't slither across that line without their knowledge."

"But how?" I persisted.

"Laser beams connected to a main monitor system linked to a small satellite that immediately shows penetration anywhere on the perimeter. We get a clear picture of man, beast, or rabbit. The satellite charts their whereabouts every second until we can reach them."

"What if there's more than one entry?" I asked. "What if they come from all sides at once?"

"You never run out of questions, do you, Princess?" Bart laughed as we finished prowling the back of the main house and headed for the swimming pool and tennis courts.

"Just curious. If someone knows your system, they've probably already figured out how to beat it."

"It's new—never been used before. Lionel and Dominic designed and tested it, and no one had seen it until I watched the final tests. I was impressed with its accuracy, and its ability to not only identify intruders, but contain them."

"It stops them, too? How?"

"They'll have it all set up tomorrow. I'll let you watch a demonstration."

The pool area was deserted, as were the tennis courts. "Where could she have gone?" I asked Bart, shivering with cold. "It's too chilly to spend much time out here unless you have an awfully good reason."

Bart called Mom on his radio. There was no answer.

"Let's check the stables," he said, wrapping an arm around my shoulder. "She may have gone back there."

"Why isn't she answering her radio? She has it on her, doesn't she?"

"Yes, she did," Bart said quietly. He was uneasy.

We hurried back to the stables. She wasn't there.

"I'm worried, Bart. Where is she?"

"Let's try the main house again. She may have gone one way while we were going the other, and we just missed her."

"But why isn't she answering her beeper?" I persisted.

This stretch of dirt road was unlit and uneven, with dark trees hugging the road edge and reaching ominously over our heads. *Perfect place for an ambush.* I shook the thought off quickly.

Suddenly I stepped on something and stumbled, saved from falling only because I'd had my arm looped through Bart's.

I stooped to pick up what crunched under my feet. It felt like . . . a radio.

"Bart, is this what I think it is?" I handed it to him, and held my breath waiting for his answer.

"Feels like it, but I can't tell for sure. Let's get it where we can see it."

We hurried toward the nearest light—over the arbor leading to the Ranch house.

A voice came quietly from the shadows. "What are you two doing out here in the cold?"

"Mom! You scared me to death. I didn't see you standing there."

"You weren't supposed to."

"Where have you been?" I asked, hugging her with relief. "We were frantic. You didn't answer your radio."

She stepped out of the shadow and began searching her pockets. "It's gone."

"Is this it?" Bart handed the cracked one to Mom.

"I think so," she said, holding it up to the light. "How did you get it?"

"I stumbled on it in the middle of the road."

"It must have fallen out of my pocket when I tripped over the dog, or coyote, or whatever it was that ran in front of me in the dark."

"Are you okay? And what are you doing out here in the cold?" I asked.

"Observing the comings and goings from the main house."

"Anyone leave in the last fifteen or twenty minutes?" Bart asked.

"Our waitress, Maria, ran from the house crying, got in her car and left."

"I'll bet that nasty Jaqueez had something to do with that," I said.

Mom lifted her radio to her ear, nodded to Bart who listened on his own, then she spoke quietly into hers.

"Good," Bart said when they'd finished their three-way conversation. "That gives us one up on them."

"For tonight, anyway," Mom agreed. "And it may slow them down a little."

"Would somebody like to enlighten me? What happened? Was that Dad?"

"They confiscated the arms and ammo, leaving the empty crates behind," Mom explained. "Lionel set up a monitor to alert us when they return. Maybe we can catch them coming back for the rest of the stuff."

"Any possibility I could have a radio? It might be nice if I could keep up on these little things, too."

"You definitely will have one—so I can keep up with you," Bart said.

At that moment, Sky and Else joined us. Else's blonde hair was hidden by a hood on her heavy sweatshirt. Sky, taller than I'd estimated when I saw him seated in the dining room, matched Else's nearly six-foot height.

"We've just checked out the Pueblo Encantados where our main celebrities will be staying. No particular security problems. Fairly straightforward, especially with the system Xavier and Lionel have worked out."

"Sky, you haven't met my wife, Allison. Princess, Dr. Rip Schyler, our behavioral specialist. He and Else are in charge of our celebrities. Sky, I'll warn you right now, Allison asks more questions at one time than most people ask in a lifetime."

"Never ask, never learn," Sky said, reaching to shake my hand.

"That's exactly what I told Bart!" I said in astonishment.

"Then it must be true." The gray-haired man laughed. "It's definitely a sign of an inquiring mind, which is a sign of intelligence, which is a sign of an interested, and interesting, personality. And I understand you speak more languages than the rest of the team combined."

"A few," I laughed. "I can converse with all of you in your native tongues."

"Let's go inside and wait for the rest of the group. They're on their way back now," Mom said.

"Did you see anything besides Maria?" I asked Mom when we were settled cozily around the fire.

"Just a guest all decked out in evening clothes, enjoying the garden. The stable was empty except for the horses. Beautiful horses. Nice stables. Thought maybe our friend on the horse would come back, but he didn't. What have you two been doing?" Mom asked.

Bart reported his activities, including the ringing telephone and search of the rooms upstairs.

"A short in the system causing the phone to ring?" Else asked. "Unlikely—but not entirely impossible. I'll check it and replace your phone. We need no kinks in our system."

When Mom asked what I'd found out, I gave a brief account of Maria's travails with Jaqueez. "He looked attractive and unscrupulous enough to take any woman he wanted. The type who keeps things hot for every female around, making life miserable for those who don't fall for him, and probably more miserable for those who do."

Dad walked in, followed by a lithe young man with a tousle of blond hair, and stopped in the center of the room with his hands on his hips. "What kind of help have I hired here? Lazing around the fire while the rest of us are working our buns off in the cold."

"We're working smart—the gray matter." Mom patted a spot next to her on the loveseat and Dad joined her, giving her cheek a peck as he settled in.

"Lionel Brandt, my daughter, Allison Allan," Dad said by way of introduction. "Lionel is our expert on protective measures. He's the mastermind behind the perimeter system we're using here."

Lionel was the Frenchman in the group. He was muscular, with the easy, graceful movements of a prowling lion, and energy radiating from every pore. Inherent strength glowed in his bronzed face.

Our FBI friend from San Francisco, Oswald Barlow, and a young man, who I guessed by his cocky but graceful swagger to be Dominic Vicente, joined us by the fire.

Oz brushed the ever-present shock of sandy hair from his forehead and winked a mischievous gray eye at me. He couldn't weigh more than 145 pounds after Thanksgiving dinner, but his small, wiry frame suggested a spry agility that bigger men might envy.

Dominic Vicente's dark brown eyes exuded an imperious confidence as he brandished an imaginary sword in the air, bowed in front of me, presenting the sword as they do preceding a bullfight, then swerved across the room like a bullfighter dodging an attacking bull.

"David and Xavier are watching things," Oz said in answer to Dad's raised eyebrow. "Hi, Allison. Glad to see you're out of the big cast. Is the arm mending well?"

"Yes. How about your wounds?"

"They only hurt when I laugh," Oz replied, his boyish grin lighting his face.

The group groaned.

"Okay, okay. It was trite." He held up his hands. "The lady addles my brains. Remind me to tell you sometime how she fingered all the players in the biggest diamond heist in history while the rest of us were still floundering in the dark."

My face flushed hot, and I felt it turning a bright shade of embarrassed red. Bart's arm tightened around my shoulder.

"And she came out barely alive, with a badly broken arm." Bart's tone was curt and conclusive. "Allison is out of the action arena. She's our eyes and ears here on the Ranch, nothing more."

The quiet in the room was broken only by the crackling of the fire. Bart quickly added, with affection in his voice, "And there aren't prettier or more inquisitive eyes and ears anywhere. I want to keep them intact."

"We'll do our best," Mom laughed. "But you know Allison. I think everyone knows my daughter but Dominic." She did belated, unnecessary introductions. I'd guessed right. Dominic Vicente was true to his name origins.

"And I'm David Chen."

I whirled at the voice behind me. Piercing dark eyes met mine as the Chinese agent moved silently into the room from the French doors. A black turtleneck hugged his slight frame. He stood stiffly erect, about five feet ten inches tall, with black, short-cropped hair and long, slender fingers that he chapeled in front of him.

Dad jumped to his feet. "What's wrong ?" he demanded.

Chapter Six

"Xavier's minding the store and everything's quiet," David assured Dad, "but we thought you should know . . . we have a weak spot in the perimeter defense."

Dad started toward him. "Where?"

"That good-sized hill at the back of the Ranch property must be made of solid granite. We're going to have to increase the security there. I came back to pick up an additional laser link. It's close enough to the road to warrant its own connection."

Dominic and Lionel were on their feet and heading for the door before Dad said a word. David gave me a quick smile and a nod, which I acknowledged with a wave of my hand before he followed Lionel and Dominic into the darkness.

Else stood. "It's getting late, and I haven't unpacked yet. I'll see you all in the morning. Sleep well." Her radiant smile shone briefly on each of us before she moved gracefully toward the front entry.

"Where's everyone staying? Are we the only ones here in the Ranch house?" I asked.

"We had some portable buildings moved in," Mom explained. "All the guys are bunking there to monitor the equipment. Else is staying in a cottage so she can keep her eye on the guests in that area."

"I don't know about anyone else here, but I've had enough for one day. No thanks to persons who will remain unnamed," Bart stared pointedly at my folks, "my nap this afternoon was interrupted." Then he looked at me. "Are you ready for bed, or is your boundless energy going to keep you up for a while?"

"Whither thou goest," I answered, unwinding from the snug comfort of the overstuffed loveseat. As we said good night and left the room, Sky, Oz, Mom and Dad put their heads together in a quiet conference.

Our room seemed more chilly than ever after being near the warmth of the fire. As I closed the French doors, Bart watched me from bed with an amused expression on his face. "What if I get up in the middle of the night and walk into those glass doors?" he asked.

"You'll just have to remember they're there. Can't you feel how much warmer it is in here already since I closed them?"

"You're supposed to rely on me to keep that body warm. That's my job. Get over here and let me demonstrate."

I snuggled down next to my husband, and he warmed me all the way through.

* * * * * *

After a quick but utterly delicious breakfast in the dining room, we embarked for Los Alamos. Frost glistened on golden foxtails in the early morning sun as we left the Ranch and headed toward the highway on the paved secondary road. I squinted into the bright sun, then turned quickly to look behind us.

"Bart, did you see him?"

"Who?"

"The man in the tuxedo. At least I thought I saw him. The sun was in my eyes, but I could swear we passed a man in a tux walking toward Rancho Encantado. When I turned around to make sure, there was no one there."

"Must have been your imagination. I didn't see anyone."

I looked back again at the empty road, cold chills sweeping down my arms. Had I been imagining it? Or were the eerie mysteries of the Southwest at work already today?

"What are we doing in Los Alamos?" I asked as we left the secondary road from Rancho Encantado and turned north on U.S. Highway 84-285. "That's where they developed the atom bomb. What's going on there now? It's never in the news."

"We're picking up a secret weapon, and they probably don't like publicity."

"Secret weapon?"

"Right," Bart said without elaborating.

"What kind? What's your connection to Los Alamos?"

"A college buddy got his doctorate at UCLA, then went to work for Los Alamos National Laboratory. Today the University of California operates it for the Department of Defense. In his spare time, Jared tinkers with specialized toys for us, sort of like 'Q' in James Bond. He called a couple of weeks ago and said he had a new one for me, but I'd have to come and get it."

"What is it?" I asked.

"He wouldn't say over the phone. But he's come up with some pretty ingenious devices in the past, so Jack decided it was worth the trip over."

"Why was Dad going to send Else?"

"So she could get checked out on it. Her specialty is self-defense and personal protection. She's an interesting lady, connected to a royal family in Europe . . . saw relatives assassinated when she was a child."

"How awful. Was she in danger, too?"

"Apparently they were only after the Duke and Duchess. The sad part is if their security had been on the ball, it could have been prevented. Else vowed that wouldn't happen to anyone else in their situation if she could help it. When she was sixteen, she approached Interpol and begged to work for them, telling them what she had in mind. They bought it as mutually beneficial, and she's been with the Company ever since."

"What did she do?"

"Interpol had her trained with a specialty in personal protection, a glorified bodyguard. She could move in royal circles where she rightfully belonged, but with a purpose."

"To protect her relatives."

"Exactly. She was privy to possible dangers through her contacts in Interpol, and passed back to the Company information gleaned from the international jet set she was protecting."

"And because of her heritage," I conjectured, "she fit in so well that no outsider would guess she was guarding someone; and unless she was on duty, she was a normal part of the coterie."

"You're a swift study, Princess." Bart pulled my hand to his lips and kissed it.

"You're pretty quick yourself," I laughed. "I noticed you wasted no time at all in slipping me into this trip in place of the lovely Else."

"Selfishness and self-preservation. I want time with you all to myself, and I didn't need your green eyes sparking with jealousy."

"Me? Jealous?" I said mockingly.

As we crossed the Rio Grande River, a huge black mesa loomed prominently behind it, a dark, brooding landmark in the middle of the flat valley floor. Just beyond was a sign directing Route 30 traffic. North to Española and Puye Cliffs. East to Los Alamos.

"Bart, do we have time for a little side trip? The Puye Cliffs aren't far. They were the dwellings of the ancient Anasazi Indians. Could we sidetrack for an hour or so?" I pleaded.

Bart glanced at his watch. "How about on the way back? I don't want to keep Jared waiting."

"Sounds good. I love to see everything when I go to a new area. Speaking of seeing, look at that view behind us." We'd passed the wide six-lane highway, and had been climbing steadily on a steep, narrow, winding road, high above the piñon- and pine-covered valley floor.

I kept waiting for just the right moment to tell Bart about my discovery in New York since I'd seen him last—about the experiences I'd had, the spiritual enlightenment I'd received, things I'd learned that were already dear and sacred to his heart. But I didn't want to approach it in casual conversation. I wanted the perfect moment— the perfect time and place and ambience to share what I knew my husband had been waiting to hear.

Suddenly Bart stomped on the accelerator. "Make sure your seat belt's tight and hang on to your hat, Princess. I'm afraid we've got company coming."

Looking over my shoulder as I checked my seat belt, I saw a white van closing the distance between us with incredible speed for an uphill climb.

"Where'd they come from?"

"Out of nowhere," Bart said as he whisked around a dangerous curve at double the posted speed. "I've been watching for them. I didn't see anyone following us; they must have kept tabs on us with binoculars so they could stay out of sight."

"Bart, they're catching up!"

"They've got lots more power in that souped-up van than we do in this little convertible."

"What can we do?"

"Not outrun them, for sure. Watch for a turnout, a wide spot, a road intersecting, anything that will give me some maneuvering room."

I watched, clinging to my seat as Bart navigated the tight, twisting turns. Stretches of the road had no guardrail, just a straight drop down the rocky cliff to the valley below.

That's probably what they had in mind. Sending us over the edge.

"There's a sign," I pointed, my pulse quickening. "Scenic over-look ahead."

"Let's hope this works," Bart muttered, glancing in the rearview mirror. I turned around. The van was on our bumper. The driver's pockmarked face was as clearly visible as the automatic weapon in the hands of the passenger.

"They're so close I can almost tell you the color of their eyes!"

"Hope you got a good look, Princess, so you can identify them. Now turn around and hang on. Here we are."

The van made its move at the same moment, accelerating with a burst of speed that brought them alongside us. The passenger's window was down, and the gunman swung the barrel of the gun out of the open window.

With the convertible top down, we were sitting ducks.

As the terrorist pointed his weapon and pulled the trigger, Bart slammed on the brakes. The van flew past us, a deafening burst of gunfire kicking up dirt and rock chips just in front of our car.

Bart skidded into a tight turn, spewing a cloud of dirt and rocks that covered us as we headed back the way we'd just come. The screech of the van's brakes was audible even as we sped down the mountain away from them.

"Mario, your driving gets better and better. Actually, that was more James Bond than Indianapolis. But brilliant. Now what?" I asked, finally able to breathe again.

"Now we need a spot, fast, that we can maneuver in and wait for them to come after us. Since we can't outrun 'em, we'll have to outsmart 'em."

I kept watch for just such a spot, but Bart flew past each one faster than I could see them coming. Finally, as he slowed for a sharp curve, I spotted a break in the rocks. In the spring, it was probably a waterfall. Now it was the perfect spot to back the small convertible into so we were hidden by the curve in the road.

"Watch for traffic. We'll need a clear road in both directions," he said.

Bart had barely maneuvered the little blue car off the road into position, in gear, with motor running, when the white van roared past. They flew right on by us.

"Traffic?" Bart asked.

"A big truck immediately on the right, with a string of cars behind."

Bart glanced to the right out my window, made a split-second decision, and spun into the road in front of the approaching truck. He tromped on the accelerator, narrowly missing the truck's giant silver grill.

A car coming down the hill careened around the blind curve to the left at that moment, barely missing our rear fender.

I sank back in my seat, spent, unable to speak. There must be an easier lifestyle than this. Something more safe and sane and reasonable, where somebody wasn't trying to kill you every time you left your bedroom.

The white van was nowhere in sight. Either they'd missed seeing us or were stuck somewhere on the road down the hill behind a stream of traffic.

I looked at Bart. He seemed totally unfazed by the whole episode.

"You're not even white-knuckled. Doesn't anything unnerve you?"

"That was manageable. I save the stress for the really tight situations. You handled it well—no screams, no hysterics. But, that's what I'd expect of you." He reached for my hand and squeezed it affectionately.

I didn't bother to tell him I was so scared I couldn't breathe, much less scream.

Minutes later we passed the old square stone-and-cement guard towers that marked the entrance to the original Los Alamos area.

It was like being on a 1940s movie set. Tall water towers on spindly legs; long, low buildings punctuated by high chimneys; four- and five-story factory-like structures, all made from the same adobe-colored brick, and all behind barbed-wire fences.

"Not very picturesque," I noted. "Actually, it's depressing. Such a drab, dismal town in the midst of this spectacular scenery. Surely they could have done better."

"Remember when this was built—and by whom," Bart reminded me. "The government wasn't into aesthetics in the middle of World War II. Now, *that's* the kind of tourist attraction I like to visit." Bart pointed to the Bradbury Science Museum, which was advertising exhibits on geothermal and nuclear energy and physics.

"There's another good one," he said, indicating the Los Alamos Historical Museum with displays on the Manhattan Project.

"I'll wander through with you, if you'll take me to the cliff dwellings."

"It's a bargain, but later. Here's where we're supposed to meet Jared."

Bart pulled off the street into the parking lot facing a lovely small lake with a fountain in the middle. The lake was surrounded by green lawn, beautiful trees, and well-shaped shrubs. Across the lake a white monument gleamed in the sun on the lawn of a long, low, modern, official-looking building. Old Glory waved in the cool morning breeze.

"Modern Los Alamos is definitely an improvement on historical Los Alamos," I said as Bart parked next to a large navy blue van with a Los Alamos National Laboratory logo.

"And the best is yet to come," Bart said, opening his door to greet a dark-haired young man who climbed from the van as soon as we drove up.

Jared was a surprise. He had the high cheekbones of a Native American, spoke with the hint of an Hispanic accent, and had light blue eyes.

"Allison. It's good to finally meet you. I've been hearing about you for years." Jared brushed aside the hand I extended, wrapped me in a bear hug and kissed my cheek. "And I brought a wedding present for you."

"For me?" I asked, regaining my breath and presence of mind.

"I've been involved in a project for some time, and when I saw the report of your explosive wedding on TV, I decided Bart needed help. So I adapted my project and came up with this."

He took my hand, led me to the rear of the van, and opened the back doors.

Chapter Seven

In the middle of the floor of the van, covered by an old wool army blanket, a three-foot square hump filled the cargo space. Jared pulled off the blanket, exposing a battered silver safe.

"Pardon the dramatics, but I've had the van broken into a couple of times, so I had the safe bolted to the floor. It's the only way I can get my personal projects to and from the lab without worrying constantly about some punk carting off months or years of work." He bent to spin the dial and open the safe.

"I assume its purpose is to help me protect Allison," Bart said, "but it's going to have to be your best effort ever. My wife has a propensity for plunging into hot spots that keeps me absolutely hopping."

Jared turned and laughed. "Are you referring solely to the volcano, or is there more?"

Bart rolled his eyes. "More. Much more."

"Cool it, you two," I retorted. "You both know I'd lead a very boring life if Bart didn't have all these low-life associations that keep trying to eradicate him. My objective is to keep out of their way, and stay alive."

"I hope this will help you accomplish that, and give Bart a little peace of mind." Jared brought forth a bundle wrapped in what had once been a shirt, but was now minus collar and sleeves. He sat on the edge of the van, spread the faded blue shirt on the van floor beside him, and opened the bundle.

Two gold watches glittered in the morning sun. Jared picked up the smaller one and held it out to me. "This should help you keep tabs on each other." He handed Bart the larger watch. "What do you think?"

It looked like a very ordinary watch. I turned it over. Nothing especially unique about it. Simple, but attractive.

Jared's blue eyes gleamed with pride. "Just an ordinary watch, you're thinking. How about this?"

He pinched the sides of the watch together and the face popped up, revealing a tiny TV screen. "This operates on the same principle as the Vehicle Navigation Device available on several cars now. It links with the Global Positioning System which beams off a satellite to tell you where you are—the exact geographical location. If one of you is out of communication with the other, you can request the location of the watch-mate and the computer chip will connect to the satellite and print the location on the screen."

"Ingenious," Bart said.

"That's not all," Jared continued. "Press the first link in the watch-band on top of the watch, and it turns into a transmitting TV screen. You can talk to each other, see each other, and view something the other is seeing. Whatever the screen sees will transmit to the other watch. Allison can show you that atrocious tie before she buys it for you."

"Or make sure no ravishing beauty is making overtures to my husband."

"That, too," Jared laughed. "Bart, I did a lock-out feature so you'll have to have a code to get in. You two can decide what it will be and program them. I know you don't need these falling into someone else's hands and having them used against you. Here's a couple of other little features you might get a kick out of. Definitely an improvement over the Dick Tracy watches I gave you before."

"You made the radio-watches we used at the estate?" I asked.

"Right." Jared walked us through the operation of the watches. "Any questions?"

"You don't happen to have another few of these lying around, do you?" Bart asked. "We could use a dozen or so."

"Sorry. I can probably have some more for you in a couple of weeks, though."

"That'll be a little late for this job, but we can always use them for the next one. What's the tab on these?" Bart asked.

"Apply it to my account," Jared said, turning to close the safe.

"Your account was paid in full a long time ago, Jared. You know that. You don't owe me a thing. These cost you a lot of time and effort, if not materials. Your time's valuable and expensive. What do I owe you?" Bart persisted.

"Lunch—and time to get to know this exquisite creature you somehow managed to make your wife." Jared slammed the doors on the van and faced us with a smile. "And I'll make it the most expensive place I can think of."

"Granted, but not today. And I'll even throw in tickets to the Three Tenors' benefit concert and the gala that goes with it. Are you still too busy to date, or has someone finally broken through that tough exterior and shown you how the other half of the world lives?"

"Actually, I have discovered there's more to life than research labs. I'll accept two tickets; and make that dinner for four. Just let me know when and where, and we'll be there."

Jared took my hand and leaned toward my ear. "Allison, you're a lucky woman. Bart's so in love with you, he never notices the gorgeous women who throw themselves at him. Take good care of him." He kissed my cheek, then turned to Bart.

Bart took Jared's hand. They stood quietly for a moment, then threw their arms around each other in a brotherly hug.

"Watch your back, Allan. That's your soft spot."

"That's my job," I said. "To protect him from all those bad guys who try to run him off mountain roads and keep taking potshots at him."

Jared raised an eyebrow, but Bart gave him a gentle shove toward the door. "Get back to work before they find out they can do without your inventive mind and I have to put you to work for me. We'll be in touch."

"Thanks for the wedding present, Jared," I said.

Bart opened the door for me as Jared backed out of his parking spot and waved good-bye.

"I sense a very interesting story behind your relationship. Do I get to hear it?" I asked as we pulled out of the parking lot and headed back to Santa Fe.

"I met Jared at UC Santa Barbara my first year of college. We surfed together when class was boring and studied together when class was hard. He had a wipeout one day, got hit in the head with his board, and I pulled him in."

"And he feels he owes his life to you."

"Yes. We've stayed good friends through the years," Bart said. "He's an electronics genius—can visualize a gadget, then devise a way to make it work."

Bart spent the next several miles extolling Jared's virtues, while I kept my eye out for the white van. It was nowhere in sight.

"Suppose it's safe to play tourist?" I asked. "The lethal white van seems to have lost interest in us for the time being."

"Anything to keep you happy, Princess. Probably the last thing they'd expect us to do is go sight-seeing. I think our boss will forgive us for taking an extra hour, especially since he is your doting father."

We followed Highway 30 north a few miles beyond the turnoff to Santa Fe, then turned onto a narrow two-lane road that climbed through rolling piñon-covered hills into a canyon to the Puye Cliff Dwellings. As the rocky cliffs became visible over the treetops, holes in the cliff face stood out black against the ochre-colored background.

We paid five dollars per person entrance fee to a bulky, plaid-shirted man with a coal-black braid extending down his back from under his battered felt hat. No park rangers here. The area was managed by the Santa Clara Pueblo.

There were already three other cars in the parking lot, but their owners were out of sight, possibly already on top of the mesa.

The bright orange brochure warned that the altitude was sixty-nine hundred feet above sea level. When we climbed the steep trail to the top of the mesa, we would be at over seven thousand feet, and would need to stop and rest often in the thin air.

The first surprise was an old stone Harvey House, one of a string of stagecoach stops Fred Harvey had populated with neat, proper single girls from back east to serve hungry, dusty travelers. Directly behind the Harvey House, the trail to the Puye Cliff Dwellings began, and around its first curve, a smiling round face was carved into the rock with three long spikes protruding from its head.

"Do you suppose that's the ancient Anasazi counterpart of today's happy face?" I asked.

"Or a message proclaiming this is a good subdivision," Bart countered.

The winding trail ascended toward the remains of masonry dwellings built against the face of the cliffs. Made of stone quarried from the cliffs, they blended perfectly, almost disappearing in their surroundings.

Poles spaced three feet apart extended from the masonry. Holes dotted cliffs where similar poles once jutted from dwellings that were now crumbled piles of stone. A long pole ladder leaned against the sheer stone cliffs, the only apparent way of getting to the second level of cliff dwellings. Climbing that would be tricky with my cast on.

Far above, a family emerged from one of the *cavates*, or cave-like rooms. Apparently the two children with them had climbed the ladder. If they could do it, I guessed I could manage.

We explored the rooms at sites three and four, trying to decipher some of the petroglyphs high above on the cliff. The view was incredible, stretching across the width of the valley to the Sangre de Cristo mountains thirty miles to the east.

Suddenly Bart shoved me into the nearest *cavate* and ducked in behind me. "There's a white van coming up the road." He positioned himself out of sight, but where he could see the winding road that approached the cliff dwellings.

"*The* white van?" I asked, searching for a means of escape.

"Too early to tell yet."

"If it is?" I already knew the answer.

"We're sitting ducks."

"Can we get down before they get here—while they're on that stretch of road where the cliffs are hidden by the trees?"

"Possibly."

When Bart's answers were short, curt, and to the point, he was thinking. I curtailed the questions and surveyed the adjoining rooms carved into bedrock, looking for a way out. Some rooms were no bigger than a small linen closet, the walls smooth and almost white. Others were large enough to hold a family and had soot-darkened ceilings and walls, blackened by fires for cooking or comfort or light.

"It's them. They must have waited for us to head back to Santa Fe, then followed us here."

"How come they stayed so far behind?" I asked. "They could have lost us."

"They probably didn't expect us to become tourists today. When we didn't come back out on this road, they came to find us."

"And my curiosity has us trapped."

"Maybe not. We'll try your idea as soon as they're below us behind the trees. If they don't know just where we are, maybe we can make it back to the car . . ."

"You know as well as I do they'll either disable the car or leave someone waiting there for us to come back. Don't try to coddle me, Bart."

"Sorry, Princess. Habit. When I'm not working with an agent, I slip into my 'save-the-damsel-in-distress' mode. Uh-oh!"

"What's the matter?"

"They just stopped on the road and let out a guy with a rifle and scope, and there's one with glasses joining him."

"Glasses?"

"Binoculars." Bart turned to me as he stripped off his turquoise windbreaker. "Take off your jacket. Your white shirt won't be quite as noticeable as that bright blue against these rocks. We've got to move before they drive to the top of the mesa, or we'll be pinned from above and below."

I tossed my jacket into the corner and moved close to Bart as he watched the pair make their way through the thick undergrowth. His warm male scent was inviting. "Anything else you'd like me to take off?" I asked as I slipped my arms around his waist.

"Anything that'll make you less visible, and don't entice me right now. If I get my mind on that irresistible body, I could get us killed. Let's move!"

We slipped out of the cave and crouched behind bushes that lined the outside of the trail.

"There must be another way down to the lower level," Bart said. "We can't use the ladder. They'll be watching that."

"The brochure says there are a dozen stairways linking the levels—stepping places carved out of the cliffs. Some have finger grips. All we have to do is find them."

"Then get those sharp eyes busy and find us some. We've only got a few minutes to get down from here."

"Where are they now?" I asked over my shoulder as I investigated several possibilities.

"The van's at the entrance. The driver's talking to the guy collecting the entrance fee. The two on foot are out of sight."

I scanned the rocks, pockmarked with holes. But which actually led somewhere, and which were simply caused by erosion?

I crawled on one hand and knees, keeping behind the bushes, to a point down the trail where I could see a crevice that looked promising. Going up the cliff, there were some faintly defined toe and handholds. But I couldn't see down the cliff. I peered through the bushes, trying to spot the approaching men. I couldn't see them, either. "Where are they now?" I asked.

"The van's still at the entrance. The two just emerged from the trees. They have a ravine to cross, then they'll be at the foot of the cliffs."

"When it's clear, follow me and pray I've found a way down, other than falling, which I may do, trying to do this one-handed."

Bart paused while the pair stopped at the top of the ravine to scan the cliffs with the binoculars. He motioned for me to lie flat. I did, and came nose-to-nose with a lizard. Black eyes darted back and forth. Its long, split tongue flicked in and out of his mouth. It stood its ground only long enough for me to move my cast to a more comfortable position. Then it flew over the edge of the cliff, its sharp, spiny claws clinging to the rocks.

I could use some of those natural climbing tools right now.

Bart scurried on hands and knees to join me. "Where is it?" he asked, peering over the side of the hundred-foot cliff.

"I think it's there, where the crevice is. It goes almost to the bottom. If I put my back on one side and my feet on the other, aren't those hand and toeholds down one side?"

I started over the edge to try it, but Bart pulled me back and slipped over the side of the cliff. "Only one way to find out, and I'll go first in case you don't have enough working hands to make it."

Just then the white van pulled into sight.

"Down!" Bart commanded. He squeezed into the crevice as far as he'd fit and froze. I flattened on the trail.

The van cruised along the narrow road, the driver searching the cliffs as he headed for the top of the mesa. Suddenly the van screeched to a stop in the middle of the road, and the driver jumped out with a rifle in his hands. I pressed against the rocks, hoping to make as small a target as possible.

The man brought the rifle slowly to his shoulder, sighted carefully with his scope, and fired.

Chapter Eight

The shot never came close. He was shooting at the family on the cliffs above us.

Before I could react, a child's excited cry echoed across the canyon. The man jerked the gun down. Even from the distance, I could see his mouth drop open. He jumped back in the van and sped up the winding road toward the top of the mesa.

"Come on, Princess. Let's vanish." Bart started down the crevice, his long, lean body barely fitting in the narrow space between the rocks.

"What if he hit someone up there? Those were innocent people he was shooting at," I said anxiously.

"That wasn't a hurt cry. The kids must have been out of sight. He probably thought he was shooting at us till the kids showed up. Follow me. You were right about the hand and toeholds."

I lowered myself over the edge and pressed my back against the smooth rock face of the crevice. The holes weren't very big, but they were evenly spaced so they were easy to find.

But you really needed two hands. I only had one since my cast extended to my fingertips. I limped along, sort of humping down from one set of holes to the next as best I could.

Bart was down. I was halfway. The men were at the bottom of the ravine. We only had a couple of minutes while they climbed the steep side to the top, and they'd be able to see us.

"Hurry, Princess," Bart urged, watching the progress of our stalkers.

"I can't."

"Then jump," Bart said.

"Right. Fifty feet." I tried sliding the length of my good arm, establishing a toehold while I located a low handhold, and sliding again. It was still too slow.

"Jump," Bart urged again. "I'll catch you."

"And if you don't?"

I slid too far, missed the foothold, and dangled by one hand, searching with my foot for the hole in the rock to support my weight.

"You'll have casts on both legs to match the one on your arm. But I won't let you fall. Alli, *now!* They're just about out of the ravine. Jump!"

It was still twenty feet to the bottom—too far to jump. But by the time I got to the ground this way, our pursuers would be on top of us. I said a quick prayer, turned to face the opening, crouched, braced with one hand and one toe, and jumped into empty space.

Bart caught me, and my cast caught him—right above his ear. He staggered, slumped to one knee, and started to pitch forward, face first into the dirt. I braced my body against him and grabbed his arm, jerking him to his feet. He shook his head, trying to clear it.

"Don't pass out on me," I whispered, pulling him behind a rock. "Just stay on your feet till we get to the car."

Bart was hurt—how bad I couldn't tell, but he was on the verge of slipping into unconsciousness. I wasn't sure what was keeping him upright.

We weren't that far from the parking lot. *If* they hadn't left someone there waiting for us. *If* they hadn't disabled the car. *If* I could get Bart there . . .

I looped his arm over one shoulder, put my other shoulder in his armpit, and started moving, keeping behind rocks, bushes, and trees as much as possible. I didn't have time to look back. Bart was barely conscious. His feet dragged along the rocks, stumbling, staggering, almost pulling me down each time he tripped. He was heavy, nearly limp, scarcely able to keep his feet moving.

Suddenly his head drooped to his chest. He sank to his knees, and I bent with his weight. "Bart, I can't support you. Stay with me. Help me get you to the car."

I managed to get him back on his feet, and we stumbled forward again to the trees at the edge of the parking lot, pausing before crossing the open space, making sure no one was waiting for us.

We made it to the car. I leaned him against the door, dug in his pocket for the keys, and eased him into the passenger seat, made easier since we'd left the top down on the convertible.

I jumped behind the wheel and was backing out of the parking space when the two men burst out of the trees, running toward the parking area. I jammed the accelerator to the floor.

"Buckle your seat belt, Bart."

No answer. I glanced at him. His head lolled to one side of the headrest, a dark red stain dripping down the white-blond hair behind his ear and into his shirt collar. "Father, please send guardian angels to watch over him until I can get us out of here and to a hospital," I prayed, watching in the rearview mirror as the man with the rifle stopped running and aimed at the car.

A bullet shattered the rearview mirror, sending glass shards everywhere. With the convertible top down, there was no protective framework around us. We were as vulnerable as you get. Jerking the wheel erratically from one side of the narrow little lane to the other, hoping to be less of a target, I barely missed a sign declaring a five-mile-per-hour speed limit. I hoped, as the speedometer climbed over forty, that the man at the entrance wouldn't try to stop me.

He didn't.

I raced past the entry shack and turned the first corner. We were temporarily out of the line of fire.

A glimpse of Bart's white face spurred me to tromp even harder on the accelerator. Where was the nearest hospital? Los Alamos? Santa Fe? Or did Española have an emergency room?

Española would be closest. I tried to picture the map I'd studied earlier, tried to remember location and distances. Seven or eight miles back to the highway, then another few to Española. Too long.

I shook Bart's arm. "Wake up. Please, wake up."

There were too many loops and blind curves here; I didn't dare take my eyes off the road or stop to help Bart. I knew our pursuers would be right behind us. But what if he lapsed into a coma because of a concussion when I should have kept him awake?

"Bart. Wake up." I grabbed his shoulder and shook him again gently, trying to keep the car on the pavement and still watch for any sign of consciousness.

Nothing.

I was suddenly sick to my stomach. *What if I killed my husband?* "Don't you dare die on me," I pleaded. "I couldn't live with myself, knowing it was my fault. And I don't want to have to live without you."

Pursuers or not, I looked for a wide spot in the road where I could pull off. Finally, I spotted a narrow dirt road leading off into the hills and spun off the pavement, stirring up a cloud of dust that blew back in my face as we stopped.

I felt for a pulse. There was one—weak, slow, but there. I lifted one of his eyelids. Bart's azure blue eye was dark, the pupil dilated. If I remembered my first-aid training, that was one sign of a concussion.

"Wake up!" I shook him again. What on earth had I done to this man I loved so dearly?

"Bart, can you hear me? Oh, Father, please let him be all right. Please," I begged. "There's so much I have to tell him. He doesn't even know I've taken all the discussions. There's so much yet we have to do, so many things he has to teach me—about the Church—about everything."

Bart moaned. Just a tiny little sound, but it was the most wonderful thing I'd heard all day. I dug his handkerchief from his pocket and pressed it against the wound. It wasn't bleeding a lot, but any was too much.

"Bart, look at me. Open your eyes. You need to fasten your seat belt. I can't do it for you with this cast on."

He was trying. His hand moved to his wound. He rolled his head toward me and groaned with the effort. I leaned over and gave him a quick kiss.

The sound of an engine gearing down on the curves behind us sent me back to my seat, panic-induced adrenaline flooding my system. Pulling back onto the paved road, I jammed the accelerator all the way to the floor. The little blue convertible responded valiantly, but it wouldn't be enough. The van was already too close. Picking up the two stalkers in the parking lot had probably slowed the driver only ten seconds. I'd been stopped longer than that.

"That's the way. Open your eyes. Don't pass out on me again. They're catching up with us." I talked to Bart, a steady stream of nonsense, trying to rouse him, to elicit a reply, to ensure that he wouldn't slip away from me again.

The posted speed limit was thirty-five miles per hour. I was taking the steeply descending curves much faster, but not nearly as fast as I needed to. I could see the white van on the hill behind us.

As we hit Highway 30, the van appeared in the side mirror, closing fast. I whipped around a line of traffic. That bought us a few extra minutes.

Bart was conscious and had buckled his seat belt. When I pointed out our rapidly approaching danger, he drew his gun, then leaned back and rested from the effort that little exertion had taken. He wasn't moving too fast, but at least he was responding coherently, and even thinking now. "Where are we going?" he asked.

"I figured the nearest hospital would be in Española. Outrunning the van will be the problem."

"You can't outrun it," Bart said. "Stomp on it, and I'll think of something—if I can get the cobwebs out of my brain and get past this throbbing headache."

"I'm sorry, Bart. I had no idea when I jumped . . ."

"Forget it, Princess. Not your fault. I'll be fine, as long as we stay out of their gun sights. We need a hiding place, fast."

We both scanned the road ahead as I pressed the little car for all the speed it could give. I glanced at the speedometer. We were going eighty miles an hour on a road that didn't allow more than sixty in most places.

All I needed was to have some farmer pull out in front of me with a piece of slow-moving farm equipment and meet a car coming in the other lane. Then we wouldn't *have* to worry about the van catching us.

Suddenly the Santa Clara Clinic appeared on the left side of the road. But I didn't dare stop.

"There." Bart pointed, wincing as he turned around to check the progress of the van. "Pull into that little farm and drive behind the barn."

The van was out of sight around a curve. After the curve, a dip in the road gave us an additional few seconds before they'd have a clear view of our blue convertible. *It isn't as if we're easy to spot or anything,* I thought ruefully. "Next time we rent a car, remind me we want a plain vanilla car—like every other vehicle on the road. Something not quite so visible," I suggested.

"But you look so great with your hair blowing in the wind," Bart said. Yes, he was feeling better.

I slowed enough to whip off the highway onto the dirt driveway lined with cottonwood trees. It led to a modest pueblo-style house with a small, weathered barn behind it. Corrals made of poles and a couple of lean-to sheds completed the spread.

We drove past an older model Chevy Impala parked by the house, and a battered pickup with the driver's door standing wide open parked by the barn. I maneuvered the blue convertible out of sight behind the barn, but a warm breeze lifted the cloud of dust we kicked up high into the air, a sure giveaway to a speeding vehicle if our pursuers noticed it.

The van roared right on by. We hadn't been seen.

I turned to Bart as soon as the car stopped moving. "How's the head? Besides hurting." I checked the bleeding. It had stopped.

"I'll live. Good job, Princess."

I leaned back against the seat, pressed my hands against my eyes, and let out a long sigh of relief.

"Uh-oh," Bart said softly.

I opened my eyes and stared straight into the barrel of a gun.

Chapter Nine

"What're you doin' behind my barn?"

I stared, speechless, into the icy, hostile, dark eyes of a tall, angular man with a big gun.

"Hiding," Bart said. "Someone's taking potshots at us."

"You can't hide here." The man squinted against the sun, his tanned face hard and unsympathetic.

"We won't stay a minute longer," I said, slipping the idling car into gear. "Thanks so much for your hospitality."

I backed away from the barn, with the man following close behind, his gun still pointed at us. "Sociable soul," I commented to Bart, thinking the old man couldn't hear me.

"You want sociable?" The gun went off, an explosion of noise and dust almost at my elbow. "I was *bein'* sociable. I didn't shoot you when I found you behind my barn. Now git, 'fore I change my mind and blast you for trespassin' on private property."

I accelerated, watching in the side mirror as he raised his gun to his shoulder and sighted.

"Thank you," I called, waving at the dour man. "You're a real misanthropist."

"I'm glad he was so sociable," I said as I put some distance between us. "I'd hate to have caught him in a bad mood when he was feeling decidedly *antisocial.*"

"Just hope he doesn't understand what you called him," Bart smiled. "At least until we're out of range."

The man didn't lower the gun until we were off his property.

"Head back to Santa Fe," Bart directed, watching for the van.

"But the hospital . . ."

"I'm fine. We don't need to run into them coming back to see where they lost us."

That made sense. "How about the clinic we passed? Can we stop there for a minute?" I was worried about Bart. He'd been unconscious several minutes. He needed to be checked by a doctor.

"No time. Get us out of here, fast."

I headed back in the direction from which we'd just come, breaking every speed limit to the junction of Highway 30 and 502. But in the midst of the construction at the crossroads, I missed the turn and ended up on the way back to Los Alamos.

We were forced to backtrack a couple of miles, giving the white van ample time to catch us. And I was sure it was simply a matter of time before it did. Could we possibly be so lucky as to have eluded them completely? No. Once they figured out we weren't in front of them, they'd turn around and be hot on our trail.

Bart checked behind us periodically, then closed his eyes and leaned back against the headrest. We passed Camel Rock and Tesuque Pueblo. "Don't miss the turnoff to Rancho Encantado," he said when he opened his eyes and saw the landmarks.

"There isn't a hospital on the Ranch," I objected.

"I don't need a hospital. The pain's almost gone. An aspirin or two will fix that. There's too much to do to spend the rest of the day sitting in some emergency room waiting for a doctor to tell me to take two aspirin and call him if I have any more problems."

"Bart . . ."

He cut me off. "Princess, if I went to the hospital every time somebody hit me on the head and I bled a little, I'd have spent half my life in waiting rooms and on examining tables. We've got work to do. There's the turnoff."

I took it. Not happily, but I headed back to the Ranch as he said. He did look better. His eyes were almost blue again, and the natural color had returned to his face.

We reached Rancho Encantado without seeing any sign of the white van. Mom and Dad were just crossing the driveway as we arrived.

"Glad you made it back in time for our meeting, Bart. Whoa, what happened to you two?" Dad asked when he saw Bart's wound and the shattered rearview mirror.

We explained.

"Are you up to keeping the appointment, or do you need to get off your feet for a while?" Dad asked. "I can always fill you in when we get back."

"Where are you going?" I asked.

"We're meeting with the local FBI and the chief of police, then with the Tenors' publicity and security people," Mom said. "Want to come along? We can have lunch and you can get a peek at Santa Fe after we have our meetings. Then we'll check the helipad at the Opera and be back in time to watch the guys demonstrate their perimeter defense system."

I glanced at Bart. He was already reaching for the car door. "Sure you feel up to it?" I asked.

"I felt better at the mere mention of lunch." He got up cautiously, making no sudden movements, steadying himself on the car door before taking the first step. I went around to help him. "Give us time to get Bart cleaned up. It'll only take a minute," I said as we headed for the Ranch house.

It took more than a minute, since we stopped to change clothes and get presentable. I exchanged my jeans for a long, flared denim skirt and a muted plaid shirt with denim vest. "Mmm. I like it," Bart smiled with approval. "Think your folks would mind if we took five minutes . . . ?" He let the unfinished question dangle suggestively as he reached for me.

"You talk a good line, Romeo," I laughed, wrapping my arms around him. "You love propositioning me when you have absolutely no intention of following through, and you know Dad would be pounding on the door saying embarrassing things if you did."

I took his hand and pulled him through the door, anxious to get out of our suddenly chilly room and back into the warm New Mexico sun.

Dad pressed for details about our pursuers as we drove to Santa Fe. Mom frowned at the descriptions of the pockmarked driver of the white van and the passenger with the gun. "I'm sure I know the passenger," she said. "We'll check when we get back to our computer, but if it is Saladin, we're up against the big boss in one of Hamas's radical groups. He's vicious, relentless, and a cold-blooded assassin."

"It's always nice to know who your enemies are," I said, snuggling against Bart. Despite Mom's depressing declaration, I finally felt safe for the first time in several hours. "Tell me about Saladin."

"You're too young to remember Dr. George Habbash. They called him the 'master of murder.' He was the first to export Middle East terrorism to Western Europe. His goal was to build history's first multi-national terrorist strike force. The first group to be trained was the IRA in 1968, and since then, most other terrorist groups in the world have been under his tutelage. He was Saladin's mentor, teaching him every dirty trick in the book. Now Saladin is known as the 'master of murder and mayhem.' He's surpassed his teacher in every ugly facet of terrorism."

I was sorry I'd asked. It was more than I ever wanted to know about our adversary.

Dad was strangely silent. I reached up and stroked the back of his head. "Anyone home today? You're awfully quiet."

"Just remembering the last time I tangled with Saladin," he said. "He's bad. Gathered Islamic radicals from Palestine, Sudan, and Egypt—undisciplined scum other terrorist organizations wouldn't even touch. They're an unstable lot, fired with a hatred of the Great Satan, as they call the United States."

"He's been establishing terrorist cells all over the country, from New York to San Diego," Mom added. "Saladin headed up the terrorist conferences in Chicago, Phoenix, and Kansas City, where he called for a holy war against the enemies of Islam. At the Kansas City conference, he even gave secret weapons training to Islamic recruits."

"You're kidding. Actual conferences to train and recruit terrorists are being held openly in the United States?" I couldn't believe it.

Bart had been leaning back, his eyes closed. "When they caught the Pakistani terrorist, Abdul Hakim Yousef, and asked him what his plans were in the United States, he said, 'Killing Americans. This is my best thing. I enjoy it.' This is the kind of men Saladin surrounds himself with. Killing machines."

"I don't like the idea of him being here," Dad said, "and making the connection between you and your mother and me. That's the whole reason I stayed out of your life while you were growing up, Bunny, so people like Saladin wouldn't get at you. Looks like all I did was delay it."

"But it gave Allison a chance for a normal childhood, which she wouldn't have had if we'd had to keep her locked away from your enemies all those years," Mom argued.

"But she's so vulnerable . . . ',"" Dad started.

I glanced at Bart. He frowned and shook his head. He'd read my mind. "You worry about the Tenors and the terrorists," Bart said to Dad. "I'll worry about your daughter."

"Dad's worries could be solved," I started, knowing full well what Bart's reaction would be.

"Princess, you promised," Bart said softly in my ear as he pulled me closer to him. He covered my lips with his, stopping my comment. He had the nicest way of silencing me and distracting me at the same time.

"How's that?" Dad asked.

Silence from the back seat.

"Bart?"

"Sorry, Jack. Your daughter's seducing me back here."

"You wish!" I laughed. "Actually, Bart was suppressing some comments he thought I was going to make."

I caught Dad's look and his raised eyebrow in the rearview mirror. "And what would that be all about?"

"Sorry. I solemnly promised my husband I would never discuss it with you in any form."

Bart groaned.

"Bart?" Dad said.

"It won't do any good, Dad. Bart won't mention it because it's something he feels very strongly about, and I won't because I would never break a promise to my husband."

Mom laughed. Bart groaned again and shook his head. I winked at Dad in the mirror.

"Anyone have any preferences for lunch?" Mom asked in her usual tactful way of changing the subject.

"I heard the French Pastry Bakery at La Fonda Hotel is a great place for lunch—and for dessert," I said, making a face at Bart, who puffed up his cheeks and made fat, round gestures with his arms.

"Sounds good. That's convenient to our meeting," Mom said.

"Guess we'll have to try the famous Frito pie at Woolworth's on the Plaza another time, Bart," Dad said.

"Don't wait too long. I understand they're closing all remaining Woolworth stores, even the old landmark ones," I said.

Everyone avoided the topic of terrorists the rest of the way to Santa Fe. But light talk of lunch didn't dispel the heavy atmosphere Saladin's presence inflicted on all of us.

The French Pastry Bakery was even better than I'd heard. My Torte Milanaise sandwich was delightfully delicious—spinach, ham, peppers, and cheese in a light, flaky pastry shell.

As we left the restaurant, we were kitty-corner from the Plaza and the Palace of the Governors, famous for its American Indian artisans' market. "I'd like to wander over to the market while we're in town," I said.

Mom agreed, and turned to Dad. "You and Bart take care of the police chief and the FBI. I'll take Allison with me to meet Else and the Tenors' people. When we're through, we'll meet you at the market in front of the Governor's Palace. Thirty to forty-five minutes?"

We met Else in the lobby of La Fonda Hotel, and proceeded together to the restaurant. Light filtering through the sunroof brightened cheerful blue tablecloths and colorful murals of fiesta dancers. Tiny white lights adorned ficus trees that almost touched pole rafters above the second-floor balcony.

A flamboyant Italian and a gloomy Greek stood as we approached. Mom introduced Else Elbert as the liaison who would be handling all security arrangements for the Tenors' entourage. She introduced me as Allison Allan, a special assistant. Whose she didn't say.

Else took charge of the brief meeting. She was impressive to watch: her professionalism, her knowledge of every aspect of the job, and the way she handled the two opinionated front men for the three famous tenors. I liked her.

Mom's portion of the meeting accomplished, we excused ourselves while Else joined the two men for lunch, plunging into all the other security details for the safety of the Tenors both at the concert and gala afterward.

Santa Fe's special ambience was in full flower today. Deep blue sky shimmered above the Plaza, which had been for nearly four centuries the hub and heart of this historic city.

We walked the short block to the Palace of the Governors. Despite its elegant name, the long, low, one-story adobe building was a humble-looking structure. Massive hand-carved wood pillars formed a portal under which the artists spread their jewelry, woven goods, and pottery every day of the year. Silver and turquoise jewelry lay on colorful handwoven squares along the brick sidewalk.

Across the street, shade trees and wrought iron benches offered respite from the warm Santa Fe sun—a place for old men to talk and read their newspapers, women to visit, and tourists to rest their feet. I waved at Bart and Dad, who were just entering the colonnade on the other end.

Inside the Palace, now a historical museum, I spotted an intriguing statue. I pulled Mom in with me, just in front of a troupe of school children flocking through the door behind us.

The magnificent wood carving of a young Indian woman holding a bird aloft in her hand stood on a pedestal in front of a huge mirror. Was she reaching up to release it, or had it just landed? The detail was exquisite, the expression on her face one of peace and serenity. I wanted to stroke the gleaming wood, imagining if I touched it, its tranquility would flow into me. The spiritual power of the carving was mesmerizing.

A disturbance outside took Mom from my side and my attention from the statue. I glanced in the mirror and watched in horror as four men jumped from the open door of a black van. Two men grabbed Bart, and the other two seized Dad from behind. Black-clad terrorists jabbed hypodermic needles into their arms through their shirts. The ruffians shoved Dad and Bart onto the floor of the van while two men inside held guns to their heads.

Then the kidnappers whirled around and headed for the door of the museum—straight for us.

Chapter Ten

Mom struggled to get out to Dad and Bart, but we were blocked by the children still streaming through the entrance. For a split-second we stared into the eyes of the terrorists over the heads of the children. They couldn't get in to us. We couldn't get out to Bart and Dad.

With an oath of frustration, they jumped into the open door of the van, and the vehicle squealed away from the curb. By the time we'd waded through the children and made it out the door, the van was out of sight.

A young Indian woman stepped in front of me, held up a necklace, and said, "Shake your head like you're telling me no, then do what I say. Both of you get back inside quickly and wait for me. We're being watched."

I stared at her.

"Do it now. You're in danger."

"Mom," I called. "Come here."

I pulled my mother back into the museum and put my arms around her while I related the cryptic message the Indian woman had given me.

Looking as if she was trying to find customers for the jewelry she held in her hands, the young woman strolled into the museum. Her manner was casual, but her expression intense, her wide eyes wary.

Long, lustrous, straight black hair hung halfway down her back. Her intense dark eyes were rimmed with heavy lashes. She was about an inch taller than I was, with a figure that filled her jeans perfectly, and a narrow waist accented by a large silver and turquoise buckle on her belt.

"I'm Pepper Marino, with the District Attorney's office. There's a man across the street watching you. I'm sure he directed the kidnapping."

Mom grabbed her arm. "Did you get a license number? We've got to call the police and go after them."

"I've called the police. They're on their way," the young woman said, holding up a cell phone. "Gave them the license number and description of the vehicle and men. I think they meant to take you, too. There's another car circling the block, getting signals from that man." She pointed in the mirror to a bearded man with dark-rimmed glasses leaning against a tree in the Plaza across the street.

"Ramadan Shallah," Mom whispered hoarsely, as though the awful name stuck in her throat.

"Who's that?" I asked, afraid of the answer.

"An Islamic terrorist your father could have killed, and didn't. He's now one of Saladin's men."

"Terrorists?" Pepper said, studying the man more intently in the mirror.

The question aroused Mom, as if it suddenly reminded her where we were and what had happened. "You said you called the police? They should have been here by now." She glanced at her watch, then looked at it again, studying it, mentally noting the time. She began questioning the young woman, but her eyes weren't on Pepper. They were taking in every detail of her surroundings, burning them into her memory. I'd watched her do this exercise many times, mentally photographing scenes so she could write about them later, but never with such intensity. "Tell me what you saw," Mom urged.

"I'd been watching the van circle slowly around the Plaza for about an hour. That's unusual. Even someone determined to get a close parking place isn't that persistent. Then I noticed a man across the street with a newspaper."

"That man?" Mom asked.

"Yes. When the van drove by, he'd signal in some way. Finally the van double-parked at the end of the street as if to unload, but they just sat there with open doors—until you got here. He signaled as you went inside. The van roared up; four men piled out, grabbed two men who had just arrived, stabbed them with hypodermic needles, and drove away."

"How did you happen to be just sitting there, watching all of this?" Mom asked.

"My grandmother sells her jewelry here every day, but she was sick today and asked me to cover for her. I'm a legal aide, working for the DA while studying to be an attorney. Since my boss was going out of town, he told me I could have the day off."

"Describe the four men."

The attractive, articulate young woman of Native American descent gave a detailed description of the four men which put my sketchy impression to shame. She was very observant.

A Santa Fe police car eased up to the curb and a short, stout, uniformed deputy rolled out. "Well, Pepper, what have you conjured up this time?" he demanded.

"Deputy Langford Mitchell." Pepper's introduction was curt.

Mom introduced us, then pointed at the bearded man disappearing into a long, dark sedan. "He's leaving."

Pepper ran to the door and spoke to the young man who had taken her place on the blanket. "Daniel, bring me that newspaper from the bench across the street. Don't smudge the fingerprints."

When he gave it to her, she returned, holding the paper by one corner, and continued as if there had been no interruption. "Their husbands were grabbed off the street in front of me. I've got to get back to work." She held out the dangling newspaper to the open-mouthed deputy, spun on her boot heel, and left Langford Mitchell fuming.

He turned to us, but before he could say a word, Mom cut him off. "Have they spotted the van yet? I assume you threw roadblocks up around the city immediately so they couldn't get out."

"No, ma'am. It was just Pepper calling in, and I had to come and see—"

"What! You had the description of the vehicle, a license number, and an eyewitness to a kidnapping, and you didn't take it seriously enough to set up roadblocks—or even take pursuit? What kind of irresponsible law enforcement is that?"

Snatching her radio from her purse, Mom thrust it into my hands. "Allison, contact the Ranch. Tell them what's happened. Get Oz here to coordinate the search with the Santa Fe police. I'm sure they have competent law enforcement somewhere in the city. Tell Sky it was Saladin and Ramadan Shallah. He can start working on that."

I was stunned. The police hadn't mobilized yet; the kidnappers were racing out of the city unhampered by anyone. I radioed Oz and Sky, the sickening feeling in the pit of my stomach mushrooming into nausea.

Mom whirled back to the now retreating deputy and flashed her Interpol ID. "Get out to your car and put out an APB on the black van as fast as that disgusting carcass of yours will move. If that van gets away . . . if my husband and son-in-law are not found . . . or are hurt or killed because of your incompetence, I'll personally peel every inch of skin from your repulsive body with that vile-looking knife at your overstuffed waist. Are you absorbing the seriousness of this situation, Deputy Mitchell?"

Nodding vigorously, Deputy Mitchell tripped over the threshold of the door as he retreated to the safety of his car and broadcast the information Pepper had given him minutes earlier. Precious minutes that had been wasted. Vital minutes.

We followed him outside.

"Pepper," Mom said, "what else can you remember? Did you tell us everything? Think carefully." Mom crouched down so she was eye-to-eye with Pepper, who sat cross-legged on the ground. "This is not just an ordinary kidnapping."

"I gathered that, Mrs. Alexander. Santa Fe doesn't have the kind of crime I just witnessed."

"The kidnappers were terrorists. Have you heard of Hamas?"

She smiled. "We do have newspapers here."

"Sorry, Pepper. I wasn't implying you were backwoods in any way. Most people don't have an interest in international terrorism, since it usually doesn't affect their personal lives."

"I'm studying law. It's important for me to know about those kinds of things. Tell me how terrorists came to Santa Fe."

"The Three Tenors are the target. Hamas needs money to fund their terrorist activities. We got word they're planning to kidnap the whole entourage, as well as many of the celebrities coming to perform, right after the benefit performance, and hold them for ransom."

"We?" Pepper asked, leaning toward Mom, her dark eyes wide with interest.

"My husband is head of Anastasia, the anti-terrorist division of Interpol. Our team is here to prevent Hamas from even getting near the celebrities."

Mom stood and shoved her hands in her pockets. "The irony of the whole thing is disgusting." She whirled to the deputy in the police car at the curb next to us. "Did you broadcast the APB?"

"Yes, ma'am," the repentant deputy said meekly, avoiding Pepper's stare.

"Have they been spotted yet?"

"No, ma'am," he said quietly, squirming under Mom's interrogation.

"Unless they find that van, and those men are unharmed, I promise you this is the end of your career in law enforcement—anywhere in the world. You won't even be able to get a job as a school crossing guard. Am I computing?"

"Yes, ma'am." The contrite deputy renewed his efforts, urging every available unit to respond, calling in reinforcements from outlying areas.

I'd only seen my mother in her official capacity at the university, lecturing or teaching stories and songs of native cultures. To watch the transformation of this gentle, loving mother-figure, who tenderly coaxed stories out of timid grandmothers in remote villages, to a hard-as-nails, no-nonsense totally professional Interpol agent astounded me.

"Tell me about Saladin and Ramadan Shallah," Pepper said, turning her little business over to the boy I assumed was her brother.

We went back inside the museum, and I sat down beside Pepper as Mom related the horrible history of the two men. I sat because my legs wouldn't hold me up anymore, my knees suddenly gone weak with the realization that my husband and father were in the hands of one of the world's most deadly assassins.

"What will he do to them?" I asked when Mom finished.

"Ultimately, kill them." Mom sat down and put her arm around my shoulder, resting her cheek against mine. "But first he'll play mind games, demanding this or that from us, make us jump through his hoops. Then he'll kill them. He won't tell us when or where, and he'll go back underground, leaving us to find them on our own. Unless we can find them first."

Oz was on the radio, on his way to town bringing Sky with him. The team was on alert and had activated the perimeter defense system. Mom tried to reach Dad or Bart by radio, but got no response.

I glanced at my watch. It had only been ten minutes, but it seemed hours.

My watch! My new watch!

"Mom. We can track them. This is what we picked up from Jared in Los Alamos. It's equipped with the Global Positioning Navigation System."

I flipped open the face of the watch, programmed the micro-computer for search, and requested the location of the watch-mate. In seconds, a miniature map revealed a blip heading north on Highway 285. "Bingo!" I shouted, jumping up. "They've just passed the Opera House and are heading toward Española."

Mom sprang toward the police car. "Come on, Allison. We'll see if Mitchell can drive."

Pepper thrust a card into my hand. "That's my phone number. Call me as soon as you know anything. Let me know if I can help in any way."

"Thanks, Pepper. You've been a great help already."

I jumped in the car as Deputy Langford Mitchell turned the siren on and pulled away from the curb. He picked up the radio, but Mom promptly took it from his hand. "You drive. Fast. I'll talk." She introduced herself and her credentials, instructing the dispatcher to patch her through to the Highway Patrol, and to Tribal Police who had jurisdiction on the reservations. Oz and Sky hadn't reached Santa Fe yet, so they were turned around and sent in the opposite direction, back where they'd just come from.

"They're turning east off 285."

"Where?"

"Just a minute. I have to figure out how to use this. Towns along that road are Nambe, Chimayo, Truchas, and Taos."

"That's the High Road to Taos," Mitchell offered.

"High Road?" Mom asked.

"The mountain road," he replied. "It's winding and picturesque. Not a logical choice for a fast getaway."

"First rule—terrorists aren't logical. They don't think like we do. The main route will have the police looking for them, and they'll think the faster they get off the beaten path, the better their chance of escaping. Which may be true."

The radio in my hand buzzed. "Yes?" I answered.

Oz reported they'd seen nothing yet.

"Where are you?" I asked.

"We passed Camel Rock a couple of minutes ago."

"They've taken the High Road to Taos—turn right toward Nambe on 520."

"No," interrupted Langford Mitchell. "Tell them to stay on 285 to Española. Then take Highway 76 to Taos. It comes in at Chimayo, and they'll make better time on the straight stretches."

I relayed the new directions to Oz and Sky.

"How are you holding up, Alli?" Oz asked, his voice full of concern.

"Fine. Thanks for asking. Just stay on the lookout. You're the closest to them right now. We're a good ten or fifteen minutes behind you. Wait!"

Mom whirled around in the front seat. "What's the matter?"

"They've stopped."

"Where?"

"Mmmm . . . the intersection of 520 and 76," I answered finally, waiting for the tiny computer to pinpoint the location. I watched the minute blip move ever so slightly. "They're moving again, faster. No." I tapped the watch. Then, forcing myself to be more patient, I programmed the question to the computer. I didn't like the answer. "They're airborne."

"They're what?" Mom said.

"They've just taken off in an airplane or helicopter."

"Will that gizmo keep tracking them?" Mom asked.

"Yes, but I don't know for how long. I don't think Jared gave us an outside range."

Mom took the radio and gave Oz and Sky new directions—take the High Road to the intersection of 76 and 520. Find and secure the van.

"Where are they now?" Mom asked.

"Heading straight north."

"What's straight north of here?" Mom asked Mitchell.

"A whole lotta nuthin'," the deputy said. "But straight north keeps them above the plain and out of the mountains. Next turn they make will give us more of an idea where they're headed. What do you want me to do now?"

"Take us to Rancho Encantado, please. We'll send someone back to town for the car." Mom turned to look out the window, but I knew she wasn't watching the chaparral or enjoying the purple beauty of the Sangre de Cristo Mountains.

I tracked the blip that represented Bart and Dad, scarcely taking my eyes from the lilliputian computer screen on my watch. Mom was formulating a plan while we drove, evidenced by the notes I could hear her scribbling furiously on a notepad.

Deputy Langford Mitchell delivered us to Rancho Encantado with no further commentary.

"Thanks, Mitchell. I'll be in touch." Mom jumped out of the police car and slammed the door. She bounded toward the steps of the Ranch house without a backward glance, leaving Deputy Langford Mitchell with his mouth open.

"Thanks for the lift, Deputy." I got out before he could ask the question that I could see was coming.

Mom was already halfway up the steps when I caught her. She stopped at the top and took her ringing cell phone from her purse.

"Hello." A pause.

"Yes, this is Margaret Alexander." Another pause. Mom motioned for me to listen with her.

"Mrs. Alexander, this is Saladin."

Chapter Eleven

"I believe I have something that belongs to you—something you'd like to have returned."

"Yes, you do. And I'd like very much to have it back—in as good shape as when you took it."

"I'd hoped to have the pleasure of your company as well as that of your beautiful daughter by now. But since that didn't happen, I have rearranged my game plan."

"Saladin, I want my husband back, alive and well. And Bart, too."

"I think we may be able to work out a deal. I am aware of your estate, and your wealth. You can have them back, in exchange for the sum of twenty million dollars by the beginning of the week."

"You know as well as I do that it will take more than three days to liquidate that amount. I'll need at least seven to ten days—and your oath that they will be returned unharmed."

"Seven days it is. The rest of the conditions are as follows. You and your daughter will leave Santa Fe immediately, and not return. You will not inform the local authorities of this. You will leave me free rein to complete my plans. If you break any one of the conditions, you will never see Jack Alexander again, alive or otherwise. Anastasia will not rise from the ashes, as the Phoenix was wont to do. Do we have a meeting of the minds?"

"Yes, Saladin. And I have your oath that if I give you twenty million dollars, you'll return my husband and son-in-law to me alive and well, unharmed in any way?"

"You have my oath. I will be in contact later to tell you how to transfer the money."

The line went dead.

Mom spun into action. She began punching numbers on her cell phone as she walked to the front desk. "Molly, will you prepare our bill? We have an emergency and we're checking out immediately."

She turned to me. "Allison, go pack your bags, and mine and Dad's. Have them down here in thirty minutes."

Then her call went through. She turned from the desk and walked toward the sitting room while she talked. "Jim, Hamas got Jack and Bart. I need twenty million dollars to get them back. I'll call you as soon as we have flight information and tell you when and where to meet us. We're leaving for Albuquerque in the next half hour. As soon as I call you, start the process."

'Jim' was Jim Allan, Bart's father, my parents' close friend, right-hand man, and manager of the Santa Barbara estate that belonged to my mother—the estate I'd grown up believing belonged to Margo, the movie star who'd vanished mysteriously during the Vietnam War. For twenty years, I'd thought Mom and I were simply caretakers on the estate—until my wedding day, when Margaret Alexander had revealed that she was Margo.

"When you're through packing, if I'm not back here, come out to the control center in the portables. And keep your eye on that blip." With that final instruction, Mom tossed me her radio and room key and disappeared through the French doors.

I hurried upstairs to pack, continually checking the Global Positioning System on my watch. The blip continued in a straight northerly direction and had just crossed the Rio de Truchas River. I radioed the information to Mom. Oz picked up my radio transmission, too. He and Sky had found the intersection of 520 and 76, but there was no van, black or white, anywhere in sight. They were searching the area.

I threw my clothes back into the suitcases from which I'd just taken them twenty-four hours earlier. Then I turned to Bart's. Tears dampened each item as I carefully folded it and gently placed it in his suitcase.

_____*Get a grip, girl. You won't be much help if you fall apart. You can do better than that.*

As I placed the packed luggage next to the honey-colored corduroy lounger, I remembered Bart's arms around me, his fingers on my bare back, the hunger in his kisses.

Suddenly a warm sensation washed over me, as tangible as had been the chill we'd experienced as we lay on the lounge. I felt eerily comforted, as though someone had put their arms around me and said, "I understand."

I shuddered. Trauma does strange things to you. Or were my psychic sensitivities heightened in the strange, enchanted atmosphere of New Mexico?

Crossing the hall, I packed my parents' belongings, then called Molly at the desk and asked her to send someone up for the luggage. As I hurried down the stairs, I met Brian on his way up to get the suitcases. I gave him the key to the little blue rented convertible and asked him to bring it to the front door and load it for me.

Then I raced to join Mom. The control center was somewhere out the French doors, so I dashed in that general direction, following the flagstone path that wound behind the Casa Piñon, and spotted the portables behind a stand of piñon pines above the swimming pool.

Except for Oz and Sky, the group was all present, receiving new instructions from Margaret Alexander, who was clearly the currently acknowledged head of Anastasia.

David Chen sat rigid in a chair in the corner, fingers chapeled under his chin. Else Elbert poured Mom a cup of coffee from the machine that was constantly brewing in the corner, and pressed it into her hands. His blond, tousled hair looking like he'd just rolled out of bed, Lionel Brandt paced the length of the control room, wheeled with nervous energy, and paced again, like a caged lion. Xavier, the handsome Arab with the interesting scar, sat quietly, his serious dark eyes studying Mom, evaluating her. The impulsive Spaniard, Dominic Vicente, placed a red rose in her hand that he'd picked on the way in, kissed an imaginary sword, saluted her with it, and sat down.

"When I'm out of contact," Mom began, "Oz will be in charge. David, your assignment is to locate Jack and Bart. Get to the Opera House. The helicopter should have been delivered to the new helipad. Follow the blip. Allison, give David the watch and show him how it works."

"Where will you be?" Xavier asked, his expressive eyes communicating sympathy.

"Margaret Alexander and Allison Allan are flying back to Santa Barbara to arrange the ransom. Margo and Melanie, a mother and daughter on holiday, are going to move into their now vacant rooms."

Mom dialed the registration desk on the secure line that had been set up in the control center. In two minutes' time, we were registered at Rancho Encantado as Margo and Melanie Murphy and established as unattached females anxious to check out the male population of Santa Fe.

"Now, we'll need some local help with the next step," Mom said.

"Pepper offered to help," I volunteered, having shown David all I knew about the GP System on the watch, and the TV monitor, before he'd silently slipped out the door to carry out his assignment.

"Good idea. Get her on the phone and see if she knows a very discreet hairdresser—and a couple of women about our size who'd like to take a vacation to Santa Barbara for a week."

I dug Pepper's number out of my pocket and called on the secure line, explaining our immediate needs.

"My sister has a shop in Tesuque, not far from Ranch Encantado. This is her afternoon off, but she'd do whatever you need if she's home. As for the other request . . . I'll make some phone calls. Give me fifteen minutes and call me back."

Pepper gave me her sister's number. Fawn was home, just leaving to go horseback riding. She gave me directions to her shop and said she'd wait there for us.

Mom was still giving instructions. "Else, use my cell phone and make reservations for two on the next flight to Los Angeles. If Saladin has my number, he also has its frequency and will be monitoring my calls. We'll use it to feed him information we want him to have." She stopped and looked at the group. "Any questions? Melanie and Margo will check in this evening. Until then, you've all got your assignments. Get to work."

Mom turned to the door, looked at me, and turned back to Xavier. "What have you got to remove a cast? Allison's recovering from a broken arm, but Melanie can't have one." Xavier came up with some long-nosed wire snips that cut through the cast, enabling me, when the time came to take it off, to simply slip my arm free.

Else handed Mom a piece of paper containing reservation information and flight time to LAX. Mom made one more phone call on the secure line. "Jim, here's the flight number and ETA. Meet two women carrying peach roses, get them safely back to the estate, and keep them there till this is over. Activate the estate alarms. Until I've got Rip Schyler's profile on him, I'm not sure what Saladin might try. You can contact me on the secure line, but don't use my cell phone unless it's something we can let Saladin overhear."

Mom listened to Jim's reply, agreed with whatever he'd said, then stood for a minute looking around the control center before she slowly put the phone down. "Else, follow us at a discreet distance when we leave, and make sure no one's tailing us. Saladin can't know about this next stop. Alli, call Pepper back. If she got someone and they can be ready, they need to meet us at the beauty shop as soon as possible."

Pepper had been busy and her calls fruitful. That portion of the plan accomplished to her satisfaction, Mom went to the door. I followed her quietly into the warm afternoon sun, and we walked briskly back through the shady bower leading to the Ranch house.

Things were happening too fast. Maybe that was good. If I didn't have time to think, if I didn't have time to worry, if I didn't have time to dwell on the empty ache in my heart . . .

Mom paid Molly, explaining we'd been called back to California on an emergency.

"Who's handling the security for the celebrities?" Molly asked as she gave Mom the receipt.

"The crew's in place and knows what to do. However, if anyone calls asking for the security people, put them off. Say they've made themselves scarce and you never see them. We'd like to create doubt that they're still here and on the job. Thanks, Molly."

I waved good-bye with my good arm, while noticeably favoring and protecting the broken one, keeping the slit cast nestled firmly against me.

Brian had the luggage loaded in the car and was waiting with the keys and my vase of peach roses. "Just a friendly tip," he said as we got in the car. He dropped his voice and looked around to see if anyone could hear him. "The next time you come, don't stay in room 109. I think there's a curse on it. Everyone who stays has to leave suddenly."

"Thanks. We'll remember that," I said over my shoulder as we drove out of the half-circle driveway. I cradled the roses, inhaling their fragrance, remembering what they stood for—our days together since Bart had returned from his five-year absence. And now he was gone again.

"Where are we going?" Mom asked, reaching to squeeze my hand. No wallowing in self-pity. Mom was in the same boat.

I read the directions to Fawn's beauty shop, and in less than ten minutes we pulled up to a charming little adobe house with roses in the front yard and lace curtains at the windows. Colorful rocks outlined the perimeters of the yard and circled purple and gold pansies, bright spots of color in the dirt enclosure.

I'd watched closely. No one had followed us. And Else had reported coast clear on the radio. Just the same . . .

A woman in her late twenties came around the corner carrying a bucket of water. While we parked she watered the roses and pansies, then turned to greet us. "I'm Fawn. Pepper tells me you need some beautifying on the Q.T. You look pretty good to me." She put her hands on her hips and flashed a genuinely friendly smile that lit her dark eyes and animated her beautiful olive complexion. She resembled Pepper—the same slender build that filled her jeans and blue denim shirt perfectly, except she was an inch or two taller, and her glossy dark hair brushed her shoulders instead of hanging down her back.

Mom introduced us as Fawn led us into her cheery shop, which inhabited the front room in her modest home. Through the door, I could see the neatly-kept room with its brown naugahyde furniture and rustic wood tables.

"We need to leave here as unrecognizable as you can make us," Mom said. "What did Pepper tell you?"

"Only that you needed a completely new look. Are you friends of Pepper's?" Fawn asked as she adjusted the height of the beautician's chair and Mom settled in.

Mom pretended not to hear the question. "I need to be a blonde. You can cut it, too, so there won't be so much to work with. How quickly can you accomplish that?"

Fawn pulled the pins from the chignon Mom wore, letting her dark hair fall about her shoulders. She ran her fingers through Mom's thick hair, loosening it, feeling the texture. "The two of you should be transformed in about two hours. How's that?"

"Good. Can we use your phone?" Mom asked. "I'll use a phone card."

"Sure," Fawn said with a smile.

"Alli, call Pepper and see how she's doing on her assignment."

While I was on the phone, Fawn snipped away Mom's long hair, leaving a fringe of short, dark curls framing her face.

"You look different already," I said.

"Not different enough. What did Pepper say?"

"Mission accomplished."

Fawn was a quick study, realizing we weren't going to reveal anything she didn't need to know. She chatted amiably about her family and the problems of trying to raise children to appreciate their Indian heritage while fitting into the outside Anglo world.

She had just finished applying the bleach to Mom's hair and had put me in the chair, draped for a shampoo, when a vehicle pulled up outside in a cloud of dust. One glance in the mirror had me on the move immediately. Tearing at the Velcro fastener that held the plastic drape in place around my neck, I ripped it off as I leaped out of the chair.

"We've got to get out of here. Now."

Chapter Twelve

"What is it, Alli?" Mom pulled her gun from her purse as she bolted from the chair.

"The white van and another car."

"Wait. It's only Pepper," Fawn called, checking the window.

"Pepper has a white van?" I asked, cautiously returning to look out the window.

"I'll find out. You get back in that chair," Mom said, replacing her gun and stepping outside as Pepper emerged from the van.

"You have the reflexes of a jackrabbit. Who did you think that was?" Fawn asked as she tilted my chair back and started the shampoo process.

"Someone I don't want to see. But don't ask questions, Fawn. When it's over, Pepper can tell you the story."

"Pepper knows the whole story?"

"She saw . . ." My throat tightened as I thought about Bart and Dad being stabbed with hypodermic needles and manhandled into a van. I fought to keep my tone cool and professional. "Pepper knows some of the story."

Pepper trouped through the door with two women in tow that were, indeed, our size, and with appropriately dark hair tucked into rakish hats. Seen from the back, they could easily be mistaken for Mom and me.

"This is Inez, my mother-in-law, and my friend, Heather." She put her arm affectionately around her mother-in-law's shoulder. "Mom thought this was a great time to get away for a short vacation. She just bought new furniture, and needed time for Dad to calm down and decide he liked it. Heather works undercover with the

Santa Fe Police Department and was getting ready for a vacation. I convinced her she needed to escort Mom to California. She's also loaning you her car so you'll have wheels."

"Let's get clothes and suitcases transferred quickly," Mom said, "and fill you in on what you need to know."

Mom explained the importance of keeping up the pretense at all times. They didn't know who might be sitting in the seat next to them, listening to their conversation, or in the next stall in the rest room. In case Saladin used voice prints to check on us, they were not to speak aloud unless absolutely necessary, and then make it as brief as possible—procedures with which Heather was already acquainted.

When they arrived at LAX, they'd be met by Jim Allan, a trusted friend and employee, and should follow his instructions to the letter. It would probably necessitate a couple of trips to the bank in Santa Barbara, where they were to do exactly as Jim instructed. The rest of the time, they could relax and enjoy the estate and the beach. Any special requests would be handled by Jim and his wife, Alma.

"Any questions?" Mom asked, studying their faces.

"Are we in danger?" Inez asked, her voice a little shaky.

"No. The man who kidnapped our husbands wants ransom. He wants to make sure I'm there arranging for it. One of the conditions for the safe return of our men was that we were to leave here immediately. We can't do that. We have a job to do. He needs to believe we're in California, arranging for the ransom."

"What if he comes to the house in California, or if he calls to talk to you there?" Heather asked.

"He won't go to the estate, and if he calls, Jim will patch his call through to me here, so it will appear that I'm answering the phone in California. If we pull this off, as I have every intention of doing, you'll each get five thousand dollars. If we don't pull it off, I won't have a penny to my name, and all you'll get will be a week on the beach in sunny California."

"Good enough for me," Inez said, the quiver gone from her voice. "I'm sure Heather can handle anything we'd encounter."

"You need one more thing." I carefully slipped the slit cast from my arm and gave it to Heather. "You're recovering from a broken arm. You have to wear this for another week."

My arm felt bare, vulnerable. Similar to the way I felt without Bart.

They exchanged luggage contents while I exchanged my long, dark, naturally curly hair for short, blonde locks.

Mom helped them put the top up on the little blue convertible, gave them keys, my peach roses, further instructions, and sent the two women on their way to the airport in Albuquerque. Mom's luggage went into Heather's black Honda Accord. She brought mine into the little beauty shop.

Pepper poked her head in to tell Fawn she'd pick the kids up from their music lessons and bring them home. "Courtney asked to stay with Brittany tonight. Is that okay, or did you have plans? Brittany could stay at our house if you're doing something."

"When do I ever have plans?" Fawn laughed. The slight edge to her voice caught my attention. "They can go riding with me. I have to exercise Mito tonight. Pick up some Taco Bell on the way home, will you?"

"Sure thing." Pepper shut the door, then popped back in to ask, "You want your usual?"

"Yup."

Pepper left, with Mom at her heels.

"What's your usual?" I asked Fawn, watching through the window as Mom poked about in her luggage.

"Mexican pizza. I love it."

"We'll need these," Mom said, returning with a change of clothes and a small cosmetic bag. "I never know when they'll come in handy, so they stay in my suitcase."

She opened it and sorted through several tiny vials, choosing two. "Until we can get you to an optometrist, I think these will do for you."

She handed me one of the vials, opened the other, and inserted colored lenses into her eyes. For years she had masqueraded as Margo, the blue-eyed, blonde-haired darling of Hollywood. Colored lenses and dye jobs were nothing new to her.

"Can I change in there?" Mom said, pointing to the living room.

"Sure, or go back in my bedroom."

She reappeared a few minutes later, totally transformed, in a chic hot pink challis pantsuit.

While the bleach on my hair processed, Mom got back in the chair so Fawn could finish what she'd started. But instead of relaxing, Mom picked up her radio. "David, report," she said in curt tones.

"The helicopter just arrived, and we're in pursuit. Looks like they're heading for Taos. It's the nearest airport. I think they're in a chopper."

"Which means they may transfer to a plane at Taos. Any possibility of catching them? You've got the best equipment money can buy."

"We'll do our best, Mrs. Alexander."

"Thank you, David. I know you will. That's why you got this assignment. Please keep me posted."

She didn't even stop for a breath. "Oz. Sky. Report."

"We found the place where they transferred Jack and Bart from the van to a helicopter," Oz said. "Looks like they set it down just off the highway. Evidence of wind from the rotors. They left a shoe behind. The van's gone, but there was lots of recent vehicular traffic in the area."

"Come on back. Sky, I'll want your report on Saladin—what we can expect from him, his probable reaction if he discovers we didn't leave here, and where you think he's taking them. What are our chances of getting them back alive if we actually broke Anastasia's no-ransom rule and paid it?"

"I'm a criminologist, not a mind reader, Boss Lady. But I'll see what answers I can conjure up for you."

"Thanks, Sky. I need you to get into Saladin's head and tell me what he's going to do. I've heard your reputation. You *are* a mind reader."

"Just a terrorist at heart, I guess." The radio fell silent.

"Mom, if Saladin can listen to cell phone conversations, what's stopping him from intercepting your radio broadcasts? And what did you mean about Anastasia's no-ransom rule?"

"We have a special frequency, and our radio units are equipped with scramblers. They'd have to have one of our radios to understand what we're saying. The no-ransom rule is just that. Anastasia will not deal with terrorists."

"But you're arranging . . ."

"I'm covering every possibility at the moment." Her tone said *subject closed.*

So I went back to the other. "But they probably have Dad and Bart's radios. Can't they hear everything you're saying to Oz and Sky?"

"Before we left Rancho Encantado, while you were packing, we changed the broadcast frequency so Jack and Bart's radios couldn't be used to monitor our conversations."

"What if they try to contact us?" I persisted. "They won't know the new frequency."

"Someone's in the control center at all times, monitoring all frequencies, so if they call, they'll be heard. I should have grabbed one of these for you. When we get back, remind me. You need your own radio. It has a feature I'm hoping one of them will be able to activate. If an agent is incapacitated or lost, pushing this button activates a homing device."

"So we could find them, *if* Saladin leaves their radios with them, and *if* they're conscious enough to activate them."

Mom nodded, prompting Fawn to gently take her chin and reposition her head. "Moving your head at the wrong time is a dangerous thing to do when I have scissors or curling iron in hand," she laughed.

"Sorry. You probably can't imagine that I forgot where I was and what you were doing to me," Mom said.

I could imagine it. Interpol did that to people. Bart easily forgot he was on our honeymoon when he was thinking about a case.

As cool as Mom seemed, I knew she was sick with worry. She not only had a husband to recover alive, but a beloved son-in-law as well. If that wasn't enough, the safety of the Three Tenors and their fellow celebrities had now fallen on her shoulders.

Where was Bart? How was he? He'd suffered a concussion just hours before, then had been jabbed full of chemicals to render him unconscious. I wondered how his system was handling that. I took time to plead in prayer for their safety, and for our success.

It was overwhelming. How could we possibly do it all? Protecting the celebrities had seemed an incredible assignment when Dad and Bart were here. Now the task was Herculean.

Mom's radio interrupted my thoughts.

"Margaret, Lionel here. They just came back for the rest of the explosives stashed in the cave. Want us to pick them up?"

"Can you do it quietly and make them disappear without a trace?"

"Sure thing."

"Don't leave anything pointing to us. Saladin has to believe we're in strict compliance with his terms. Remove all traces of your surveillance equipment and lay a false trail for him to follow looking for his men."

"Oui, mon commandant."

I envisioned blond, lithe Lionel Brandt, executing a Baryshnikov bow, and leaping off to capture the terrorists. A ridiculous image, but somehow I perceived the Frenchman as a dancer, graceful and filled with fiery zeal for his role.

"Are we about through?" Mom asked, attempting to mask the impatience in her voice.

"Just have to spray you down good, then do Allison. It won't take long, though I'm sure it will seem like hours to you when you want to be somewhere else," Fawn said good-naturedly.

"I do want to be somewhere else. Anywhere besides Santa Fe, New Mexico. And doing anything but what I have to do." Mom suddenly sounded weary, burdened.

I watched my mother in the mirror. She closed her eyes for a minute, pain and distress etched into every character line on her face. Then she took a deep breath. Her head came up straight, then slowly, almost imperceptibly, her shoulders squared, and she caught my eye in the mirror. She smiled and stood up. "I'm through, Fawn. Please finish Allison as quickly as you can. We have a lot of very important things to do."

Suddenly David's quiet voice broke in. "Mrs. Alexander. The blip just disappeared."

"Can you see the helicopter?"

"We do not have a visual. We'll continue to the Taos airport and see what we can find."

"How far out are you?"

"Five minutes from Taos. But there are three other airports within twenty miles of Taos, around what they call the Enchanted Circle. It's possible they were headed for Eagle Nest, Questa, or Angel Fire. Or none of them. They could set down anywhere it's flat enough with clearance for the rotors."

Mom turned to me. "What would cause the blip to disappear?"

"Deactivating the unit, or destroying it." Neither was anything I wanted to contemplate. Bart wouldn't deactivate it, knowing we could use mine to locate them. And he certainly wouldn't destroy the only link we had to him.

David Chen's voice came once again over the radio, quiet and understated. "We'll keep looking, but from Taos, we get into rough terrain. This is ski country—eleven- and twelve-thousand-foot peaks."

"Thanks, David. Keep me posted. Fawn, would it be inconvenient for Pepper to take Allison to the Ranch when she comes back?"

"If she can't, I'll take her."

Mom turned to me. "When you get to the Ranch, remember you've never been there before. Change your clothes and remove everything from your suitcase that you wore there. We don't want to take anything anyone could recognize."

Mom's radio stopped her as she went to the door.

"Madame X. I have some bad news."

Chapter Thirteen

"Something went wrong when we went in." All cockiness was gone from Dominic Vicente's voice. No more pretend bullfighter.

"Dominic, what happened?"

"I don't know if they suspected we'd been there and were on the lookout for us, or . . ."

The radio was mute. Silence smothered the little shop.

"Or what?" Mom asked, her face a mask of cool control, but the hand that gripped the door was white-knuckled.

"It was messy. Instead of quietly taking them for interrogation like we'd planned, there was a shoot-out. Xavier was hit, one got away, and we now have three to dispose of."

"How bad is Xavier hurt?" Mom asked, leaning her forehead against the edge of the door.

"Leg wound. He'll be off his feet for a couple of days."

"Can you handle the cleanup of the cave? And the casualties?"

"*Sí*. While Else disposes of the late terrorists, Lionel and I'll empty the cave and leave a couple of clues to lead Saladin on a wild-goose chase."

"Who's taking care of Xavier's wound?" Mom prepared to leave as she talked, dropping a hundred-dollar bill on the little shelf by the sink. She gathered car keys, sunglasses, and the cosmetic case which was her personal, portable disguise unit. She was out the door before Dom answered.

What did they do with a bullet wound? Doctors ask questions and are required to report bullet wounds to the police. Would the team take a chance on Saladin tracing them through the doctor?

Fawn finished transforming me into a blonde and I changed clothes, trading my jeans skirt and vest for a multi-colored broomstick skirt and turquoise silk blouse. Wincing with pain as I used my nearly-healed arm, I noted I'd need to be very careful for a few more days until it was completely healed.

I looked in the mirror. Even Bart wouldn't know me at first glance.

Pepper drove up, and two vivacious little girls bounded from the white van. Every time I saw the vehicle, my first reaction was fear, my second was flight.

"Here's your dinner, Mama. We couldn't wait. We ate ours in the car." The child stopped when she saw me. "We didn't get any for her. You'll have to share," she said, handing the box to Fawn.

"That's okay, sweetie," I laughed. "I'm having dinner with my own mother later tonight. Your mom can have hers all to herself. You must be Brittany."

She nodded.

"I'm Courtney. Who are you?" the other child asked with precocious innocence.

"Melanie Murphy. I'm happy to meet you, Courtney." I turned to Pepper. "I need a ride to Rancho Encantado. Do you have time to give me a lift? Mom had to leave."

"Sure." She turned to her daughter, who had climbed in the beautician's chair. "Give me a hug, and be good for Aunt Fawn. I'll pick you up in the morning."

"Thanks, Fawn." I slipped a generous tip on the shelf beside Mom's money, grabbed Heather's suitcase which now contained my clothes, and followed Pepper to the van.

"I'd never have recognized you as a blue-eyed blonde," Pepper said.

"Good. I hope no one else does, either."

"Have you ever been to Santa Fe before, or is this your first trip?" Pepper asked, waving to the little girls as we pulled away from the house.

"I was here once before as a child, when Mom was studying the songs and stories of the Navajo nation. I remember one family, a grandmother who took a special interest in me. There was a girl about my age . . ."

Pepper slammed on the brakes and pulled the van to the side of the dirt road.

"You're the Gifted Child!"

"Gifted Child?"

"That was my grandmother! I was the girl — I remember you, probably because grandmother talked about you a lot. And she told me you were coming back."

"When?"

"A couple of weeks ago. She said you would come back, and you'd need our help to do some very important thing."

"She was certainly right. I don't know what we would have done without you so far."

"Allison . . . ," Pepper started.

I interrupted her. "I'm Melanie from now on. Actually that's my name—Melanie Allison—but you need to call me Melanie, even when we're alone."

"Okay, Melanie, do you have a few minutes before you have to get back to the Ranch? I'd like to take you to see my grandmother."

I glanced at my wrist. No watch. Mine was tracking my husband. "Will it take long? I'm anxious to see what's happening, and if David has located the helicopter with Bart and Dad."

"Not long." Pepper whipped the van around and we headed back down the dusty street we just traveled, turning a block before the beauty shop.

Grandmother's house was another small, neat, adobe structure.

Pepper hopped out and I followed, a butterfly suddenly flitting about my stomach. Pepper's words resounded through my head. "The Gifted Child." What did that mean?

"Grandmother, it's Pepper," she called, gently knocking before she opened the door. "I've brought someone to see you."

Sunlight streaming through the open door fell on an ancient woman sitting in a rocking chair, hands folded in her lap, eyes closed.

"You've brought the Child to me." Her voice was barely a whisper. "I knew she was coming."

"Yes, Grandmother."

"Bring her here." She held out her hands. I knelt on the woven rug at her feet and took her outstretched hands.

"Yes," she whispered. "You have come back. I knew all those years ago that one day you would return. What have you done with your special gift?"

"Gift?" I looked up at Pepper. Was she thinking of my link with Dad? If so, how did she know about that?

"Do you know what her gift is, Grandmother?" Pepper asked quietly, settling down on the rug beside me.

"A gift of sight, of vision, of things not present. Isn't that right, child?"

"Yes." It was incredible. How could this woman know about my extraordinary connection to my father? I wasn't really aware of it when we were here before.

"What have you done with it?" she repeated, clutching my hands tighter. She leaned forward as if to study my face, but her gray eyes were glazed and sightless.

What have I done with it? I thought.

"I saved my father's life once, which then enabled me to save my mother's."

"Do you use it only for good?" she demanded in her soft, throaty whisper.

"Yes," I stammered. "In fact, I hardly use it at all."

"Why?"

"I guess I don't know how. I don't know what to do with it. I'm not sure why I have it, how it works, or how to develop it."

"That is why you are here. I will teach you. You will need your gift, with all its power, to help those who are very dear to you. If you do not use your gifts, you will lose them."

I glanced at Pepper, wondering if I should tell her grandmother what we were involved with. Anticipating my question, she nodded.

Briefly I explained that my father and my husband had been kidnapped by a man who reputedly killed his victims, ransom or not. We had to find them as quickly as possible.

The old woman settled back in her chair, tightly grasping my hands. She closed her eyes and was still and silent. I wondered if she'd gone to sleep.

"Your link to your father will show you the way to him," she finally whispered. I strained to hear the rest. "You will need another gift to find your husband."

"What kind of gift?"

"You will know." The old woman leaned forward. Her long white braid fell across our joined hands. "But you are not ready yet. You must tune yourself to Mother Earth and Father Sky. Listen, and the wind will tell you. Watch, and the creatures will teach you. If you prepare, your gifts will serve you. If you do not . . ."

She released my hands and leaned back in the rocking chair.

"Morning Dove, bring me the necklace."

"Your necklace, Grandmother?" Pepper's voice was filled with disbelief.

"Yes. It will give life to the Gifted Child. My life is gone. I am old and ready to join my ancestors. I don't need it anymore. With her special gifts, the necklace will be in the proper hands."

Pepper went to a carved wooden chest on a small table in the corner of the room and brought back a roll of soft-looking buckskin which she placed in her grandmother's lap. The old woman stroked the roll of leather with affection, then slowly unrolled it. An elaborate squash blossom necklace of turquoise and silver tumbled into her lap. Ancient fingers caressed the necklace, touching the large, smooth stones as if to ascertain they were in their proper setting.

"Here, child, put this on." She held the necklace up.

"I can't take that. It's far too valuable," I protested.

"The value of the necklace is in its power. Put it on."

Pepper touched my arm and nodded.

I leaned forward, reluctantly allowing the old woman to slip the necklace over my head. It was heavy. The cold of the silver chilled me through the silk blouse.

"You have a gift of uncommon sight. The power of the necklace will strengthen that gift. Use it wisely, and only for good."

The sightless eyes closed, and the old woman slumped back into her chair.

Was that all? Were there no instructions with the necklace?

"How do I use it?" I asked. "How do I access that power?"

The old woman silently began rocking, her hands gently stroking the buckskin in her lap. I looked at Pepper.

"Grandmother, she needs to know how to use the power of the necklace," Pepper said softly, taking her grandmother's wrinkled, veined hands in her young, smooth ones.

"As she seeks the gift that will save her husband, she will find the power of the necklace." She sat up straight, opened her clouded eyes, and leaned forward as if to look me in the eye. "You must not take the necklace off. Wear it until the danger is over." She touched it, traced the *naja,* the crescent, with bent and crooked fingertips, as if bidding farewell to each stone, then whispered, "It will save your life. You must not take it off. Now go, go."

Her hands dropped in her lap and her head fell back on the rocking chair. Pepper jumped to her feet, feeling the side of her grandmother's throat for a pulse. "I thought she'd left us. She's been waiting to give the necklace to someone who could use its power. I've felt she was holding off death until she did that. But now I think she's just exhausted. Let's go. I'll check on her on the way back." Pepper kissed her grandmother's wrinkled cheek, and we quietly left the little house and returned to the van.

"I can't take this necklace, Pepper," I protested. "It's too valuable to be given to a stranger. It should stay in your family."

"It was to have been mine. Grandmother tried to teach me how to develop the gifts in me so I could use the power of the necklace." Pepper hesitated, pulled out on the dirt road, and continued, "But I chose to develop my spiritual gifts in a different way."

"How?"

"I joined The Church of Jesus Christ of Latter-day Saints."

"You're a Mormon?"

"Yes. You sound surprised," Pepper said. "Why?"

"My husband has been converted and wants to be baptized. I've been taking the discussions in New York while we've been apart, but I haven't told him. I didn't want him to get his hopes up that I'd accept his newfound religion, in case I decided against joining."

"And have you decided?" Pepper asked, taking her eyes from the road to scrutinize me.

"Actually, I think I have. Although, it all seems so . . . I'm not even sure of the word. Peculiar? I mean, an angel appearing to a boy and telling him none of the churches on the earth was true, and that he would be the means of restoring Christ's true gospel? Then finding ancient gold plates in the earth? And all the biblical prophets returning to restore their priesthood power? It seems such a stretch of reality."

"Have you read the Book of Mormon?"

"Yes, all the way through, twice."

"Did you follow Moroni's admonition?"

"Yes."

"And?" Pepper persisted.

"When I'm praying, I know it's true. I *know.* Then later, doubts creep in and I'm not sure I really did get the witness I thought I'd received."

"Have you been to church yet?"

"Yes, but only once. I'd been gone from my job for several weeks and had a lot of work to catch up on before I decided to quit and be with my husband."

"Your impression?"

"I felt good there, the people were friendly and seemed sincere, and the sermons—no, they were called talks—were excellent. I really felt a special spirit that reached out and touched my heart."

We pulled into the driveway of Rancho Encantado and Pepper turned the car off. "Would you like to go with me on Sunday? It might help you decide what you're really feeling."

"I'd like that, if . . ." I stopped. I couldn't bring myself to say *if* I've found Bart and Dad, *if* we've found a way to get them safely out of the hands of Saladin, *if* any of us are still alive on Sunday. "I've got to find out if they've had any word on Bart and Dad. But I need your help with the necklace. I really didn't understand what your grand-mother meant by its special power and how I should use it."

"I can teach you what she taught me. But in the meantime, I wouldn't take the necklace off. And remember what she said. Spend some time thinking about it—ponder—meditate. Get in tune with what she called Mother Earth and Father Sky. I'll be in touch."

Just then Oz and Sky burst through the front door, heading for the parking lot. I started to call to them, then remembered I wasn't supposed to know who they were. This wouldn't be as easy as I thought.

Dominic and Lionel bounded around the corner, heading for the parking lot.

Suddenly a blonde whirlwind spun down the front steps with open arms and a dazzling smile. "Melanie, I'm so glad you finally found this wonderful place. It's teeming with good-looking men, and there's so much excitement going on right now. We're going to have a *wonderful* time here."

Her manner was light and funny and exuberant, but the message in Mom's eyes clearly spelled disaster.

Chapter Fourteen

I flew into Mom's arms. "What's the matter?" I whispered, hugging her as if I hadn't seen her for days.

"Tell you later. Make your entrance, then go to the control center as soon as you can. Xavier will fill you in."

"Where are you going?"

Mom avoided my question. "I'll be back as soon as I can get here. Do your assignment—make sure everyone on the Ranch is trustworthy." With that instruction, she ran to the little black Honda Accord Heather had loaned her and peeled out of the parking lot, leaving a cloud of dust behind.

"Is it always like this?" Pepper asked, watching the three cars disappear down the dirt road.

"Since Bart came back into my life, yes. And speaking of my husband, I've got to find out the latest developments on tracking the helicopter. Thanks so much for the lift, Pepper, and for all you've done." I fingered the necklace. "I'll be in touch, very soon. I need to know what to do with this."

I turned to the front door and took a deep breath. Time for the charade to begin.

Molly stood behind the registration desk. I dropped my suitcase by the door and gave an exuberant greeting, circling the tiny foyer enthusiastically.

"This is wonderful. Mom said we'd love it here. I do already. I'm Melanie Murphy. Mom just flew out of here and told me to get settled and explore this delightful place. So I'm going to."

Molly chatted while I signed in. I watched carefully for any sign of recognition in her warm hazel eyes, but there was none. Good. Over the first hurdle.

Brian was again summoned to take my luggage to room 109, the same room Bart and I had shared. Brian performed the same strange ritual at the door as before, plopping my suitcase in the middle of the floor, whirling from the room and standing in the hall waiting for his tip while dispensing friendly, helpful information.

As soon as I shut the door, I was overwhelmed by an eerie feeling of melancholy. Was it because I was here alone, without Bart? Because I had no idea where he was or how he was, or if I'd ever see him alive again? Each one alone was sufficient reason for depression. I wanted to throw myself on the bed and have a good cry. But that wouldn't get Bart back, or my father, and my energies needed to be expended in that direction.

Glancing in the mirror as I headed for the door, I was startled by the reflection I saw there. It was a total shock to see a blue-eyed blonde with short, curly hair staring back at me.

I examined the necklace, heavy but no longer cold, around my neck. The workmanship was exquisite. Inch-long silver trumpets depicting the blossoms of the pomegranate, or the life-giving squash plant (depending upon which expert you consulted) extended from the heavy silver setting for each of ten quarter-size turquoise stones. A horseshoe-shaped pendant, called a *naja,* the size of a child's fist hung from the bottom center of the necklace, with a nickel-sized chunk of turquoise at the top. Six smaller stones graduated in size to the tips. Dangling in the center of the *naja,* or Arms of Allah, hung a single tear-shaped turquoise stone which trembled as I breathed.

Why did Pepper's grandmother think I should have this? And why must I wear it constantly? The power ascribed to it was probably just the superstition of an old woman. Then again, I certainly didn't have anything to lose by following her advice.

I missed Bart acutely, and almost succumbed to the temptation to fling myself on the bed and wallow in self-pity for the rest of the afternoon. Instead, shaking off the melancholy, I hurried from the depressing room.

Trying to look like I was just exploring my new surroundings in case anyone was watching, I headed for the control center. When I opened the door that proclaimed, "Private. No Admittance," Xavier's dark eyes showed no sign of recognition. "I'm sorry. This is a private area. You can't come in." His bandaged leg was propped on a chair, and he looked like he couldn't decide whether to endure the pain involved in getting up to put me out or hope that I'd leave on my own.

I stepped inside the control room and shut the door. "I'm Allison Allan, Bart's wife. Didn't you see Margaret's new look? I assumed she'd tell you that I'm also a blonde now."

"Sorry. Come."

"What's happening? Where did everyone fly off to in such a hurry? Did David find the helicopter? Have you had any word on Bart and Dad?"

"Stop." Xavier held up his hands, a smile flitting briefly at the corners of his mouth. "Bart told me about you, but I thought he was exaggerating. You do ask more questions than anyone else."

Then solemnity captured his dark eyes and the smile disappeared. He watched me for a minute, measuring me. "David lost the helicopter he was following," the Arab said simply.

"Yes. The blip just disappeared. Does he know why?"

He paused only briefly. "It flew into a mountain."

Just like that. No warning. No softening of the blow. Cut to the chase.

Inhaling sharply, I reached out to the desk for support. "And?"

"David found the site of the crash. The others have gone there."

"What did he say? What did he find? Were there survivors? What about Bart and Dad?" I fought for control, to keep my voice down, to keep from shaking the information out of this maddening person calmly tearing my life apart.

"He couldn't land. It was on a steep slope. They're going to have to go on foot or horseback. I'm sorry, Mrs. Allan."

I turned quickly away so Xavier couldn't see the tears that spilled down my cheeks. Taking a deep breath, I wiped my eyes and turned back to the Arab whose name meant brilliant and splendid. I hoped he was brilliant enough to do whatever needed to be done right now.

"What now? Obviously, I can't go help any more than you can. What can we do here?"

"I'm monitoring the defense perimeters around the Ranch, and the radios. I think you had an assignment also."

"Yes. I'm the mole, the spy, poking my nose into everyone's business to make sure they really are who they seem to be." Suddenly I had a distinct distaste for the job.

"And it's even more important now than before. We are two less to do the work."

I winced visibly at his words.

The dark, serious eyes softened briefly. "I'm sorry."

"I didn't even ask how your leg is," I said. "How serious is it?"

"The bullet didn't hit the bone. The man shot wild, or he could have killed me."

For an instant, I saw a look of pain in Xavier's eyes that I felt had nothing to do with his wounded leg. "What happened at the cave?" I asked, watching his guarded expression.

"The perimeter defense cameras spotted them coming in. We thought we could take them for interrogation. They must have heard us, or had some warning system we didn't know about. I was the first one in. The guy was surprised, shot wild, and got my leg instead of my heart."

"What happened to him?"

That look again. Xavier turned back to the panel in front of him, avoiding my eyes.

"He got away."

"How?"

"Ran out of the cave and disappeared."

"You were down, I understand, but how did the others miss him?"

"You have an assignment, Mrs. Allan. Time is critical. If you'd like to read my report when I've finished, I'll be sure you get a copy."

With that, he dismissed me—as if I was a little girl asking questions I had no business asking. As if I had no interest or stake in any of this.

I stared at the back of his head, wanting to mess up the thick, black, neatly styled hair. No. Wanting to smash something over his thick Arab skull. His problem was that I was a woman, therefore inferior, and not worthy of the time and trouble an explanation would require. I would have thought he'd have a little more enlightened attitude than his brothers of the Middle East, now that he could see how other nationalities treated their women.

"Yes, I would like to see a copy of your report when it's finished. Since I'm an official member of this team, I need to know as soon as you hear anything. I'll take this radio with me so you can contact me immediately."

I scooped the small radio up from the table and walked out into the dusk of late afternoon. Long shadows stretched out along the path back to the Ranch house.

But I didn't want to go back to the Ranch house. I wandered without a destination, numb with shock. I tried to block out the mental picture of helicopter wreckage strewn over a hillside and Dad and Bart trapped somewhere inside, hurt, bleeding, unconscious. Doing so brought a flood of questions. What kind of drugs had they been given when they were kidnapped? How much? Were they conscious when the helicopter flew into the mountain?

And the worst one of all—had they survived?

"Howdy, ma'am. What can I do fer ya?"

Startled, I stared up into deep-set, dark brown eyes peering out from under a stained, faded Stetson.

"For me? Nothing." I looked around. I'd wandered to the stables.

"Can I help ya?"

I stared at the man under the hat. He was of average height and build, but that's where average ended. He had a handle-bar mustache that drooped over his mouth, down to his chin, and scrolled back up, ending in tight circles on his tanned cheeks. His nose was red and bulbous, exaggeratedly so. He had a straw sticking out of his mouth, and a twinkle in his eye that may have been caused by either an early beginning of his evening libation or his sense of humor. A faded plaid shirt and jeans tucked into scuffed, well-worn boots completed the picture before me.

I stared at him. "Can I ask you something?"

"Sure, darlin'."

"Are you for real, or just a prop for the guests?"

"I'm fer real. Name's Wade. Obvious ya didn't come ta ride, so what brings ya out here at supper time?"

"Exploring. We checked in this afternoon, and I wanted to see the place. Do you run the stables?"

"I work 'em."

"Have you been here long?"

"A few years. Got hurt rodeoin', so I had ta find a job. This wuz as good a place as any. Good food, good weather, good people, good pay."

I leaned against the fence. "Are you from around here?"

"Riudoso, down near the border."

"Are you ready for all the celebrities about to descend?"

Wade leaned on the fence and pushed his hat back, revealing an ample forehead. "If they're as pretty and friendly as you."

Chatting with Wade, I pried into his personal life till I was embarrassed, and came away with the feeling that this cowboy was no threat to anyone but the local barmaids. He even told me about Jake, the terse, lean cowboy we'd encountered last night, or at least Wade's opinion of him. And that there really was no big black horse on the ranch.

"There is a local legend of a big black with silver mane and tail that appears just 'fore a calamity hits," Wade explained. "The devil opens corral gates and spirits away the mares, which in itself is often the calamity," he chuckled.

New Mexico was full of superstitions, I thought, touching the necklace that lay heavy on my breast.

We'd watched the sun set as we talked. Now it was almost dark. I headed back to the Ranch house, suddenly starving. Mom would have come looking for me if she was back. Why was there no word from anyone?

I checked the radio in my hand. *It has to be turned on to work. Dummy.*

Else was in the middle of a report when I clicked it on. "The heliport is finished at the Opera. Everything looks good here. How are you doing there?"

Mom's weary voice answered. "We need several more hours of daylight. David got some high-powered searchlights, but I don't know if it will help."

"Mom, where are you?" I interrupted.

"Hovering over the crash site, trying to see something, anything. We got the men as close as we could, then they jumped and are hiking the rest of the way. It'll take them another few minutes to reach the site. But by that time it'll be dark."

"What can I do?" I felt helpless. There was probably nothing I could do if I was there, but at least I'd know what was going on.

"Complete your assignment." Mom's professional voice faltered. "And pray," she added softly.

I hurried toward the Ranch house, feeling the chill now that the sun was behind the mountain. Suddenly the hoofbeats of a horse pounding down the road sent me scampering into the chaparral. I turned around in time to see the big black horse fly by, a rider crouched low on his bare back.

This was certainly no ghost horse. This animal was flesh and blood, ridden by someone with long, dark hair streaming behind him in the wind. But why had no one else seen them? We'd nearly been trampled twice in the two days we'd been at Rancho Encantado.

I hurried to the Ranch house and met Else going into the dining room. She glanced at me, then looked again. "Would you be Melanie Murphy?"

I nodded.

"I'm Else Elbert. Your mom told me to look for you. I was afraid I was going to have to eat alone. Will you join me?" Else's lovely face broke into a genuine smile, and she held out her arm to wrap around my shoulder.

"Thanks. I'm starving. I guess no one else will be around for a while." I swallowed hard, not wanting to appear weak and weepy in front of this seemingly perfect being.

"No. Not for a while. Melanie, are you okay?" We sat across from each other at a small table by the window.

"Other than being worried sick, I'm fine," I smiled, but the effort was less than successful.

"Do you know what a lucky woman you are? Bart loves you so much. Did he tell you I tried to seduce him when I first met him?"

I was speechless. I dumbly shook my head.

"It was before you were married. Bart sat me down and explained what an extraordinary person you were, that he'd proposed to you, then had to leave and hadn't seen you for over four years. But he was confident that you were waiting for him, as neither of you had ever loved anyone else."

I nodded, holding tears at bay, unable to speak.

"Of course, that really presented me with a challenge, and I tried every trick I knew to get him into bed. I figured he was too good to be true, and he had a weakness somewhere that I'd be able to find. I couldn't. I've never met a man who was so loyal to his woman, nor one with such high moral standards. He's unique. But you know that, don't you?"

"Yes. But thanks for telling me someone else appreciates him, too."

We were interrupted by the radios. Else and I grabbed ours at the same moment and heard Lionel's terse report.

"Madame X, I'm sorry to report . . . there are no survivors."

Chapter Fifteen

I felt like I'd just been hit by a rampaging buffalo. Else reached for my hands and held them tight.

Mom's quiet voice broke the silence on the radio. "Are you sure?"

"Yes, ma'am." The energy was gone from Lionel's voice. It was flat, dull.

"How many bodies are there?" Mom asked in a near whisper.

"Four."

"You've identified them all?"

"No, the light isn't good enough for positive identification on all of them, and some of them were . . ." The Frenchman's voice trailed away.

"Were what, Lionel?" Mom asked when the silence on the radio became unbearable.

"Were pretty badly mangled. I'd rather not describe it."

"Don't describe it. Just identify every one of those bodies in the next two minutes, or I'll jump out of this helicopter and do it myself."

"Yes, ma'am." Vigor returned to Lionel Brandt's voice. We could hear him giving orders to those on the ground next to him and directing the chopper pilot how to position the lights.

I put my mind on pause during those excruciating minutes. I didn't want to think, blocking the mental pictures that burned into my mind of pieces of my husband flung across a dark, cold hillside.

Then something pushed the horror aside—an image, an impression, of Dad, bound and gagged. I closed my eyes and concentrated, calling to him. My concentration was broken by the radio.

"Margaret, we've identified the pilot. He's still in the cockpit with the stick in his hand. The man riding next to him is in one piece, but his face is not familiar. A pine tree pierced the cab right behind the pilot. The two passengers in the back . . ." The radio went silent.

"Lionel, what about the two passengers in the back?" Mom questioned.

"Ma'am, it's bad. I'd rather not . . ."

"Tell me," Mom said, her voice crisp, hard, and determined, "or I'll come and see for myself."

"They have no faces, no clothes. The branches stripped them from head to foot, skinned them."

"You can't make an identification? Hair, remaining clothes, watches, rings?"

"Can't see hair color because of blood. There is a watch and a gold wedding band on one."

"Describe them."

"Let me clean them up enough to see." More instructions for light placement, then an agonizingly long silence.

I *needed* to hear the description of the watch and ring—as much as I dreaded hearing it.

"The ring is a plain gold band, quarter of an inch wide. The man was wearing it on his pinkie finger. The crystal of the watch was smashed in the crash. The band is made up of links."

"Lionel, this is Allison. Squeeze the first two links of the watch-band on top of the watch. Does anything happen?"

The next few seconds were the longest of my life.

Then Lionel Brandt voiced the words I'd been praying not to hear. "The watch just opened up. There's another face of some kind underneath—like a computer or miniature TV screen."

I couldn't speak. I couldn't breathe. Constricting bands tightened around my throat like hands squeezing the very life out of me.

Bart's watch.

"Allison." Mom's voice came over the radio—quiet, tender, firm. "Can you identify that watch?"

Nothing happened when I tried to speak.

Else put a glass of water to my lips and urged me to drink it. "It's Bart's watch?" she asked softly, her eyes filling with compassionate tears.

I nodded, having trouble breathing. My body seemed to have stopped functioning automatically. I had to force air into my lungs, then out again. My heart alternated between pounding in my chest and barely beating at all.

Else spoke quietly into her radio. "It was Bart's watch."

A strangled sob on the radio cut off abruptly. Then there was silence. Heavy, deafening silence.

I clenched my hands to my aching heart and touched the necklace, grasping the pendant. *This was supposed to protect me.* From what? No one could hurt me physically more than I suffered at this minute. I'd rather be dead than feel the agonizing ache that spread through me like a disease, eating away all the love and joy and happiness I'd felt a few hours ago, and leaving a hollow shell behind.

I wanted to fling myself off a cliff into oblivion. But I couldn't move. I closed my eyes and sank into black despair. What would my life be like without Bart?

Suddenly, through my misery, I was aware of the pendant still clutched in my hand. It grew colder, almost freezing my fingers. I stared at it, expecting to see it turn into a snake and slither off the table, or coil in front of me and strike. Neither happened.

Letting go of the pendant, I leaned my head against clenched fists, kneading them into my burning eyes. There were no tears. I hurt too much for tears. I blanked my mind, forcing every image into oblivion, driving out the mental pictures of the mountainside strewn with wreckage, and pulled a black velvet curtain over my thoughts, leaving only an empty stage.

On that stage came the unbidden impression again, of my father, bound and gagged in a cave. Dad was alive!

I concentrated on the image, opening my mind to receive whatever impressions would come. The link to my father had not been broken. Jack Alexander did not die in that helicopter crash.

Maybe, just maybe, Bart . . .

I concentrated on my father, banishing my own hopeful thoughts. He was still foggy with sedatives, but he projected enough rational thought to inform me that he and Bart had been separated when the helicopter met them. He'd been transferred to a car. That was all. He lost his concentration, and I lost him.

So Bart had been on the helicopter.

I opened my eyes when an arm slipped around my shoulder. Else moved next to me and gave me a hug.

I reached for the radio. "Mom, Dad wasn't on the helicopter. He's alive, tied up in a cave. Do you read?"

"Are you sure?" The hope in her voice brought tears to my eyes—the tears I hadn't been able to shed for myself, or for Bart.

"Yes."

"And Bart?"

I couldn't answer.

"Allison?" Mom pressed gently.

"Bart and Dad were separated when they met the helicopter. That's all I got before I lost Dad — probably the drugs they'd given him. I'll keep trying."

"Thank you." Those two simple words spoke volumes of relief and gratitude. I wished someone could give me the same gift I'd just given her.

Concentrating again, I tried to reach Dad to find out what else he might tell me, what hope he could give me. All I got was the impression of my father slumped against the wall of some dark, cold cave.

My thoughts returned to the watch. Maybe—no. If the watch had been something special, something that looked valuable or unique, I could easily see one of the kidnappers stealing it. Since it was so very ordinary looking, it would probably not attract anyone's attention.

I opened my eyes, almost surprised to still be in the dining room with Else at my side, I'd been so totally immersed in that hillside scene.

"Are you all right?" she asked, her eyes luminous with tears.

"No." *I'll never be the same again,* I screamed inside. I took a deep breath. "But I will be, eventually," I heard myself say. "Thanks for the support. I'm glad you were here."

"Allison, how do you know that wasn't your father—that he's alive and tied up in a cave?"

"We have a unique link, or bond, between us. Some call it ESP. I don't know what it is, except that it's a special gift. He knows when I'm in serious trouble and has helped me, through mental images and impressions. We've never had time to explore it scientifically. It's just always been there. That's how I knew he was alive all my growing-up years, when I was supposed to believe he was dead."

"When he was supposedly killed in Vietnam and had to go undercover?"

"You know the story of Anastasia's beginning?" I was a little surprised Else knew.

"Of course. Everyone in the business knows about Anastasia and her Phoenix-like director who has more lives than a cat and survives one assassination attempt after another. Do you think you could eat something?"

Else motioned to Maria, who had apparently been waved away and had been hovering just beyond earshot, waiting to take our order.

"No, thanks. I need some time alone. I need to concentrate, to reach Dad and find out if Bart . . ." The words welled up in my throat and wouldn't come out.

"Can I do anything?" The offer came from a genuine desire to aid and comfort, apparent in Else's compassionate eyes.

Shaking my head, I rose, unable to speak without opening the floodgates, and squeezed her outstretched hand, then hurried from the dining room, away from the curious stares of half a dozen diners scattered throughout the room.

I wasn't fully aware of the Spanish tile staircase, of changing clothes, or even of leaving the Ranch house. I found myself back at the stables, leaning on the fence, urging Dad to wake up and talk to me, with a horse nuzzling my hand.

But the horse wasn't in the corral. It was outside, standing next to me. And it was big, and dark.

The moon was just coming over the mountains and the stable light was too far away to show the horse's true color, but there was no mistaking the silver mane and tail. The ghost horse.

"You're pretty tangible for a ghost, boy. Want to take me for a ride? Maybe that's what I need right now." As the horse was standing next to the pole fence, I simply climbed it and mounted him. He stood perfectly still as I settled onto his back, as if this was something we did every day.

I'd grown up riding with Bart on the estate, and had ridden horses in Central Park during the last few years living in New York, but with a saddle. Bareback on a strange horse could be dangerous.

If Bart was dead, it didn't matter how dangerous it was. I had nothing to live for. *If.* I clung to that "if." If Dad hadn't been put on the helicopter, maybe Bart hadn't been either. I wouldn't do anything drastic—yet.

Grasping the long, silvery strands of the horse's mane, I gave him his head to go wherever he wanted. I was just along for the ride, quiet time to follow Pepper's grandmother's admonition to meditate on Mother Earth and Father Sky, to reach Dad, to ponder, to pray.

With a start, I realized I hadn't done that since receiving word of the crash. I hadn't called on the one power in the universe who had control over all things. So I did, begging, pleading for the life of my husband. He was a good man, and there were far too few really good men on the earth. The world needed this one. So did I. I was perfectly willing to share him, even help him, while he battled evil, and I had some specific evil in mind I wanted to battle right now. Saladin.

If Bart was . . . My mind wouldn't finish the thought, but instead carefully rephrased it. If Bart wasn't alive, I vowed to devote my life to making sure Saladin paid for this.

As the possibility of never seeing Bart again, of having to face life without him overwhelmed me, the heavy silver necklace flopping rhythmically around my neck summoned my attention. I pressed the pendant against me to still its bouncing rhythm, and felt it turn icy-cold in my hand—the second time I'd felt this phenomenon. Retracing my thoughts, I discovered that both times I'd been devastated by the thought of life without Bart, the necklace had reacted in this particular way.

Not possible.

I just hadn't noticed the temperature of the pendant at other times. Necklaces don't react. Then again, this wasn't just another piece of jewelry—or so I'd been led to believe. And this was the Land of Enchantment. Anything was possible here, I'd been told. Something else to ponder. But just how do I connect with Mother Earth and Father Sky and find the answers Pepper's grandmother seemed sure would be waiting for me? While a trillion bright stars shimmered overhead, I pondered heavily on these things.

As we wound our way silently through piñon and chaparral in the moonlight, the quiet thud of the horse's hooves was lost in the soft dirt of a little trail. This horse wasn't wandering. He knew exactly where he was going—where he was taking me. But was that where I wanted to go?

I kept concentrating on reaching Dad, but could get no other impressions than those already received—he was unconscious in a cave. I needed him conscious. I needed him to tell me about Bart, and prayed constantly that Bart had not been on that chopper.

I prayed for the opportunity to carry out the plans Bart had for baptism, and for an eternal marriage—for that sealing of our special relationship so that no matter what happened, we'd not have to fear an eternal separation. He'd quoted someone who called it "being joined under a covenant that time could not destroy and death could not break." With death constantly hovering so close since Bart had come back into my life, that seemed like a very desirable covenant to make.

Suddenly the horse stopped. He raised his head, snorted softly, and pawed the dirt with one hoof. Someone or something was out here in the desert. The horse sensed it.

Chapter Sixteen

There wasn't a sound in the moonlit night, except the chirp of an occasional cricket. Seconds ticked into minutes while the horse stood, head alert and ears up, as if waiting for someone. I didn't particularly want to be there to meet whoever it was, but if I got down and hid, I might not be able to mount the horse again. I'd never find my way back to the Ranch alone and on foot. I was stuck.

A piercing whistle rent the still night air. Without warning, the horse reared on his hind legs, dumping me off his back. I hit the ground hard, too surprised to even try to break my fall.

That was the good part. Breaking my fall would probably have broken my arm again. Only my dignity was damaged. And a couple of places that would be bruised from the hard, sun-baked earth.

Another whistle, and the huge horse reared again. I rolled under a piñon, out of the way of the flashing hooves. Then the big black horse took off down the trail, silver mane and tail flying in the moonlight. Scrambling to my feet, I raced after it. The last thing I needed right now was to be left out here alone. And the last thing *Mom* needed was to have to worry about a lost daughter, in addition to everything else she had on her mind.

The trail was fairly easy to follow where the vegetation was low and the moonlight illuminated the path. Where trees and bushes grew high and close together, I tried to follow the sound of the horse, zigzagging around and through the pungent undergrowth.

I stopped, unable to hear the horse anymore. I was alone—lost in the crisp, chill night at the foot of the Sangre de Cristo Mountains. Blood of Christ. I shuddered.

Now what? Try to find my way back, or try to follow the horse and see if I could discover who the reckless, mysterious rider was? No contest. Mystery always won.

The horse followed a track he'd used before. His hooves had worked the dirt, loosening it slightly, making it easier to trace when the brush thinned and there were several possible trails.

Just ahead, a deep arroyo slashed the path in front of me. The big horse had plunged over the side, crossed the dry, flat bottom, and climbed up and out the other side. I caught a quick glimpse of his silver mane just before he disappeared into the trees beyond. Picking my way carefully down the first four or five feet of the steep embankment, I slid the remaining six feet to the bottom of the gully, landing, miraculously, on my feet. The ascent up the other side was fairly easy because of jagged slices cut through the soil by erosion.

But now where? The horse was far ahead of me. I could no longer see or hear him. The piñon grew thick and close together. Which of the few nearby openings had the big black taken?

Coyotes howled in the distance, strange, mournful calls that raised goose bumps on my arms.

Then some sound, I wasn't sure what, directed me to the right. A few yards down the bank, a narrow opening in the pungent piñon led me through a winding maze of trees so high it blocked the moonlight almost entirely. But the narrow trail was easy to follow. It was the only passable way through the trees. Ahead, that same sound, unidentifiable as yet, led me on.

Suddenly the narrow trail opened into a small clearing. A coyote fence of tall, prickly juniper spikes tied close together sagged against heavy growth on the far side of the moon-drenched scene. A small lean-to drooped next to it, both looking like a heavy wind would blow them over.

A silvery mane and tail flashed as the horse bobbed his head in my direction behind the fence. But as I started toward him, a rope snaked through the air and silently dropped over my head, pinning my arms at my sides. In a single second, before I could turn around, see my captor, or wriggle free, the rope looped three more times. I was thrown to the ground and hog-tied.

In that instant, a single foolish question filled my mind: What was the maneuver called in rodeoing when a cowboy rides out of the chute after an animal, has to lasso it, bring it down, and tie its feet? Bulldogging?

Well, I'd just been bulldogged. And blindfolded. And gagged. And left on the ground where I'd fallen. My captor silently ignored my attempted objections to this treatment.

Footsteps quietly crunched away from me toward the corral. The clickety-clack of wood on wood drifted across the clearing, then suddenly hoofbeats, fast and heavy, pounded straight toward me, flew over the top of my head, and disappeared in the dense vegetation behind me.

Now what? I was already chilled, and the night would only get colder. Do snakes come out at night? And what about spiders? The desert had some nasty ones. And lizards. And scorpions. My desert survival training was nil. Non-existent. Not being able to see, I strained to hear even the slightest sound to know what might approach me in this vulnerable position. But spiders and scorpions wouldn't make any noise.

To say I was in a predicament was an understatement. I couldn't call on Dad for help; he needed help of his own. In the past, I always had the hope that Bart would appear, like a knight in shining armor on his mighty charger, to rescue me. He'd effectively done that many times. Would he ever again?

I rolled over, trying to wriggle free of the ropes. That only served as a painful reminder of my nearly-mended arm. With hands and feet tied together behind me, I had a better understanding of the term hog-tied. I tried to loosen the blindfold, rubbing my head against the hard-packed earth, but it wouldn't budge either. All I accomplished was scraping my cheek. Nor could I dislodge the cloth stuffed in my mouth. Being tied up out in the wild was bad enough, but not being able to see was terrifying. Irrational thoughts raced through my mind, but I pushed them aside.

My purpose in taking this ridiculous, ill-fated ride in the moonlight had been to contact Dad. So I concentrated on him now, trying to reach him, trying to see how he was, where he was, and what he could tell me about Bart. But only the impression of a cold, dark cave and my father tied, much as I was, came to me.

My thoughts turned to Bart. To the helicopter smashed into the mountain. To the repulsive scene Lionel had reluctantly described. To the possibility Bart had been so horribly injured that he could not even be identified. My mind balked at the thought. Not Bart. Not my tall, blond, blue-eyed, suntanned husband. Not the only man I'd loved my entire life—my best friend in all the world.

Somehow, I couldn't accept his death. Denial? Possibly. But the abject grief I'd felt when I first heard of the crash had vanished. The more I thought about it, the more certain I was Bart was not on that helicopter. Would God take my husband from me when we'd had a scant twenty days together?

I could almost hear Bart's voice: *"This life is a time of testing. Bad things happen to good people, but God will be there to help us through them. The faith we have in him and his promises will determine how we come through those tests and what we learn from them. If we're humble and say, 'Thy will be done. Help me learn what thou wilt from this,' we'll grow and progress. If we curse God and are bitter through our trials, we may not learn anything and the blessings will be denied."*

"Dear Father," I prayed, "Please help me learn whatever it is I need to know from this experience. And, please, *please* bless Bart to be alive. There are enough tests and trials at his side I can learn from, without having to be schooled alone."

Alone.

I was really alone out here, without even my hands and eyes to help me. I suddenly had a new appreciation for the trials of the blind. But strangely, I didn't feel bereft and abandoned, either by Bart or by God.

I tried to wriggle into a more comfortable position to ponder this surprising revelation, but no matter which way I turned, I couldn't get comfortable with my hands and feet tied together behind me and my face in the dirt. My arm throbbed with a dull, deep pain.

The beautiful necklace was probably being ruined. Turquoise is a soft stone, and the large turquoise pieces would be grinding in the dirt with every movement. The least I could do was not disfigure it before I returned it to its rightful owner. I rolled onto my side, turning the necklace out of the dirt.

How do people come to ascribe certain attributes to inanimate objects? What had happened in the history of the necklace that

Pepper's grandmother felt it could offer any kind of protection? And why did I need it? Heaven only knows, I always seemed to need protection from something or someone, especially since Bart had come back into my life. But Pepper's grandmother should have had no inkling of that.

My mind went back to what Bart had said about learning from our trials. What was I supposed to learn from this particular one? Definitely to think before I acted. But what else? How dependent I really was upon heavenly watchcare? How fragile life is? Those weren't new lessons; there must be something more. Of course, since it was apparent I hadn't really learned to overcome my impetuousness, maybe it was just part of an ongoing heavenly tutorial.

Or possibly I was missing something completely. What should I be gleaning from this frightening experience? I pondered the prospect of having to live my life without Bart. Not pleasant, but possible. I pondered the decision to leave my job at the United Nations in order to be with Bart and work at his side as an Interpol agent. Wise? Possibly not, but it was the best solution I'd discovered to be with my husband—and certainly, I hoped, a productive one for Anastasia. Besides, it was something I felt a deep need to do.

But what else? Surely there was a greater lesson than these.

Suddenly a sound from the direction of the corral startled me from my reverie. At least, I thought that's where it came from. The lean-to was also in that direction. Was someone else here? Was I not alone in the middle of nowhere after all? As a thousand scenarios flashed through my mind, I decided I might really rather be alone.

Someone *was* there. Footsteps crunched quietly across the clearing toward me. Two sets of footsteps. Different footsteps.

I held my breath. They stopped. I could hear the low pant of an animal's breathing close to me. A dog? A coyote? A wolf? Wild or domesticated?

I lay perfectly still, waiting. Friend or enemy? Had I been in Santa Fe long enough to make friends or enemies? The pockmarked face of the man in the white van loomed vividly in memory. I did have enemies, not of my own making.

The footsteps crunched again, closer, stopping in front of me. I sensed rather than heard movement near me. As someone touched the necklace, I was aware of a masculine scent of sweat and tobacco. Jerking away, I tried to roll free from his touch.

The man uttered a single low oath, then grasped the rope behind me. I felt a tug, a pull, and suddenly my legs were not tied to my arms. He'd cut the rope. It was a friend. "Who is it?" I mumbled, choking on the thing stuffed in my mouth. He removed the offensive article and I shuddered, almost gagging with relief.

He touched the blindfold. I expected him to undo it, to give me my sight back and reveal himself. But he simply loosened it, then walked away.

"Wait! Don't go. Don't leave me. I'll never find my way back to Rancho Encantado."

By time I rubbed the blindfold off, the man was gone. Vanished. I strained to hear something that would tell me which way he'd gone and if he was on foot or horseback, but never heard another sound. He'd silently abandoned me.

My hands and feet were still tied, but not together. I could stretch out in the dirt, and even managed to sit up, but I couldn't stand, couldn't walk, couldn't go anywhere, and couldn't get in a position that eased the throbbing pain in my arm. I could see. That alone left me greatly indebted to the man, whoever he was.

Now what? How do I get out of here? How do I get back to the Ranch? Mom must be worried sick by now. My radio was in my jacket pocket, but there was absolutely no hope of using it with my arms tied behind me.

A coyote howled in the distance. Another answered, closer to me. I shivered. The cold night air seeped through my jacket into my bones. I realized I was freezing, except where the necklace hung around my neck. I'd expected to feel the silvery cold through my thin silk blouse, but it was warm where it touched. Why was it warm now, in the cold night air? Why had it been icy cold when the air was warm? I'd been acutely aware of the necklace when I was overcome by thoughts of facing the rest of my life without Bart. The necklace had been frigid. Did it, in fact, have special properties? Maybe Pepper's grandmother was right about the necklace after all. I pondered that until the acute cold reminded me that even if *part* of me was warm, the *rest* of me wasn't, and I needed to get out of the chilly night air.

I began inching my way across the clearing toward the lean-to, using an exercise my high school gym teacher called the duck walk: legs straight out in front and thrusting forward first on one buttock and then the other. I hoped the seat of my jeans would withstand the friction.

The radio in my pocket vibrated. Someone was trying to reach me. Probably Mom, but I couldn't figure out how to activate even the 'locate' button to tell anyone where I was. I couldn't manipulate the radio between my arm and my body to press anything.

I was halfway to the lean-to, smack dab in the middle of the clearing, when I heard the approach of horses' hooves. Was it the big black horse, returning with the man who'd tied me up? Or rescue?

Or worse.

Chapter Seventeen

I couldn't move fast enough to get back to the tree line to hide. I was stuck, spotlighted in the center of the clearing by the moonlight, so I twisted to face the approaching horseman and waited, my heart pounding.

At treetop height, a hatless head bobbed, occasionally visible, coming ever closer, but not close enough yet to identify. Was it my captor? Had he had a change of heart? What would he do with me now?

A horse with a wide, white blaze from forelock to nose stopped just short of the clearing. Not the big black. In great relief, I exhaled the breath I'd been holding.

"Allison. Is that you? You look so different."

"Oz?"

Oswald Barlow emerged from the shadows and jumped from the horse. He gently raised me to my feet, then wrapped his arms around me in an embrace of relief. "Are you okay?" he asked softly in my ear, still holding me tight.

"I will be as soon as you get these ropes off and I can move again. How did you know where I was?"

"Did you forget about the defense monitoring system around the Ranch?" he asked as he started on the ropes. "Xavier spotted you riding a horse alone toward the perimeter and notified us. I was on my way back from the crash scene, so I grabbed the first transportation available." He motioned to the horse as he bent to untie the ropes binding my legs.

"But how did you find me?" I asked, rubbing the circulation back into my wrists and hands. My arm hurt.

"Xavier talked me here with directional headings to your location." Oz finished and tossed the rope aside. He stood with his hands on my shoulders, looking into my eyes. "How are you doing?" His voice was soft, gentle, filled with loving compassion.

"Better, now that you're here and I'm free."

Even in the pale moonlight, the look of delighted surprise on Oz's face was apparent. "Alli," he whispered as he embraced me. "Oh, Alli." He held me close, stroking my hair, murmuring my name over and over.

I was stunned, unable to move, to pull away, to protest.

Oz drew back to look at me. "I'm so sorry about Bart. But I promise I'll do everything in my power to take his . . ."

I put my fingers to his lips to stop the flow of words I couldn't bear to hear. Words that should never be spoken. "Oz, wait. Don't say any more. Bart is *not* dead. Bart was *not* in that helicopter. You're a wonderful friend and I'm so happy to see you, I could kiss you. But my husband is alive, somewhere. We just have to find him."

A flash of confusion crossed his face, then pained enlightenment. I took his face between my hands and brushed his lips with a quick kiss. "Thank you. For rescuing me, for being my friend, for being Bart's friend. You're a special guy. Now, do I have to walk back or can I hitch a ride?"

Oz stood, silent, immobile, expressionless, for a long moment. "You can share my transportation anytime you want," he said finally, with a gallant bow. "I'll even walk, and you can ride."

"Not necessary. I'll ride behind you."

Oz climbed into the saddle, then gave me the stirrup and an arm up. I settled behind him, trying to keep some distance between us, acutely conscious of the body contact, as I'm sure he was, each time I touched him.

Our radios vibrated, and we answered them at the same time.

"Xavier here. There's more activity at the cave, and you two are the closest. Can you take it?"

Oz started to protest. "Allison shouldn't . . ."

"We'll take it," I interrupted.

"Allison, you be careful." Mom's voice wasn't professional now, it was all motherly concern.

"Just tell us what you want us to do, and we'll do our best. Right, partner?" I said, trying to elicit cooperation from Oz.

"Margaret, are you sure Allison should be involved in this?" he protested. "Bart was adamant . . ."

I cut him off again. "Bart will give his permission to anything after we rescue him. That's the next thing on the agenda, as soon as we handle this."

There was absolute silence on the radio. They thought I was in denial. I'd address that issue later. Now we had work to do.

Oz spoke into his radio. "Xavier, is it faster to follow the gully or cut cross-country?"

"Stay in the arroyo. You'll be hidden till the last minute. Just be careful. I think they have some sophisticated equipment; they shouldn't have seen us coming last time."

"Copy."

"How far is it?" I asked.

"Ten or fifteen minutes. We'll leave the horse and go the last bit on foot. Are you sure you're up to it?"

"Of course."

"Do you have a gun?"

"Not with me. Bart gave me one, but I didn't bring it."

"Don't leave your room again without it. I know Bart didn't want you involved in any of the action, but since you have a way of getting yourself right in the middle of it anyway, please keep the gun with you all the time." He reached in his jacket pocket and pulled out a small pistol. "I brought this along. Figured you wouldn't have one. Bart said you're pretty good. Where'd you learn to shoot?"

"For a birthday present while I was still in high school, Mom gave me a year's worth of self-defense lessons. Looking back, I can see why she felt it was important. At the time, I just thought I had a wonderfully unique mother who gave great, unusual presents."

"Do you get much practice?" Oz asked as he urged the horse down the steep embankment into the bottom of the gully. I fell against him and had to wrap my arms around his waist to stay on.

"Nice," he commented. I hastily moved back on the horse's rump and put distance between us as we leveled off at the bottom.

"In answer to your question, yes, I've stayed current. I have a friend in the New York Police Department who takes me to the practice gallery once a week when I'm in the city. What're we supposed to do when we get to the cave?"

"Catch some bad guys so we can interrogate them."

"What do you want me to do?"

"Stay out of the way."

"Oz, I'm serious. What can I do to help?"

"Whatever I tell you, when I tell you. You have to know, Alli, working with a new partner is, to put it in highly technical terms, really scary."

"You're a funny guy, Oz."

"That wasn't meant to be funny. First time out with a new partner is bad news. Never know how they'll react. Will they be cool-headed and use good judgment, or lose it and get you killed? Protect your back, or leave you open to the enemy?"

"I'll try to be cool-headed and protect your back."

"Thanks; I'd appreciate that. I have to tell you, though, taking you into the thick of things may be the scariest thing I've ever done."

"Why?"

"Your propensity for trouble. I'm prepared, when you're around, for double trouble."

"You don't know me well enough to say that. Bart exaggerated, and you believed him. It's not true."

"We'll see." Oz turned slightly and grinned. "I know a lot more about you than you think."

My radio tingled against me. It was Xavier. "You're approaching the cave. Two inside."

"Copy."

Oz halted the horse and I slid to the ground. He wrapped the reins around a rock, then we drew our guns and crept forward, staying in the shadows and out of the moonlight.

Voices ahead stopped us. They spoke in Arabic, joking about what they were doing. I put my lips to Oz's ear. "They're laying explosives around the cave. Setting a trap for us," I translated.

Oz motioned for me to stay in place. He would go down the gully and come up on the other side. At the signal—his raised arm—I'd come up on this side and catch them between us. We wouldn't use the radios until we were in place—in case they had monitoring equipment that might pick up a transmission.

His agile, wiry silhouette crept silently down the arroyo and disappeared around a curve. I panicked. I couldn't see Oz, wouldn't know when he was ready.

I stepped out of the shadow, toward the center of the gully, just as one of the men came out of the cave. His voice was clear on the night air directly above me. Flattening against the steep dirt wall, I tried to make myself invisible in the shadows. If he'd seen me, he'd have a clear shot from eight feet above me. The man came to the very edge of the arroyo, so close that rocks and dirt dislodged by his steps showered down on my head. I didn't breathe, trying to make myself as one with the hard-packed clay. He stood in that spot until I was going to have to breathe or burst, before finally answering the call of his partner and turning around.

As their voices faded into the depths of the earth, I ran back to the center of the gully. Oz was there, signaling. I picked a spot where erosion had cut deeply into the earth and washed away the softer soil, leaving jagged stairsteps to the top. Oz reached the top as I did, a hundred yards away.

The men were returning, their vulgar laughter at what would happen to Anastasia because of this night's work preceding them into the moonlight. I dropped to the ground and rolled behind a rock, gun in one hand, radio in the other. Pain shot through my arm.

The bare-headed man backed toward me, unrolling wire from a spindle. I peered around the rock, checking his progress. The second man, wearing the traditional handkerchief called an *iqal,* held in place by a twisted cord, unrolled his spindle toward Oz.

"Now." The radio spoke a one-word command to move. As I jumped to my feet, I was horrified to see a man with a gun creeping up behind Oz. A third man.

"Quif! At lak la!" "Stop! Don't shoot!" I cried in Arabic, pointing my gun at the third gunman as I smashed my radio hard against the bare head of the man in front of me. My man staggered and fell to his knees.

The third man paused momentarily at the command. I'd hoped it would give Oz a chance to protect his back. But Oz's target, the second man with the *iqal,* pulled his gun and whirled to face Oz. FBI and terrorist confronted each other, guns drawn, three feet apart.

As shots rang out, the third man raised his gun and pointed at Oz. I fired. The bare-headed man at my feet lunged toward me. I aimed and fired again, hitting him in the shoulder.

The silence of the night, shattered by ear-splitting shots reverberating off rocks, returned as suddenly as it had fled.

Disarming the writhing man nearest me, I ran to check Oz and the other two terrorists.

Oz knelt over the man he'd shot. Dead. I went to the third man, the surprise. The one we hadn't been told about. He lay very still, face down, arms stretched out on the rocks, his gun clutched in his left hand. As I reached to take it, he raised his left shoulder and arm, pointing the gun directly at me.

I pulled the trigger again. Pure instinctive reaction. Too close to the edge, the man rolled and plunged into the arroyo below. He lay very still, face up, at the bottom. Peering over the edge, I could not believe what the light of the full moon glowing above revealed eight feet below. I collapsed in a heap on the edge of the gully.

"Nice work, Allison. Are you okay?"

I couldn't answer.

"Alli? Are you hurt?" Oz asked, kneeling beside me, keeping his eye and his gun on the first man, the bare-headed one I'd hit in the shoulder.

I shook my head.

"What's the matter? After-battle jitters?"

I pointed to the bottom of the gully. "I just killed Xavier."

Chapter Eighteen

"You *what?*" Oz took one look down into the arroyo and scrambled to the bottom. He looked up wordlessly.

I tested my radio, fully expecting it to be non-operable after clobbering the terrorist with it. It still worked. "Mom, where are you?"

"Allison, what happened?"

"Everything's under control. Where are you?"

"At the control center."

"Who's with you? Who's monitoring the equipment?"

"Xavier. Why?"

"Because I just shot someone who's a dead ringer for him."

"He's still alive," Oz said, kneeling by the wounded terrorist. "You didn't kill him."

"Did you hear that, Mom? Ask Xavier if he has a brother—a twin brother. Tell him he's still alive. And ask him how come we didn't know there were three instead of two, like he told us."

I was quivering all over. I really didn't make a very good special agent. The thought of shooting someone made me nauseous. The thought of killing someone was too horrible to contemplate. The fact that I'd actually overcome two of the terrorists was incredible.

I threw up. Not very professional.

"Report." Mom's professionalism returned now that she knew her only daughter was safe.

I deferred to Oz to relate the tale while I considered my options. Did I really want to become an agent? If I accomplished my goal, would I be the only agent in the organization to throw up after every confrontation?

"What do we do with them now?" I asked, rubbing the arm that throbbed painfully from all the activity.

"They have a car in the gully around the corner. We'll take them back in that."

"I'll take the horse," I said, getting unsteadily to my feet. "In fact, I'll go get it right now, unless you have something else for me to do."

"Allison . . . ," Oz began.

"Yes?"

He looked up from the gully floor where he held a gun on the terrorist. "Thanks. Thanks for being cool-headed and protecting my back."

"Thanks for pretending you didn't see me get sick."

"You're welcome. You can be my partner anytime."

"Only until we find Bart. Will you help me do that?"

"Alli . . .," Oz stood and looked up at me so piteously in the moonlight that I wanted to take him in my arms and rock him, like a child who needed comfort.

"Don't say it. No one will believe Bart's alive until we find him. But I believe it. And I will find him. Now, what do you want me to do before I go for the horse?"

"Make sure the guy up there won't bleed to death and tie him up. Stay away from the cave and the explosives. I'll get the car while you keep an eye on them. It's uncanny. If Margaret herself hadn't said Xavier was with her, I'd have sworn this was him."

Oz tied Xavier's look-alike securely, then took off running down the arroyo. I checked the man I'd bashed in the head with my radio, then shot when he wouldn't stay down. What a horrible thing to do to another human being.

What unspeakable things they had planned to do to us! And to the Three Tenors. And had already done to my father and husband. My misplaced sympathy dissipated instantly. The man got what he deserved, maybe much less.

Curled in a fetal position, the terrorist rocked back and forth, clutching his shoulder. He didn't seem too badly injured, but I was careful to keep my gun on him as I pulled the shoelaces from his expensive athletic shoes. Docilely, he held out his hands while I tied them in front of him, so he still could hold his bleeding shoulder.

Oz parked next to Xavier's evil twin and put him in the trunk.

"Can you get that guy over to the edge?" Oz waited at the bottom of the gully, about eight feet below. The terrorist, obedient and cooperative, walked in front of me to the rim of the arroyo. Then, in a blur of unexpected motion, he whirled away from me, spun in a full circle to get behind me, and hit me across the shoulders with his outstretched hands, propelling me into space.

I flew headfirst into the gully, the terrorist's fleeing footsteps pounding in time with my rapidly beating heart. Oz caught me before I hit the ground, but the impact bowled him over and we rolled to the gully floor. For a split second, as I lay on top of him with his arms wrapped around me, his eyes flashed a message I didn't want to see. Then he pushed me aside, jumped to his feet, and took up the chase.

The man in the trunk began banging on the lid, kicking it, and cursing in Arabic, calling insults and threats to the infidels. I walked a short distance away so I couldn't hear him, but where I could still keep an eye on the cave and the arroyo in both directions.

Hard-learned lesson number one: These men were filled with unreasonable hate, wouldn't stop for a simple bullet wound, would do everything in their power to kill us, and would fight to the death.

Oz returned on horseback, following the staggering terrorist. "I brought your transportation," he said. "Are you sure you want to ride the horse back? We could tie him to the bumper."

"No, thanks. I came out here because I needed to do some thinking. I got interrupted. Maybe I can finish on the way back to the Ranch."

"It's too dangerous out here for you alone," Oz protested.

I took the reins from my reluctant friend. "I have a watchguard, remember. Xavier can see me on the monitor. Funny how he didn't see the third guy, though. Remember to press him on that."

As I gripped the saddle horn and put my foot in the stirrup to help hoist my aching body into the saddle, I felt a stab of pain in my arm. A lot of help I'd be if I'd rebroken it.

"Xavier," I radioed. "If I get headed in the wrong direction, correct my course. I'd like to make it back to the Ranch sometime tonight. And please inform me if I'm about to intersect with some bad guys—before I get to them."

"Copy."

That was all. No explanation of the look-alike terrorist. No explanation of the surprise appearance of the third man who could easily have killed Oz. It left me with a bad feeling.

At the spot where they'd driven the car into the arroyo, Oz and I parted company. I rode his horse through the trees, over the hill. He took the winding dirt road that led to the pavement, and then to the Ranch.

Emotions surged and ebbed as we ambled through the moon-drenched landscape. I tried to reach Dad. Still nothing but the impression of him tied and unconscious in the dark, cold cave. They'd been kidnapped around three o'clock. Dad had only tried to contact me twice, both times being barely lucid. They must be giving him additional sedatives to keep him out. I needed him to be fully conscious. I needed him to tell me about Bart. Why had the kidnappers separated them? So they couldn't work together to escape, and it would make it much harder for a rescue?

The moonlit landscape brought memories of other nights with a sky full of stars and moonlight-drenched scenery. I remembered the joy at Bart's proposal after my high school graduation on a night with a moon like this. At least, I thought it was a proposal at the time. It was the year he graduated from college, just before he disappeared—dropped out of sight completely for five years.

I'd finally convinced myself he hadn't been serious when he asked me to wait for him. Five years without so much as a postcard was asking a bit much. I accepted an engagement ring from Milton J. Hollingsworth III, a dear friend and junior ambassador at the UN, but I'd never been able to bring myself to set a date for the wedding.

Bart was truly the only man I'd ever loved, and I'd secretly clung to the notion that he would come back and hope to find me waiting for him. He had come back—and my life had been one wild, dangerous adventure after another.

Was this the kind of life I wanted to live, never knowing from one hour to the next when our lives would be endangered? Never having quiet evenings at home to sit and talk and dream and plan for our future? Never knowing from day to day whether there would even *be* a future? Was this really how I wanted to spend my life?

I contemplated the alternative—being pampered and spoiled by my millionaire ex-fiancé and having to contend with his very proper, socialite, possessive mother. That held no appeal for me, not even the security and quiet routine or the prestige that life with Milton would bring.

As I tried to peer into my future, I couldn't imagine anyone there but Bart. He was my closest friend; he understood me, loved me in spite of my foibles and failures, and accepted me just as I was. I could talk to him about anything, and he listened and cared. He was my soul mate. My life. I understood his driving desire to rid the world of men like Saladin and make it a safer place. I wanted to be with him as he did that. If it meant not having a normal home life, I could live with that. Wherever Bart was would be my home.

Reining in the horse, I listened to a sound in the distance. Hoofbeats, coming closer, fast. I edged my mount close to a large piñon and waited in the shadows, stroking the horse's neck and telling it to be quiet. The big black horse thundered by, his flowing silver mane and tail gleaming in the moonlight, the rider crouched low on his back. My horse snorted, whinnied, and pranced nervously, but the big black and his rider were gone without being aware of our presence.

Who was this mystery horse that no one claimed to have any knowledge of, but one I kept running into at every turn? Were all of New Mexico's ghostly mysteries as solidly flesh and blood as this one? One hoped so.

I arrived back at the stables with no further encounters, ghostly or otherwise. No one was in sight, so I led the horse into the corral. Unbuckling the girth, I pulled the saddle to the ground next to the tack room and left it. With my arm throbbing painfully, I didn't dare lift the saddle to put it away.

Mom appeared as I left the corral. Stopping under the light, she held me by the shoulders at arm's length, scrutinizing me as she spoke. "How are you?"

"Tired. Worried. Aching. Other than that, I'm on top of the world." Then I realized what she meant.

"Mom, I know what you believe right now, but Bart's not dead. He wasn't on that helicopter."

"How do you know?"

"I can't explain it. I just *feel* it. I've tried to reach Dad, but he's still unconscious. He's only come out of it just enough for me to know he's alive, that he wasn't on the chopper either."

"But he's told you nothing about Bart?"

"No. Actually, he hasn't told me anything. I get an impression of him tied in a cave. I tried to connect it to the Puye Dwellings where we were today, but struck out. I'm sure it's not the same place, though the caves were similar. The feel of the place was different."

"Allison, I know you don't want to consider the possibility of Bart's being gone, but Lionel described the watch and the ring. They were Bart's. The build was the same. Honey . . ." My mother wrapped her arms around me and held me tight, tears streaming down her face.

"Mom," I said, tears stinging my own eyes, "why would Bart be wearing his wedding ring on his pinkie finger? That doesn't make sense. I'll make you a deal. If you won't talk to me about Bart being dead, until there is a positive identification of that body, I'll forgive you for your lack of confidence in my intuition, or whatever it is."

Releasing me from the embrace, she stepped back and stared at me for a long moment. "Okay. Deal. Until we have a positive ID, we'll assume nothing."

"No. Until we have a positive ID, we'll assume Bart is alive and, like Dad, is being held somewhere. You said we had to find them before the ransom deadline because they wouldn't be returned alive. I didn't really believe you until I saw the terrorists up close tonight. I couldn't believe the hate they have for infidels, for us. You're right. We've got to find them—immediately."

As we walked back to the Ranch house, I related everything that had happened, beginning with my first encounter with the big black horse at the corral, and ending with our last encounter after I left Oz.

We reached the steps as Else and Sky were leaving, duffel bags in hand. "Where are you going?" Mom asked.

"To spend the night at the Opera," Else said. "Someone was over there after we inspected the heliport this afternoon. The guards didn't catch them, but found where they'd come over the fence and entered the Opera compound. Sky offered to keep me company."

"Good idea," Mom said.

"You've probably already thought of it, but how would some guard dogs work inside the compound?" I asked.

"We did think of it. We have some coming in tomorrow," Else

smiled. Then, as if she suddenly remembered my situation, her expression turned to one of pity and compassion.

I held up my hand to stop whatever she was going to say. "Bart isn't dead. He wasn't on that chopper." I took her outstretched hands. "Believe me."

Rip Schyler's eyes studied me from behind his horn-rimmed glasses. I faked a bright smile and said lightly, "You can analyze me all you want—my denial, my motives, my behavior. But you'll see."

Sky smiled. "I'll save the analysis. And we'll go save the Santa Fe Opera from whomever shouldn't be there. Come on, Else."

They left, but before we had even climbed the front steps to the Ranch house, Lionel called Mom on the radio. "Madame X, we got *gros* problems with the bodies from the helicopter crash."

"What problems?" Mom asked. "Won't the coroner's office cooperate? I know it's the middle of the night, but we need a positive ID immediately. They're used to being dragged out of bed at all hours. It's their job."

"Mrs. Alexander—there are no bodies to ID. That is the problem," Lionel said softly.

Chapter Nineteen

A deadly silence fell. An oppressive, smothering silence that extinguished the very air I needed to breathe.

"Lionel, repeat, very slowly, your last transmission," Mom said, sagging against the white wrought-iron stair railing.

"There are no bodies to ID."

That simple statement made my already off-keel world spin right out of orbit.

"What happened, Lionel?" Mom asked, her voice barely a whisper.

"We called the sheriff's office, notified them about the crash, asked them to send someone for the bodies. A helicopter with deputies and the coroner arrived, loaded the remains, and flew away. We stayed at the site a couple of hours, sifting through the debris, until a ground crew came, sealed off the area, and kicked us out."

"Then?"

"David flew us to the place the deputies said they were taking the bodies. No one there had heard of the crash, seen the report, or received the bodies."

"Impossible," Mom said, shaking her head slowly. "Maybe you got the wrong directions."

"No, Mrs. Alexander. The deputy wrote it down for us, and told us to stay with the crash until their ground people could come in."

"Maybe they didn't have the proper facilities there, so they transferred them somewhere else."

"There isn't an official agency anywhere from Santa Fe to Taos that knows anything about it," Lionel said quietly, his voice filled with the patience of someone trying to explain a difficult concept to a nonbeliever. "Even the sheriff's office that took the original call denies receiving it, and there's no record of it on their log."

"That's impossible," Mom insisted. "Someone has to know something. Did you find the deputy who took the call in the first place?"

"Would you believe that person had a family emergency and has left the state?"

"Saladin! This is Saladin's work. He's got the bodies. Better tell the sheriff to start looking for the deputy. I'm afraid they'll find there was no family emergency. Saladin has disposed of a witness." Mom sank to the steps, her head in her hands.

I sat down beside her. "It doesn't matter. They were all Saladin's men. Let him have them. We've got to find Bart and Dad. There's no time to waste worrying about Saladin's scum."

Mom gave me a long, probing stare before she spoke into her radio. "Okay, come back, Lionel. We'll regroup. Everybody listening? Check in."

One at a time they answered. Else and Sky had just arrived at the Santa Fe Opera and were checking the place before settling in for the night. Xavier was monitoring the radios and equipment in the control room, with subtle supervision from Dominic. David Chen and Lionel would start back immediately. Oz was interrogating the terrorists, and would probably be doing so the rest of the night. "When you've finished, don't turn them over to the sheriff as we'd planned," Mom instructed. "We'll keep them so Saladin won't get his hands on them. Everybody who can, catch a couple of hours of sleep. I'll see if the kitchen will set up a little breakfast buffet for us in the control center. See you all there at eight. Any questions?"

"What about Bart? Aren't we going to . . ."

I broke in over the top of David Chen's quiet question. "Bart wasn't on the helicopter, David. And neither was Dad. Those bodies don't mean a thing to us. Finding where Saladin is keeping our men and getting them back is our prime concern."

As I expected, there was a heavy silence on the radio. They didn't believe me. They all thought Bart was dead. And probably that I was looney. It didn't matter what they believed. It only mattered that *I* believed he was alive. And to prove it, I had to find him, fast, before he actually was dead at Saladin's hands.

Mom got slowly, wearily to her feet and offered me a hand. "Ready for a little shut-eye? We've got a big day tomorrow—I guess I should say today. The sun will be up in a couple of hours." We climbed the stairs arm in arm, lending moral as well as physical support to each other. We were exhausted—the weariness that comes not from physical exertion, but the complete energy depletion that great emotional upheaval brings. The bone-deep fatigue that sets in after trauma.

"Want to bunk with me tonight?" Mom offered as we reached our rooms.

"Thanks, but I'd probably just keep you awake with my tossing and turning. I'd better stay in my own room so you can get a little rest."

She took my hands, looking into my eyes as mothers are wont to do, probing for things unspoken. I kissed her on the cheek and hugged her. "I'm fine," I said. "Or will be, as soon as we get our men back. If you haven't heard me stir by seven-thirty, wake me. That's probably about the time I'll fall asleep."

I turned the key in the lock and pushed open the door to the empty room. Thirty-six hours earlier, Bart and I had entered this room and filled it with laughter, love, life, and light. Now it was quiet, lonely, cold, and dark. I didn't bother to turn the lights on. Moonlight lent just enough illumination to see where I was going without seeing myself in the mirror. I washed my face, shed my clothes and the necklace, and dropped to my knees for a quick plea to my Father in Heaven to please watch over and protect Bart and Dad—and to lead us to them as quickly as possible. Then I fell into bed, knowing I wouldn't be able to shut my eyes.

But I did. I guess I did. The dream was so real I expected to reach out and touch the little boy who stood at the side of my bed. The little boy who cried and said he was scared, and asked me to find his mommy and daddy. The little boy who shed frightened tears on my sheet. He seemed so real I felt for the spot where he had been.

It was wet.

Were those my tears? I shivered and pulled the blanket over me.

The dream had been so vivid I could remember everything about the little boy: his sad, dark eyes, sandy crewcut hair, yellow and blue striped T-shirt, even a bandage on one finger.

I sat up in bed and hugged my knees, resting my chin on them. Sleep, had it ever been here, fled. I was wide awake, and troubled. Why would I dream about a little boy when my entire focus had been on Bart and Dad?

Trying again to reach Dad, I put the dream from my mind and concentrated. He didn't respond, but I had the impression he was in a different place. It was no longer a cave, more like an empty room. He was tied up, and either asleep or unconscious.

I wished I had the same connection to Bart. I had no real knowledge that he was alive. Just a gut feeling that he wasn't dead. But how could I find him? What had Pepper's grandmother said? *"Tune yourself to Mother Earth and Father Sky."*

Native Americans revered Mother Earth for providing them an abundance of wealth in the form of plants to survive and raw materials for arts and crafts to sell and enjoy. Father Sky provided light, heat, and rain to nourish Mother Earth. How could that help me? Plants, raw materials, light, heat, and rain?

I pondered another phrase: *"Listen to the wind and watch the creatures."* But again, I couldn't imagine how doing such things could lead me to Bart.

Then I remembered something else. *"You must not take the necklace off until the danger is over. It will save your life and lead you to your husband."*

How could the turquoise and silver necklace save my life? Did I have to believe that it could, before it would? Or, if Pepper's grandmother believed strongly enough, did it matter if I didn't? Would it still work?

Suddenly I remembered the man in the clearing when I'd been tied and helpless. He'd seen the necklace, had touched it, then swore under his breath, cut my ropes, and loosened my blindfold. What would he have done to me if he hadn't seen the necklace?

Had it already saved my life?

I climbed out of bed and retrieved the necklace from the settee where I'd casually discarded it with my clothes. As I draped it around my neck, expecting the heavy silver to feel icy on my bare skin, I was surprised to find it just the opposite—warm to the touch. It never was as I expected it to be. Almost as if it had a life of its own.

Maybe the Indians were right. Maybe every natural object did have a spirit living within it that gave it power of some sort. They believed strongly in the power of the turquoise. If it had any, I certainly needed it now. I guess it was a little like what the missionaries said during the discussions—I could lean on their testimony and Bart's that the gospel was true while my own testimony was developing. Well, I'd accept Pepper's grandmother's belief in the powers of the necklace and lean on that until my own belief was full-blown.

Tumbling back into bed, I glanced at the clock and groaned. Dawn was beginning to lighten the eastern sky already, and I was wide awake. I fluffed my pillows, stacked them behind me, and lay back to ponder the grandmother's strange words. *"Your link to your father will show you the way to him. You will need another gift to find your husband."*

Concentrating, I shut my eyes, willing my father to wake and respond, projecting my thoughts to him, my fears for Bart, our need to find them as quickly as possible.

A large, dark shape filled my mind. A faintly familiar shape. Ebony shadows rimmed the crown of the flat top. Black Mesa. We'd passed it today, on the San Ildefonso Reservation, just beyond their pueblo, near the Rio Grande River.

I sat up in bed. But Dad couldn't be there; that was sacred ground. Even terrorists couldn't get away with violating sacred ground, could they? Of course. Terrorists are a law unto themselves. They can get away with anything.

Fluffing the pillows, actually pummeling them, I projected my frustrations on them. I *was* frustrated. Big time. I lay back, trying to quiet the distractions that spun around in my head: Oz's attempted declaration of devotion; the mystery of Xavier and the look-alike terrorist; the helicopter crash, then the missing bodies.

I still couldn't associate Bart with the crash or the bodies. During the initial shock, those first traumatic moments, I assumed he was on the downed helicopter; and there were the small doubts during my ride on the black horse. But since then, I'd felt confident that Bart was alive. Why, when all the evidence contradicted my feeling?

The wind crooned outside my open window, a gentle, soothing lullaby. *Listen, and the wind will tell you. . . .*

I jerked up with a start. The boy was back, crying, at the foot of my bed. I was awake. The little boy wasn't a dream. He was real. Throwing back the covers, I reached for him. He vanished. Disappeared. Evaporated.

But he had been there. I could have sworn he was there. Sunshine had filled the room. It had highlighted his hair, glistened on the tears streaming down his cheeks.

Suddenly, the room was very cold. Goose bumps flushed down my arms and shivered up my spine.

I jumped out of bed, crossed bedroom and sitting room in four steps, but my fumbling, frantic fingers couldn't unlock the door. Finally it clicked, and I burst from the room. "Mom. Let me in." I knocked on her door four feet from my own. "Hurry."

She threw open the door and gaped at me. "Allison! What's the matter? Where are your clothes? You look like you've seen a ghost." Her arms opened and I flew into them.

"I think I did. I'm sure I wasn't dreaming. It was too real for a dream."

"Here's my robe. It must have been scary to drive you into the hall with nothing on but your undies and a turquoise necklace."

"Oh." I hadn't even thought about not being dressed. I shrugged into the silk robe, then snuggled into the pillows piled on one side of the bed while I described the little apparition who cried at the side and foot of my bed.

Away from the room, it seemed silly. But Mom pressed the issue. "Tell me again — describe the feelings you were having when you saw him. What were you thinking?"

I recited the details again, both times feeling I was awake but acknowledging I couldn't have been. "I'm either getting kooky or I must just be stressing out," I offered lamely.

"My guess is that your senses are heightened by the 'magic,' the 'enchantment,' the 'spiritual aura,' or whatever you want to call it that New Mexico is so famous for. You're certainly not kooky. The stress I can believe, but I think you're picking up on something else here. Too bad we don't have time to look into it."

As I agreed, I realized Mom was fully clothed. "What are you doing dressed?" I questioned. "It's only six o'clock. We have two hours before we're supposed to meet everyone."

"I couldn't sleep. I was thinking about Xavier. I questioned the terrorist, but he said nothing. And Xavier is being just as tight-lipped, denying he knows anything about a look-alike."

"Did you ask him why he only saw two on that wonderful monitoring system, when there were three—the third being his evil twin?"

"Oz pounded that point in, stressing that if it hadn't been for your marksmanship, he'd be a dead man right now. Good shooting. It's nice to know you can keep a cool head under fire, though I wouldn't have expected anything less."

"Did Oz also tell you I lost my cookies?"

Mom laughed. "No. But that doesn't surprise me, either. I did the same thing my first few times in the field."

"That's hard to believe, watching you in action now. You're the epitome of cool, calm, and collected. And hard as nails."

"All a facade. I earned my living and my fortune as an actress, you'll remember."

The cell phone on the table rang, disrupting our conversation.

"This is Margaret Alexander." She motioned for me listen in.

"Mrs. Alexander, I'm disappointed in you."

"Saladin. Why is that?"

"I thought you wanted your husband back enough to follow my orders and keep your part of our agreement."

"You know I want him back, and my son-in-law, too. What part of our agreement have I not kept?"

"You left Anastasia in place. They have decimated my organization."

"You specified that Allison and I would leave immediately and that we would not inform the local authorities. You said nothing about the security team we brought in. I assumed you thought they were not a threat to your superior mind and cared nothing about them."

"Ah, yes. Well, I want them out. Call them off. Send them back to wherever they came from."

"You're adding conditions, Saladin. That's not fair. We made an agreement, and it had nothing to do with your men or my men."

"It has *everything* to do with my men. I've lost ten men. Ten good men. Men I paid a lot of money to train."

"What makes you think Anastasia had anything to do with your missing men? Maybe they got a better offer and deserted you."

"Enough! You have three days to put twenty million dollars in my hands. If I do not have the money seventy-two hours from now, Mrs. Alexander, not only your husband will die, but you will watch your daughter die, too, before you join them."

"Saladin, you gave me your oath I would have seven."

"I changed my mind. It is not expedient . . ."

"You dishonor your fathers by breaking your oath."

"Silence, woman. You may not lecture me. Have the money ready in three days, or I have the delight to exterminate a formidable foe."

The line went dead.

Chapter Twenty

"Now what?" I asked.

"Now we've got big trouble." Mom flopped back on the bed, one arm over her eyes. "I wasn't sure we could do it in seven days. Three days is . . ."

"Imperative."

"Impossible was the word that came to mind." Mom sat up and looked at me. "Okay. Let's start with what we know. You had the impression your father was in a cave, but didn't think it was the Puye Cliff Dwellings, just someplace similar. I did some research in the sleepless hours of the morning." She went to the table and brought back a handful of maps, tossing them on the bed in front of me. "Do you have any idea how many 'similar' caves there are in the area? Bandolier is full of them; so is . . ."

"Mom," I interrupted. "I think he's been moved. When I couldn't sleep this morning and tried to reach him, I had the feeling he was in a room—an empty room. It felt old. Like a ruins, but the walls were smooth like the cave."

"Old, smooth, empty—sounds like one of the pueblos." Mom grabbed the maps. "Oh, no," she groaned. "If I draw even a twenty-mile circle around Rancho Encantado, there are at least half a dozen: Teseque, Pojoaque, Nambe, San Ildefonso, Santa Clara, and San Juan. That's right here, close. Just up the road are two more, Picuris and Taos." She stalked to the window, staring silently out, then dropped her head and clutched her forearms.

"I might be able to narrow it a bit," I said. "I had an impression of what I think might be Black Mesa, near the San Ildefonso Pueblo. The only problem is, all the literature I read on the plane said that non-tribal members are prohibited in many places in the pueblos, since most of them are inhabited. So these men, obviously out of place, couldn't keep Dad a prisoner where they had no business going."

"Unless they had an insider helping them." Mom turned from the window. "It would be possible to smuggle someone into the pueblo in a car after dark. I don't know how they'd be able to keep them hidden for very long, but it probably could be done for three days."

"What do we have to do to get permission to search a pueblo?" I asked.

"I'll look into it."

We were both silent. I was thinking about Bart. It was one thing planning to rescue people when you had a vague idea of their whereabouts. Something else entirely when there wasn't even an inkling of where they might be. *Or if they are still alive*, a horrible little voice whispered in my ear. I didn't listen. If you take away hope, you take away everything.

"I'll get dressed and probe the employees," I said. "Maybe somebody has ties to San Ildefonso and can help us. With only seventy-two hours to do this, I can't waste a minute of it sitting around 'what-if-ing.'" Bouncing off the bed, I headed for the door.

Mom put her hand on my arm. "Alli, what about Bart?"

I looked at her, not knowing how to answer. "I haven't a clue where he might be. Only that I really feel he's alive."

Mom took my hands. "Sky says . . ."

"What Sky says doesn't matter," I interrupted. "No one believes Bart is still alive. They think I'm in denial, or some such psycho-babble. I'm sorry we couldn't ID the bodies so *you'd* know Bart wasn't on that helicopter. I don't need that. I don't know how, but I'll find him. Pepper's grandmother said I could do it. And I will."

"Pepper's grandmother?"

"Oh. I didn't tell you. Remember our trip here when I was little? The woman you interviewed was Pepper's grandmother. She remembered me as "the Gifted Child" and felt I'd return someday. Yesterday she gave me her turquoise necklace—said not to take it off till the danger was over, that it would protect me and help me find Bart."

"Cerelia? You saw her? Pepper must be Morning Dove. Interesting we'd run into them again."

"Pepper's grandmother didn't think it was a coincidence. She knew we were coming, and told Pepper we'd be here soon and would need their help."

"I'll have to see her. What a remarkable lady. She was afraid the songs, stories, and dances of their Tewa culture might be forgotten, so she made it her personal quest to teach every child who was interested. She's left quite a legacy to her people."

"Maybe we ought to go today. Pepper said she felt her grandmother was living only to give the necklace to someone spiritually sensitive enough to use it properly. When she gave it to me, she promised me she'd teach me how to use it. I need to know."

"Then let's go right after the briefing."

I hurried across the hall, leaving both doors open. I was convinced the little boy was a dream, but, this being New Mexico, the Land of Enchantment, one never knew.

Rifling through my suitcase, I found a white cotton tee and a full blue chambray skirt with a single ruffle around the bottom. That looked Santa Fean and would properly show off the necklace, which I took off only long enough to shower.

It was now seven o'clock. I had an hour to pick and pry.

The magnificent strains of Pavarotti's "Nessun Dorma" greeted us as we separated at the foot of the Spanish-tiled staircase. Mom was heading for the control center, and I rounded the corner to the kitchen.

I never made it past the swinging door. Jaqueez burst through, nearly bowling me over. He thrust his arms around me to keep me from falling, but he didn't let go. At first I was afraid he recognized me from the dining room with Maria during their little scene, but it was apparent he didn't. And he shouldn't have. Then I'd been a brunette; today I was a blonde.

"Good morning. I'm so sorry. I should have watched where I was going. But then, I wouldn't have had the opportunity to bump into you, thus." His boldly handsome face hovered inches from mine. He knew he was good-looking, wearing self-confidence like most men wore expensive cologne, acting as if I should swoon at being held in his arms.

My first reaction was annoyance, my next repugnance, and then, just before I bopped him in his handsome chops, I remembered who I was supposed to be. "Then I'm glad I wasn't watching where I was going either," I flirted, easing his hands from below my waist where they were creeping lower and lower as we spoke.

"You have just arrived at the Casa? I haven't seen you before? I would have noticed one so lovely."

Gag. "We just got here last night. Mom and I are studying the—night life—in Santa Fe."

I could actually see his heart rate increase at the pressure point on his throat. "Ah, yes, I heard about two adventurous beauties who wanted an exciting vacation." He stepped back and bowed at the waist, a deep, dramatic flourish he completed by clicking his heels together and kissing my hand. Very continental. And his accent was Castillian, not Hispanic.

"Do you know someone who might like to show me the high spots of Santa Fe?" I said suggestively. I wasn't very good at this. When was the last time I'd flirted with anybody?

"Could I offer my services? I am well-equipped to fulfill your every desire."

The innuendo was too brazen. I felt my cheeks flame bright red.

"You have a car?" I stuttered. *Lame. Couldn't you think of anything better?*

"I have a car, Señorita, and everything else to make your vacation your most unforgettable yet." The tone was sexy, seductive—and nauseating.

He took one step closer and reached out a finger to stroke my arm, while he undressed me with his eyes. "What a striking turquoise necklace. Have you seen where they get this beautiful stone?"

"No. Is it around here?"

"It would be my honor to show you where they mine the turquoise. Have you heard the legend of the stone?"

"No. Tell me." I stepped back, but bumped into a waist-high chest and couldn't retreat further. He advanced, standing so close I had to lean back against the chest and look up to see into his dark, sensuous eyes.

"The Acoma Indians believe turquoise has a special power to make one attractive and to be loved. You don't need turquoise for that, *mi amor*, but your turquoise has woven a powerful spell over me." He slowly tilted his head as he lowered it toward me, lips apart, eyes holding mine, daring me to look away, to break the spell.

"Is that why you wear that turquoise pendant under your shirt?" I asked, putting my hand on his chest to stop the progression of his lips to mine. "To weave a powerful spell on all the women you meet?"

"This," he laughed, stepping back only far enough to pull the necklace from his shirt, "is from the place I will take you."

The necklace wasn't just a pendant. There was one large piece of turquoise, attached to a silver finding, hanging from the chain. But there were at least twenty other small chunks, not as highly polished, that had been bored through the center and strung on the chain.

"You found this turquoise in the mines?"

"Yes. Each time I go there, I search until I find another to add to my collection. Each has particular significance for me. When I take you, we will find a very special piece for you, and one for me. You will love the—mine." He paused, dropped his voice, and swayed toward me, breathing the last word softly as his lips brushed my ear.

Enough. I ducked out from under the arm that leaned against the chest and whirled coquettishly away. At least I hoped it seemed coquettish. I was about to say thanks, but no thanks, and leave this Lothario to someone who might appreciate his unwanted attention, when I suddenly had a little intuitive flash.

I fingered the tear-shaped turquoise stone dangling from the *naja* on the necklace around my neck. Necklace. Turquoise. Mine. Tingles trickled down my arms to my fingertips. "When can we go?"

"I shall pick you up here at seven o'clock." He grabbed my hand, held it to his lips in a long, languid kiss, and I really think he was going to touch it with his tongue, before I snatched it away.

"I'll be ready at seven."

"Until then, my every thought will be of you."

I'll bet it will be. One more conquest, one more bead for your trophy necklace, I thought as I whirled out of the lobby—and straight into Oswald Barlow's hands.

"Tell me I didn't see what I thought I just saw," Oz said as he grabbed my elbow and guided me, not gently, out of the French doors onto the patio.

"What did you think you just saw?" I responded, trying to catch my breath and regain some measure of composure.

He propelled me into the corner in front of the fountain and grabbed me by the shoulders.

"He was putting the make on you right there in plain sight of everyone," he hissed, "and you were enjoying it. You were egging him on. You let him kiss you." With each accusation, his fingers gripped more tightly into my flesh and he shook me more violently.

"Whoa, boy." Bringing both arms up, I snapped them against his wrists, breaking the grip he had on me. Mistake. I felt like I broke my arm as well as his hold on my shoulders.

"First of all," I said, trying to keep my voice low as I tapped his chest, attempting to contain the fury I wanted to unleash, "who do you think you are to talk to me that way? You are not my husband, nor my father, nor my brother, nor my guardian. Second, what you saw was me carrying out my assignment. Third, he did not kiss me. Fourth, I was not enjoying even one second of that interplay. And fifth, it's none of your business if I had been. *Comprende, amigo?*"

The only sound was the gurgle of the fountain behind me. Oz stood without moving, mute and unmalleable. A bird flew to the adobe arch above the carved wooden cross at the entrance and warbled a maddeningly cheery song that was entirely out of place at the moment.

"And sixth, if you need another, there wasn't a single other soul who saw that little scene except you. I was watching. Do you think I wanted anyone to see me being a brazen hussy? Do you think I liked doing that? I almost threw up when he leered at me. He was nearly drooling."

"The strangest things upset your delicate system," Oz said finally, the trace of a smile playing about his lips. Pulling a verdigre patio chair away from the table, he offered me a seat. "Sorry, Alli. How I feel about you—is certainly no secret."

I held up my hand to stop him. "No, Oz. I don't want to hear this."

"This, dear Alli, is just an apology. Not for feeling the way I do, but for acting like a possessive boor. I just went crazy. You repel my advances, but you were cozying up to that creep like a . . ."

"I don't want to hear that, either," I said. "I have a hunch that I have to follow through. I may need your help, though. I'm not quite sure I can handle Lothario by myself, especially with a bad arm."

"You're not really going with that guy? Allison, he'll have you . . ."

"No, he won't," I interrupted, "because you'll be there to rescue me. But I have a feeling he has a very important key to this puzzle. I just don't know what it is yet."

Chapter Twenty-One

Oz leaned across the table. "What does that Romeo have to do with the kidnapping?"

"There's something flitting around in the back of my mind, something I can't quite put my finger on yet, but I feel he has something—knows something—can give us something very important. I truly don't know what it is. Someone had made a remark, and when Jaqueez started his moves, it triggered my memory. My burst of epiphany was too brief to do any good, but too strong to ignore. It'll come, sooner or later."

"Better be sooner. Margaret said she'd had another call from Saladin."

"Seventy-two hours." I glanced at my watch. "Correction. Seventy hours. Seventy hours to find Bart and Dad, and wrest them out of the terrorists' hands before Saladin tires of his game and . . ." I couldn't finish.

Oz reached across the table and took my hand. I winced.

"Was that physical pain I just saw, or emotional angst at my unwanted touch?"

"Pain. My arm really hurts. I just can't be careful enough, I guess, without the cast."

"Then you'd better go get another one, pronto."

"Right. Just take off and forget the fact that my father and my husband have only seventy hours of life left unless we can find them."

"Point made. At least baby it, will you? Tuck your thumb in your belt and don't use it. Come on." Oz stood and pulled my chair out for me. "We'd better get over to the control center. It's time for the briefing."

We left the patio to the melodious warbler, exiting on the sidewalk behind the kitchen. Through the open window I could hear Jaqueez, in lilting Castillian Spanish, bragging about his latest conquest and his big date for tonight. What had triggered the notion that he had something important to contribute to the solution of our immediate problems? What was it that led me to believe he played an important part in this?

Everyone was crowded around the monitors when we arrived at the control center. "What have you got?" Oz asked, looking over Sky's shoulder.

"It's not what we've got, it's what we haven't got. We just drove in from a night at the Opera. On the way there late last night, we passed a man in a tuxedo walking toward Rancho Encantado. Didn't think much about it, until we saw him again this morning in about the same spot, heading in the same direction. It's an area covered by the monitors, but Xavier hasn't seen any activity there, except our car and a delivery truck—neither of which stopped to pick up the man."

"I saw him when Bart and I were on our way to Los Alamos," I broke in. "At least, I thought I saw someone all decked out in a tux. The sun was in our eyes, and the glare on the windshield prevented a good look. When I turned around, no one was there. Bart didn't see him at all, so I decided I was hallucinating."

"I've seen him," David said quietly. "Twice."

"No one has ever seen a lone walker on the monitor?" Mom asked. "With all the sightings you've just mentioned, sounds like he should have shown up half a dozen times. Dominic, doesn't this system record all entries within the perimeter and give time and location?"

"*Si, mi comandante.*" He did a graceful pirouette, as if dodging a bull with the cape, then faked a sword plunge. "I will disinter the records you need."

"Wonder if he confused that with disembowel," Oz whispered. "That looks like what he was doing to that poor bull."

Mom called the group to order. "Enough on the mysterious overdressed hitchhiker. While Dom does his research, I'll drop the latest bombshell. Saladin is a little upset about losing ten of his highly paid men. He's given us seventy-two hours to have the cash in his hands or—you know the scenario."

"Seventy-two hours from six o'clock this morning," I corrected. "We're now down to sixty-nine hours and forty-five minutes."

All eyes turned to me. I hated the pity I saw there.

"How many of Saladin's men have you got?" I asked.

"We terminated three yesterday afternoon," Dominic answered, "and one got away."

I glanced at Xavier. He quickly averted his eyes.

"We captured two last night, and erased one," Oz added. "Thanks to Allison's eagle eye, I'm here to report it."

"And two in the helicopter crash." Lionel spoke the words no one else would.

"And how many is that?" I asked, holding up eight fingers. "I only count eight. Saladin said we'd taken ten of his men. Which means that there were *four* of Saladin's men on the helicopter. Not two. Jack Alexander and Bartholomew Allan did not plow into that hillside with Saladin's men. And we now have," I checked my watch again, "sixty-nine hours and forty-three minutes to find them."

Oz whistled quietly. "You did it again. Thought circles right around the rest of us whiz kids."

"No, you just believed the obvious. I didn't."

Else reached out and squeezed my hand, her eloquent blue eyes communicating what there was no need to vocalize.

"Now that's established," Mom cut in brusquely, "and tabling the more immediate problem for the moment, Else, how did you and the Tenors' personnel decide to handle the increased security at LAX and JFK for the special celebrities' flights? And did they agree on the train from Albuquerque or a fleet of private jets?"

Else replaced Mom in front of the group. "Since this is now officially an international terrorist threat on U.S. soil, the FBI is involved, so they're handling the airports." A murmur of approval and relief met her announcement. "However, they didn't make this part as easy. After much heated debate, the Tenors' two front men decided a special train will carry those attending this benefit concert, which includes every celebrity you can name, plus every political and society headliner in the country."

Groans met that part of the plan.

"How are you handling that?" Mom asked.

"Not the way the Tenors' people planned," Else said. "The logistics of moving all the guests off their champagne flights and to the railroad were unacceptable. We've issued everyone special IDs that will get them on their planes in New York and Los Angeles. Since we'll have so many government dignitaries aboard, the Air Force is accommodating us with escorts all the way, utilizing the opportunity as training flights."

"How did you solve the railroad transfer?" Mom asked.

"By eliminating the train. It will be standing by, ready to receive its illustrious passengers, but they'll never show up. We've arranged for the jumbo jets to set down on the end of one runway, where a fleet of intermediate jets that Santa Fe's runways can accommodate will be waiting. The passengers will disembark from their luxury flight, flash their special tickets, and get on the connecting flight to Santa Fe."

"No one will go near the terminal?" Lionel asked.

"No," Else said with a conspiratorial smile. "The paparazzi will wait at the Albuquerque terminal and at the railway station, along with anyone who may have had any nasty little plans for the passengers, without ever getting close to their quarry."

"How many people are involved in the new plan?" Xavier asked, speaking up for the first time.

"Only one airline official—the president of the carrier we're using. He's treating this as an emergency evacuation exercise, testing to see how many of their planes and crews could be ready at a moment's notice to evacuate the city. He'll issue the alert with only enough time for the crews to assemble and have the planes ready."

"*Maravilloso!*" Dominic exclaimed, looking up from his computer printouts. "This was your idea?"

"Yes. It's going to cost a pretty penny for the reserved train we won't use, but the additional security makes it worth it. Only ten people know the real plan, and nine of them are in this room. If there are breaches in security, we'll know where to look."

I glanced at Xavier, then quickly looked away.

"Good job, Else," Mom said. "Then how about from Santa Fe airport to the Opera House?"

"We hoped to use only helicopters, but the numbers made it impossible. Everybody who is anybody seems to think they have to be seen at this event, coupled with the fact that the new Opera House now seats twenty-one hundred and twenty-eight."

Mom glanced at a paper in her hands. "I have a guest list of twenty-five hundred."

"I know," Else said. "There are more coming than can be seated for the performance. So we're using buses as well. We've separated Hollywood and Washington as much as possible, trying to keep senators, governors, and cabinet members assigned to the helicopters to get them here as quickly as possible. Unfortunately, the President and Vice President insist on traveling with their Hollywood friends. They'll make a fuss, but even the President of the United States doesn't get his way all the time."

"How do you plan to separate them, and where, since they'll all be flying together?"

"Celebrities have blue tickets, along with those we didn't feel had a need for additional protection. Certain political figures, anyone we felt might be a target for the terrorists, received red tickets. As they get off the planes, red ticket holders will be directed to the waiting helicopters, blue tickets to the buses."

"And the President's party?"

"The Secret Service insisted that they use the fleet of helicopters the President always uses. We agreed. They'll arrive just before the planes land and will be waiting. Your social butterfly President wasn't too keen on the separation, but he had to bow to his security people's wishes."

"I'll bet you did a little arm-bending to make sure they stood firm against his insistence," Mom laughed.

"Actually, it took a personal visit to the President himself to convince him. He was adamant that he be treated as one of the guests until I pointed out the reason Anastasia was involved."

"Send a pretty face to get the job done. Did he even know what Anastasia is?" Oz asked with a sardonic grin.

"He does now," Else smiled.

"Any questions?" Mom asked. "Any problems anyone can foresee? You all know where you're supposed to be that night, and what you're supposed to be doing."

She turned from us and deposited her notes on the table behind her, arranging the pages with studied precision. Taking a deep breath,

Mom then faced the group with folded arms and leaned against the table with one hip.

"Now. The immediate problem—how to find Jack and Bart and get them back. Alive."

Only the hum of the computers was audible in the room. No one moved. No fidgeting, no rustle of papers, no refilling of coffee cups, no smart asides that were the normal part of briefings.

"I think you're all aware of Allison's special tie to her father," Mom continued. "I'm going to let her tell you about it, and what she's seen, which is basically all we've got to go on."

This caught me off guard. I stood, uncertain, in front of this group of trained professionals, not knowing how they'd receive my very non-professional offering.

"I can't explain exactly what happens. I receive thought patterns from my father, pictures, impressions, almost like he's talking to me, but it's not really words. We can be separated by many miles, even hundreds of miles. You've probably heard it called telepathy, or thought transference, or extra-sensory perception, and I guess that's about as good a way to describe it as I can come up with."

Affirmative nods from my rapt audience.

"What I received, as Dominic was trying to identify the bodies on the hillside, was an impression of Dad, bound and gagged, in a cave. I think the trauma I felt at the thought of losing him and Bart triggered a response in him, because he was very groggy from the sedatives, but came out of it enough to assure me he was alive."

"What about Bart?" Else asked. "Did he tell you anything about your husband?"

"No. Only that they'd been separated when the van met the helicopter. I haven't been able to 'talk' to him since then. I think they're keeping him totally sedated. But I did see, feel, know, somehow, that he's been moved." I described the impression of the small, smoothed-walled, ancient room I could see him in, and the large, dark silhouette of what I believed to be Black Mesa.

"San Ildefonso Pueblo is just below the Mesa," Mom added. "I think that needs to be our first priority. Oz, work with the local authorities and get permission to seal off and search the area. I haven't had time to research all the agencies necessary to go through, but I guess the best place to start is the tribal governor. If they won't allow outsiders in, maybe they'll assign it to the tribal police. Do whatever it takes, but we've got to have the search done by nightfall, in case they try to move him again."

"Will do." Then Oz turned to me. "About Bart—you feel strongly that he's still alive. Why? What have you got?"

"Absolutely nothing," I admitted. "At least, nothing concrete. I'm not even sure of the source of my feeling."

The promise of an old Indian woman that I could find Bart alive didn't seem like something I could hang my hopes on. My hand went to the necklace as I addressed the rest of the group. "I'm going to visit what I believe may be the source of that assurance this morning. Maybe I'll have something more to tell you by noon. I'm following a lead tonight, with some backup from Oz, that I hope will produce something, but I'm not even sure where it's going, so—I'm sorry. That's really all I can give you."

I felt impotent, ineffective, totally unqualified to work with people who spent their lives dealing in absolutes, with fact and figures and concrete evidence.

Else laid her hand on my arm. "Every one of us has relied on intuition at one time or another, on a gut feeling that hard evidence said just couldn't be. Follow your feelings." She winked, and in a stage whisper said, "We have an advantage over mere men. We have woman's intuition. Trust it. It'll rarely lead you astray."

Her facetious comment relieved the tension in the room. The men loudly objected to being demeaned by a mere woman, and chaos reigned for a brief minute before Dominic's astounding announcement brought the clamor to an abrupt end.

"There's nothing here. I've been through every hour of printout since we set up. There's been no foot traffic on that road since we turned the monitors on." Dominic flashed the printout. "No man in a tuxedo. Nothing."

Chapter Twenty-Two

Sky motioned for the papers. Dominic tossed the stack across the table. Else and David leaned over his shoulder, and the three of them scrutinized the entries.

They finished in silence. Sky pushed his horn-rimmed glasses onto his forehead and thoughtfully massaged the bridge of his nose with his thumb and forefinger.

Else studied David. "You said you saw him twice. When?"

"The first night we were here. I was riding the perimeter on a horse, and as I crossed the road I saw a man and woman walking toward the entrance to Rancho Encantado. Their backs were to me, but the tails on his tuxedo were obvious, and she was walking in high heels and a formal, filmy gown. As if they'd just come from the Opera. I assumed their car had broken down, but they were at the gate, so I rode on."

"And the second time?" Else pressed.

"On my way to the Opera helipad to get the helicopter. He was alone, still in his tux, further down the road, but headed for the Ranch."

Mom broke the silence that followed. "I've seen the woman." She walked to the window and stared out before turning to speak. "Her dress is black, with an organza skirt that comes almost to her ankles in handkerchief points. She has red hair and wears it high with an ornate comb and a Spanish mantilla."

"Where did you see her, and when?" I asked, amazed that Mom hadn't mentioned her to me.

"The first night we were here, at dusk, when I was watching the Ranch house. She put a flower in the hand of the statue of the child just off the driveway, then disappeared along the flagstone path into the little park. I thought she was a guest. She was there again this morning, in the same clothing, just before sunrise."

"Then why doesn't the printout show it?" Lionel strode to the door and back with the graceful energy of a caged cat.

"Could there be some kind of glitch?" Xavier asked.

"The system checked out perfectly. It's picked up every single intrusion into, and every movement in, the perimeter."

"I think it malfunctioned one other time," I said quietly, looking at Xavier. "When Oz and I went to the cave, there were only supposed to be two men. A third one materialized out of nowhere and nearly got Oz."

No one spoke. Dominic grabbed the printout, flipping pages until he found what he was looking for.

"There were three. Why did you think there were only two?"

"Because Xavier *told* us there were two," Oz said, grabbing the handsome Arab by his shirt and hauling him to his feet, despite the wounded leg that Xavier still kept propped on a chair.

"What's going on, Xavier? No more pussyfooting around. Why did you tell us two, and who is the mirror image of you that Allison shot, just before he got me?" Oz slammed the Arab back into the chair and bent over him. "Traitors pay certain penalties where you come from. It would be my pleasure to make sure you follow the customs of your people."

Mom put her hand on Oz's shoulder. Oz glanced at her face and stepped aside. Diminutive Margaret Alexander, all five feet four inches of her, stood before Xavier and asked quietly, "Were you simply protecting your twin brother? He is your twin, isn't he? Your soul mate, in everything but politics. That's how you got shot. You didn't expect to see him at the cave, nor did he expect to see you. He shot you in the leg so he wouldn't have to kill you, and you shot wild to let him get away. Are you a traitor, Xavier?"

Xavier shook his head, his lips pressed tight in a thin line, his dark eyes defiant, pained.

"Why didn't you tell Oz and Allison about the third man?" When he didn't answer, Mom continued. "Because you recognized your brother on the monitor. You chose at that moment not Oz's life and possibly Allison's, but your brother's. Admirable under some circumstances. Not here. Not now."

Xavier looked up at Mom. "I am no traitor. Your cause is my cause to the end. I would have warned Oz in time, but I could see that Allison had spotted my brother. I let Allah decide between them. I am no traitor," he repeated fervently. "What will you do?"

"To you? Nothing. I'm going to walk out of this room and find my husband. I believe your custom is to leave the punishment to those who were wronged. Your fate is now in the hands of those whose lives you put in jeopardy, whose lives you swore to protect when you joined Anastasia."

Sky broke in. "May I handle this?"

Mom nodded her consent, turned and walked to the door, pausing with her hand on the knob. "Allison, will you come with me?"

I followed her into the dazzling New Mexico morning. We walked silently along the footpath that led to the pool, but instead of turning back to the Ranch house, Mom crossed to the Cantina.

The sun was warm on the long, low porch that surrounded the Cantina, but the interior was dark and cool and empty. I stood in the doorway and watched as Mom walked aimlessly around the room. She ran a finger along the piano keys, absently checked book titles on shelves across one wall, then dropped, dejected, into a rattan chair at one of the round tables that filled the comfortable, intimate room.

"What will they do to him?" I asked, joining her.

"I'm not sure. I was surprised at Sky's interference. Normally in those circles, especially in Xavier's culture, when there's been a betrayal, those betrayed determine the punishment."

"They won't kill him, will they?" I thought of elegant, compassionate Else; quiet, serious David; exuberant, golden-haired Lionel. Dominic, with his graceful matador moves, and mature, scholarly Rip Schyler. And Oz. They couldn't possibly do that. Could they?

Mom didn't answer. She was so far away, I wasn't sure she even heard me. I took her hands in mine. "What are you going to do now?" I asked softly.

She closed her eyes and leaned back in her chair. "I'm going to sit here for another minute, then I'm going to drive over to see Cerelia." Mom opened her eyes. "Do you remember where she lives?"

"I'm sure I can find it."

"Many people believe that medicine men, diviners, shamans, wise old village women, even witches have no special powers or abilities. But in the twenty years I've studied cultures the world over, I've come to believe that we 'educated, civilized' people can learn much from those who stay close to their earth origins and practice their cultural beliefs."

"You think there really is power in the turquoise necklace? And that Pepper's grandmother can teach me how to use it?"

"I would be the last one to say no, given the gift you possess. At any rate, she's our best hope for the moment. Let's go talk to her."

Ten minutes later, we pulled up in front of Cerelia's house. Pepper's white four-wheel drive vehicle was parked out front beside a disreputable-looking pickup. She came to the door as we approached, tears streaming down her face.

"I'm afraid you're too late. Grandmother is slipping away. She doesn't know me anymore."

Mom put her arms around the young woman and hugged her close. "I'm so sorry, Pepper. I hoped to tell her how many times I've thought of her over the years, and how grateful I was that she shared her cultural heritage with me. She was a very special person."

A tall young man with black hair streaming over his shoulders stepped through the door. The scowl on his face abated the tiniest bit as he heard the last part of Mom's consolation, but returned when he noticed the necklace around my neck.

Pepper turned, saw his expression, and put her hand affectionately on his arm. "This is my brother, Tomas." That she adored him was written all over her face. That there was an unsettled issue between them was evident as she looked at him.

"Tomas, this is . . ."

"I know. The Gifted Child. Grandmother told me she was coming. But I didn't know she was going to give . . ."

"Hush. It's all right. That's what Grandmother wanted." Pepper turned to us.

"Thank you for coming. I appreciate your kind thoughts."

"Pepper, did she say anything more?" I asked. "Anything that would help me?"

"No. I'm sorry."

"Then I might as well give this back to you. She said she'd teach me how to use its power, but without her guidance, it's only a beautiful piece of jewelry. And it belongs to your family." I started to remove the necklace, but Pepper stopped me.

"No. Grandmother wanted you to have it. She said you could learn to use it. And you do need it. Any word on your husbands?"

"No," I said.

Mom corrected me. "What Allison means is we've had nothing official. Through her connection to her father, we think he's being held somewhere on or near the San Ildefonso Pueblo."

Tomas exchanged his scowl for an unreadable expression. When I looked at him, my mind saw a youthful Indian brave, clad only in buckskin breeches, a leather thong tied about his tan, muscular arm, racing bareback across the river bottoms on a pinto pony, dark hair flying in the wind. Too many Hollywood westerns, I guess. But there was something wild, untamed, and angry about this handsome young man who looked poised to either run or attack at the slightest provocation.

He did neither. He simply stalked to his pickup and drove away.

"Tomas is caught not only between the struggles of childhood and adulthood, but the struggles Native Americans have living in two worlds," Pepper explained. "He's pulled between the materialism of America and the traditional pueblo life with its deep ties to the earth and the natural rhythm of life. This difficult time is made worse because he was very close to Grandmother."

"And he resents my having the necklace."

Pepper looked away. "Yes."

Grasping the turquoise pendant that dangled from the *naja*, I knew I must speak to Tomas, alone.

"Where's he going? Will he be back soon? I need to talk to him."

"He often goes to the house of a friend near the San Ildefonso Pueblo. They spend hours training a horse there when they're not working. I could ask him to call you."

"Please do." I hesitated before adding, "I think he may be able to help us find my father."

Pepper stared at me. "Why?"

"The thought came to me as he was leaving. Probably because he knows the area so well, I guess." I wasn't sure just why I felt that way. Explaining hunches and feelings was getting more complicated.

"Can we see Cerelia?" Mom asked. "To say good-bye, if nothing more."

Pepper hesitated a little too long in replying.

"Forgive me, Pepper. I know in your culture this is a very private time for your family. I shouldn't have asked. Is there anything we can do for you?"

"No, thank you. But please stay in touch."

We headed back to Rancho Encantado, silently lost in our own thoughts. "What are you going to do now?" I asked Mom as we approached the Ranch.

"We have two immediate problems. Find out where the glitch is in the perimeter defense system, and hope Dominic and Lionel can fix it so this area is totally secured for the Tenors' arrival on Monday, and locate our men. Saladin broke his oath, a serious offense in his culture, which means he has no bounds. No parameters. He's volatile and unstable. If Jack and Bart become a problem in any way, he'll dispose of that problem."

"While you work on securing the Ranch, I'm going to drive up to San Ildefonso Pueblo and see if I can find Tomas."

Mom pulled into the parking area and left the car running. "Want me to send someone with you?"

"No. They all have their assignments, and we're three short already. I don't anticipate any problems talking to Pepper's brother, so I certainly don't need to take them from their job just to go along for the ride."

Mom covered my hand with hers. "I wouldn't let you go alone if I didn't feel you could handle whatever you run into. But please, be very careful."

I touched the necklace. "Pepper's grandmother said this would protect me from danger as long as I kept it on. I'm not about to take it off now."

"Don't take that promise too literally. She could have had one thing in mind, and you could run into quite another."

We got out of the car and Mom hugged me, holding me very tight for an extra second. "I love you. Be careful," she said softly as she let go.

"I love you, too, Mom. And you be careful. Remember, Saladin is full of nasty surprises. If he thinks the new blonde guest at the Ranch has anything to do with Anastasia . . ."

Mom shut the door and waved me off.

I thought about that as I pulled back onto the highway and headed north on 285-84. What would he throw at us next? What would he think we'd be least likely to expect?

I buzzed Mom on my radio. "I'm sure you thought about the possibility that Saladin might decide to kidnap Margaret and Allison from the estate in California, just to ensure that he got his money. Then he'd have everyone and could do away with Anastasia once and for all."

"The thought had crossed my mind before our doubles were even on the plane," Mom replied, "so I put Jim on full alert at the estate and told him to bring in extra guards. If Saladin found out those two gals are plants, and we're here, I don't even want to think what he'd do."

"I should have known you'd have covered all the bases."

"Having been at this business longer than you, I'd certainly hope so," Mom laughed.

Passing the turnoff to San Ildefonso Pueblo, I drove slowly across the Rio Grande River, then backtracked on Highway 30 north toward Española, where we'd been chased by the white van and eluded Saladin's men at the 'sociable' man's farm.

The most outstanding geographical feature in the area, Black Mesa loomed dark and shadowy over the picturesque San Ildefonso Pueblo, with ranches and rural subdivisions spread on the flatlands below its slopes. Pulling off the highway on the west side of the mesa, I rolled down my windows to breathe the cool, clear mountain air. I studied the mesa while I tried to reach my father, tried to get some clue as to what I should be doing here.

Turning onto the access road that ran along the highway, I drove slowly past the village, then followed the country road to see how close I could get to the mountain. A stand of cottonwoods, tall and green, outlined the course of the Rio Grande, which wound between me and Black Mesa.

Suddenly a horse reared above the sagebrush, tossing its magnificent head and pawing the air with its hooves.

Chapter Twenty-Three

I pulled to the side of the narrow road, opened my door and stood on the door frame to see over the high clumps of blue-green sagebrush. The gorgeous pinto horse reared again.

Someone had a rope on it. Standing on tiptoe, I could see the top of a head with long black hair. Slim chance that I'd stumbled across Tomas, but I'd check it out, just the same.

I found a dirt driveway up the road a few hundred yards and followed it back through sagebrush and piñon to a fork in the road. One lane seemed to wander toward Black Mesa, the other to a couple of huge cottonwood trees shading a diminutive, square, ancient-looking adobe house.

Tomas' pickup was parked under the trees near a small herd of sheep enclosed by a jagged coyote fence. The corral, behind the house, was a rickety-looking affair of juniper poles and crooked fence posts.

I parked my car next to the pickup and got out. The haunting sound of a native flute drifted across the hot, bare earth. Following the sound toward the corral, I skirted a large cage made of chicken wire and weathered plywood. The dilapidated affair seemed to be standing only because it leaned heavily against the side of the house.

On first glance the cage seemed empty, but as I passed the end, a vicious snarl, then an angry roar emanated from the shadowy interior. A huge cat shook the flimsy-looking structure as it raised on its hind legs and hit the wire, roaring with displeasure at my presence. Or its confinement. Or both.

I backed carefully away from the cage, afraid to take my eyes from the tawny-colored cat. A cougar. A fully-grown, adult mountain lion.

It roared again, dropped to all four feet, paced a couple of angry turns in the cage, then hurled its length against the puny chicken wire.

Whirling from the cage, I ran smack into a tall, bare-chested, irate Native American. "What are you doing here?" Tomas demanded.

"I came to find you."

"Why?"

"Because your grandmother's necklace told me you could help me find my father."

"How did it tell you that?" he asked, pulling me around the corner, out of sight of the enraged cat.

"I'm not really sure. When I met you, the presence of the necklace around my neck was intensified, and when I touched this piece," I showed him the dangling turquoise in the center of the *naja*, "I just felt that I had to talk to you, that there was some way you'd be able to help me find my father."

"You said my grandmother had not instructed you in using the power of the necklace."

"No, she gave it to me, but was exhausted after our short conversation, so she said to come back and she'd teach me. I'm so sorry we were too late to talk to her. Mom was especially disappointed. She loved Cerelia."

Tomas stepped toward me. I couldn't read the expression on his handsome face, but it didn't look especially friendly. He reached for the necklace. I stood perfectly still, staring into those unfathomable dark eyes.

"When Grandmother called on the power of the turquoise, she grasped this stone, and this stone only. She did not show you this?" He fingered the turquoise pendant dangling from the *naja*.

"No, Tomas. She placed the necklace on me and told me not to take it off until the danger was over—that it would increase my own gift, and help me find my husband and my father. Did Pepper tell you what happened?"

"Yes." The tall, tan young man stood still, an arm's length away, and stared, his expression still unreadable.

"If we don't get my father and Bart out of Saladin's hands in the next two days, he'll kill them. With those two out of the way, he'll then be free to kill many other people—not just in some remote part of the world, but right here where it could be someone you love."

Still Tomas didn't speak. But his eyes left mine and he cocked his head, gazing into the distance, as if listening. Then I heard it, too. A car was coming. We peered around the corner.

A white van.

The vehicle, not Pepper's, approached the fork in the road, coming from the direction of Black Mesa. It slowed, began the turn to the highway, then stopped. The man at the window pointed toward the house.

"Do you know them?" I asked.

"No. Do you?"

"I hope not, but I'm afraid I might. That man looks like the terrorist who tried to kill my husband and me, and was one of the men who kidnapped him. They're not close enough to tell. But they can't be after me. I'm in Santa Barbara."

Tomas pulled me back behind the house.

"I mean, I'm supposed to be in Santa Barbara. No one should have recognized me as a blonde. Unless they've discovered that Mom and I are still here at Rancho Encantado, they wouldn't be interested in me."

The van started moving again. Tomas looked around the corner. "They're coming this way. Stay here. I'll find out what they want, and what they've been doing on the sacred mountain."

Long black hair streaming behind him, the tall, lean, young man strode purposefully toward the advancing vehicle. The cat growled as Tomas walked by. What on earth was he doing with a wild cat in a cage? Somehow, that didn't seem totally incongruous. As I watched Tomas wait for the van, his feet spread wide, hands on his hips, I imagined his jeans as buckskin and his boots as moccasins. The image was incredibly powerful. All he needed was a bow and a quiver full of arrows, and the vision of the young warrior would be complete.

Tomas stood straight and tall and defiant as the driver leaned out of the window and pointed at my car. There was an interchange of comments, but I couldn't hear what was being said, though it was apparent the man wasn't pleased about something.

I groped for my gun. No purse. No gun. I'd left them in the car. *Great anti-terrorist agent I make*, I thought. *Unarmed and defenseless.*

Suddenly Tomas shouted and ran. He leaped over the top of a waist-high clump of sagebrush and disappeared in the undergrowth as the driver pointed an automatic weapon out the window and fired it. The driver and the gunman on the passenger's side burst out of the van and took off after Tomas. A third man, weapon drawn, ran toward the house.

There was no place to hide—unless I could make it to the piñons before he got to the back of the house.

I whirled toward the trees. I'd only made it the few steps to the end of the house when I heard a whistle from near the sheep pen. Tomas, hidden behind the coyote fence, pointed at the roof of the adobe house, then did a curving motion with his hand. *Go around the house and get on the roof.* I raced around the corner.

A pole ladder leaned against the side of the house. I lost no time in climbing it. As I flung myself over the top and lay still on one side of the house, the cougar roared on the other. The third man had reached the cage.

The caged animal went crazy. The two men chasing Tomas ran toward the house and I could hear the men taunting the cougar, gathered around the flimsy cage. Didn't they know that was a stupid thing to do?

The ladder creaked next to my head. I rolled away, but had no place to go. The flat roofed adobe was too small. There was no place to hide.

Suddenly Tomas appeared on the ladder, leaped silently, gracefully to the roof, and dropped down beside me. He removed his boots, crawled to the edge of the house where the three men were noisily harassing the cougar, and untied a rope that led over the side. With a powerful jerk that sent him tumbling backwards, he released the door of the cage. The big cat was loose.

Piercing screams rent the air. An automatic weapon crackled in a staccato burst of deafening noise. The roar of the angry cat echoed across the sun-baked earth. Sheep bleated plaintively, helplessly trapped as their mortal enemy attacked just outside their pen. A dog barked somewhere in the distance.

Then it was quiet. The only sound was the pastoral melody of the Indian flute drifting up from the corral, a paradox to the violence below.

Tomas crept to the edge of the roof. I joined him in time to see the cougar flee through the undergrowth toward Black Mesa.

The engine on the van kicked over. One man was escaping. Two others were down, badly mauled. The driver jerked the van in gear, spun the wheels backing out of the driveway, and kicked up a huge cloud of dust as he sped toward the highway.

"There's loyalty for you. He didn't think twice about his companions. Guess we'll have to take them into custody," I said, wondering where Anastasia had stashed the other terrorists. I knew they hadn't been turned over to the sheriff.

Tomas looked at me with a question in his eyes that went unasked. I asked mine. "What did they want?"

"They said they were camping by the river and saw your car. Wondered if it belonged to a friend of theirs who was supposed to meet them."

"What did you say that had them shooting at you?" I got to my feet and brushed the dirt from my skirt and tee.

"I told them they could not camp there. Non-tribal members are not allowed on sacred ground. They didn't like that."

"You sure move fast. I'm glad they didn't hurt you."

"I saw their guns. I was ready to run."

"Tomas, what about the cat? What were you doing with it? What will happen now that it's loose?"

Tomas held the ladder while I descended, explaining as he followed. "She'd been killing sheep in the area. I captured her, but I couldn't find her cubs. I hoped to get them together before the babies starved, then take them all into the mountains and set them free where they couldn't get to the sheep."

"How did you come to have that ingenious cage rigged to open from the roof?"

"It is an old cage. I have trapped many things, observed them, then turned them loose. It isn't wise to open the cage on a wild animal while you are standing next to it."

We rounded the corner as one of the claw-ravaged terrorists tried to get to his feet. Tomas simply pointed to the ground and the man sat back down, holding his torn, bleeding arm. The other wasn't moving at all. He had a bullet hole in his head, victim of his partner's wild shooting.

"What will you do with these men?" Tomas questioned.

"Some of their group have been captured and are being held for interrogation. This one will be put with the others, and the coroner can have that one."

"How can I help you find your father?" Tomas asked, dragging the dead terrorist to my car and directing the tall, mauled one to walk ahead of us.

I opened the trunk. "I thought you could tell me where he might be." I described the place where I felt my father was being held.

Tomas shook his head. "It would not be at the pueblo. But there might be an old deserted house like this one that is not used anymore. No one lives in this house, but we use the buildings and the land." He smiled for the first time. "We like running water and electricity."

Suddenly I felt my father was trying to reach me. The message was weak and unclear, as if he were struggling to come out of a drugged state. "Bunny, I feel you're near."

"Dad, where are you?"

He was gone. It was as if a thick veil had lifted momentarily, giving me a brief glimpse of my father, then had fallen again, hiding him from me.

"What is it?" Tomas asked as he turned from depositing the body in the trunk.

"I just had an impression of my father, but not in the room. He was in a car. It was fleeting; he was there, and then he was gone. They've been keeping him sedated, and it was as if he was finally able to come out from under the influence of the drugs long enough to contact me."

Again he came, a brief glimpse, still tied, hand and foot, struggling to see out the window of a car. "Allison, can you see me? Can you hear me? I feel you are somewhere near."

As I felt his words form in my mind, my heart sank.

"Tomas, my father was in that van!"

Chapter Twenty-Four

Tomas shoved the tall terrorist into the trunk, thrust his long legs and large feet over the edge, and slammed the lid. "Follow them in your car," he ordered. "I'll get on the roof and tell you which way he went on the highway. I can't leave the horse until I've secured the corral."

Tomas raced for the house. I jumped in the car and jammed it into reverse. My father was here! I couldn't believe it.

Slamming on my brakes at the paved road, I paused only long enough to check traffic, then sped toward the highway. Tomas was plainly visible on the roof over the top of the sagebrush, pointing back to the junction of 30 and 502. I bit my lip and jammed the accelerator to the floorboards. If they'd gone toward Española, there was a minute chance I could find them. But this way . . .

No van in sight. How far was it to the junction? Five, six miles. I glanced at the speedometer: ninety-three. I had to catch them before the junction. Or at least be able to see which way they went.

"Dad, can you hear me? Where are you now?"

Nothing.

I concentrated, willing him to hear me, willing him to overcome the drugs and tell me what he could see, where he was, where they were going.

No answer.

The junction was coming up, with its construction zone all the way down the hill. *Please don't let there be a problem*, I prayed.

But there was.

A man in an orange hard hat and shirt, waving a stop sign, stepped into the one open lane. *No. Turn it around. Let me just slow down. Don't stop me.*

I considered ignoring him. Driving right on by. But ahead, a huge belly-dump truck and trailer filled with gravel pulled into that same single lane, slowly, effectively blocking all progress. There was nowhere to go. Not even a shoulder where I could illegally bypass the tortoise-paced truck and the traffic following it.

"Dad, where are you? Please answer me."

Nothing. Just the impression of my father slumped in the backseat of a moving vehicle.

Had he been given another injection? Why could he reach me before and not now? Or had he started to revive, and the driver not being able to take time to sedate him, had knocked him out? Or worse, shot him?

I shook off the morose mood I was plunged into by that last thought. *There must be something I can do besides sit here, helpless.* But I couldn't think of a thing.

Morning gone, the afternoon grew hot. Melting sun beat down on the new blacktop, creating heat waves that shimmered across the highway. The wounded man, stuffed beside his dead companion, pounded on the inside of the trunk and kicked the backseat. The only thing that prevented the flagman from hearing him was the approach of the huge, slow-moving truck that drowned out every other sound in a grinding of gears and roar of engine on the uphill climb.

My arm hurt. The pain had escalated from a dull, throbbing ache before I climbed up and down the high-stepped ladder to deep, penetrating, teeth-clenching pain. I dug in my purse for a couple of aspirin and finally found the little tin I carried them in buried in a corner in the bottom. Empty. I tried to console myself with the nasty thought of swallowing aspirin without water, but at this point, I'd have gladly done it.

"Dad, where are you? How are you? How can I find you?"

Just a dense, dark void.

Why had they moved him so often? Did they know about our connection and think I'd find him? Were they also moving Bart daily?

I leaned my head on the steering wheel as the line of traffic crawled slowly by. How could I possibly find Bart? How could the necklace help me?

Please, Father, I prayed. *Help me find them before it's too late.*

The car behind me honked impatiently as the last vehicle in the line moved out of the way and the flagman signaled it was my turn to creep slowly forward. Lot of good it did now. The white van had long since disappeared, and I had no way of knowing which way it had turned— toward Santa Fe or toward Los Alamos.

I headed back to Rancho Encantado to unload the unpleasant cargo in my trunk, alternately trying to contact Dad and praying for help in finding him and Bart. I couldn't believe I'd been so close, and had let them get away.

Oz met me as I drove into the parking lot. "Was this coincidental, or were you waiting for me?" I asked as he opened the door.

"I was watching the monitors, waiting for you to come back."

He was interrupted by pounding from the trunk.

"Oh, I should have radioed you," I explained. "I have a dead man in my trunk and another who needs to see a doctor. He was mauled by a mad mountain lion."

Oz stared, dumbfounded. "What're they doing in your trunk?" He slid into the passenger seat.

"It's a long story. Do we let this one out here, or drive somewhere away from the Ranch house to unleash the torrent of obscenities that will flow when the trunk is opened?"

"Where did you get them? I can't believe you. Margaret should never have let you . . ."

"No lectures," I interrupted. "Do you want them here or somewhere else?"

"Let's go back out to the road, and I'll direct you from there." Oz shut the door and buckled his seat belt.

"They had Dad in the van. I let him get away."

Oz radioed for Sky to meet him at the "holding pen," then turned to me, ready for an explanation. As I began to recite the morning's events, he stopped me and shoved the radio into my hand. "Sorry," I said. "I can't hold that and drive, too. I only have one good arm at this point."

Oz held the radio up while I reported so everyone could hear. He just shook his head when I finished, his gray eyes filled with concern. "Allison, you can't just go running off by yourself."

I held up my hand. "Don't even start. Mom knew I was going and said she thought I could handle it. I did. End of discussion."

Oz opened his mouth to protest.

"Didn't I prove anything to you the other night at the cave? I'm not a total novice at this business, you know."

He clenched his teeth and fists and sat silently stewing as we wound up over a hill, through an area of private residences, then turned off the pavement onto a tiny dirt road that was no more than two dirt tire tracks. A ramshackle cabin crouched under a rocky cliff at the end of the trail.

"This is the holding pen?" I said, not believing the rickety-looking place could hold itself up much longer, much less contain anyone bent on leaving.

"This is it." Oz opened his door. "Stay in the car. Lock the doors, then punch open the trunk when I get back there. Wait in the car till Sky gets here. He'll take care of the other guy. Then you go back to Rancho Encantado and get that arm looked at."

"I don't get to come in?"

"Absolutely not. Don't you dare get out of that car." He locked the door, slammed it for emphasis, and signaled when he was in position with gun drawn. I punched the "open trunk" button and the lid popped up.

Neither of us was prepared for what happened next. The wounded terrorist launched himself like a jack-in-the-box the minute the lid opened, ramming Oz full-force in the stomach.

They rolled in the dead, dry weeds, the tall terrorist straining for Oz's gun, and Oz struggling to keep it out of his reach. They both were handicapped. The terrorist only had one good arm. Oz had two, but his were short, much shorter than the man who was trying to reach the gun.

I grabbed my purse, retrieved my own gun and jumped from the car as they wrestled back toward me, rolling over and over with grunts and snarls and language no lady should ever have to hear.

Oz was losing. He couldn't keep his gun out of the long-armed terrorist's grasp and couldn't bend his arm to use it, so he dropped it and rolled away, slugging his attacker in the jaw.

The terrorist immediately lunged for the gun, reaching past Oz's outstretched hand. As his fingers closed around the handle of the pistol, I stomped on them with all of my one hundred and twenty pounds, jabbing my gun to his forehead. "Roll off him," I commanded. "Then don't move another muscle, for any reason."

Oz was on his feet in a flash, prying the gun from the terrorist's hand. "You disobeyed orders," he said, securing the man's hands behind his back with his own belt.

"You wanted me to stay in the car while a wounded, desperate creature attacked you?"

"That was the idea."

"Hey, remember I'd seen this guy. I knew he had at least a foot and a hundred pounds on you. Even though he only had one hand, you were outmatched. And he didn't want to be caught. I'm supposed to stay in the car through that?"

Oz stood up and looked me in the eye. "Yes."

"Why can't you macho men admit that just every once in a while you could use a little help?"

"I didn't want you in any danger," Oz said, enunciating his words slowly, clearly, in an exaggerated manner. "Do you understand me? I want you out of here, out of trouble, out of my life forever. I don't want to baby-sit you, I don't want to worry about you. I don't want to . . . ," he grabbed me by the shoulders and spun me into the driver's seat of the car, ". . . love you," he finished quietly as he slammed the door.

He grabbed the body from the trunk, dropped him on the ground next to the shackled man, and pointed down the trail. "Go."

I left.

Was he embarrassed because I'd saved his life again? Was he ashamed because he hadn't been able to handle the guy? Or was he upset because I had stepped in just before he had the situation under control, and it made him look bad?

Not bad. He just needed a little help. Why was that so hard for guys to accept from the female gender, especially when it was under circumstances like this? I didn't want to think about his last statement, blocking it from my mind, pretending it had been drowned out in the slamming door.

Sky arrived on cue and motioned me to stop as I reached the pavement. I rolled down my window and faked a casual smile.

"Everything under control?" he asked, arching his eyebrows to notify me that his analyst eye had caught my distress.

"Everything except rampant male hormones," I said. "Oz is waiting for you. Sky, they had Dad in the van, not one hundred yards from where I was, and I didn't know it until the man drove away. Please make him tell you where they're taking Dad, and where they're holding Bart."

Sky nodded, waiting expectantly for the rest of the outburst.

"And find out why they've moved Dad so often. Are they moving Bart, too? What's going on?"

"We'll see what we can do," he said, removing his horn-rimmed glasses and leaning out the window to ask with fatherly concern, "How are you holding up? Need a listening ear or a sympathetic shoulder?"

"Thanks," I sighed, shaking my head. "I just need my dad and my husband back, alive and well."

"We'll work on that," he said reassuringly, and drove away with a wave.

I headed back to Rancho Encantado, exhausted. I was drained, emotionally and physically, and didn't have any idea how to replenish either my energy or my enthusiasm.

Two o'clock. We'd lost eight of the precious seventy-two hours. Only sixty-four hours left before Saladin . . .

Don't think about that. Think about how to find Dad. And Bart.

I hadn't come up with any good ideas by the time I arrived back at the Ranch. I was not only too tired to think anymore, I was numb. Everywhere but my aching arm, which by this time had begun to swell. I was in trouble. If I told Mom how much it hurt and that I'd damaged it again, I'd end up at the hospital to have it reset. That would take me out of the action for another few hours, at the very least, and as much as a day if it had to be x-rayed and I ended up in the huge cast I'd had before.

No time for that.

I parked the car, waved at Molly as I went through the lobby, and headed straight for my room. I stripped off my dirty clothes, got in the shower, and let the water stream over me, washing away dirt and grime, hoping it could wash away weariness and despair and pain at the same time.

The colorful, hand-painted designs on the bathroom window didn't cheer me, nor did the noisy bird singing his fool head off on the shady patio by the fountain. I wrapped a towel around my wet hair, swallowed twice as many aspirin as a doctor would have prescribed, and dropped on the honey-colored corduroy lounge.

Where had they taken Dad? Was he all right? Where was Bart? How could I possibly find him? My hand reached for the necklace. I hadn't put it on. I got up, pulled on jeans and a T-shirt, and slid the heavy turquoise and silver necklace over my head. Not that wearing it made a difference, but now at least I had something to play with. To finger. Like worry beads.

Concentrating on reaching Dad was useless, so I tried to imagine where Bart could be, forbidding the thought to creep into my mind that I'd never see him again.

I fell asleep clutching the turquoise pendant. And I dreamed.

Bart was chained to a post in a cave half-filled with rising water. Dad slept the sleep of the drugged, his arms filled with needle marks from the sedatives administered every few hours.

Then I dreamed of a little boy, scared and alone, crying for his mommy and daddy. I wiped his tears away, and when I woke up, my hand was wet.

Chapter Twenty-Five

And my phone was ringing.

I looked at the clock. Six o'clock. Standing too fast, I nearly passed out from the pain in my arm as I reached for the wall to steady myself.

It was Mom. She couldn't reach me on the radio. Was I all right? Hungry? Ready for a bite of dinner?

Hungry? I was ravenous. I'd missed lunch, couldn't remember eating breakfast, and, yes, I was ready. She'd meet me in the dining room in fifteen minutes.

I sat on the edge of the bed, then rolled back onto the pillows and hugged my arm to me. Maybe room service would be better. At least she wouldn't see me babying my arm. I rubbed it and felt a shock of dismay. It was twice the size it should be. I'd never hide that from my observant mother.

Rummaging through my clothes, I finally found a long-sleeved peasant blouse with lace around the elastic neckline and wrists. Easy to get into without passing out from pain. The voluminous sleeves would hide the arm. I wiggled into a cotton gauze tiered skirt, difficult to do one-handed, and slipped on soft leather loafers.

The only problem now was my hair, which had been wrapped in a towel for the last four hours. Sticking my head in the sink, I turned the water on and dampened my hair, fluffed it with the fingers on my good hand, tweaked it here and there. That would have to do. A fashion model I wasn't, but natural curl did its own thing anyway.

The turquoise necklace was the last thing I donned before I left the room. I felt I was leaving something behind, but since I was only going downstairs for dinner, it couldn't be too important.

Mom met me in the lounge as she came in from the control room. She had dark circles under her eyes and her step was slow and deliberate, as if it was a chore to put one foot in front of the other. A pang of guilt stabbed me. I'd slept the afternoon away while she'd shouldered our burdens alone.

"How are you doing?" I winced as she squeezed my shoulder. She eyed me as mothers do, peeling away the surface layers and getting to the heartcore underneath.

"I'm handling it," I said. "How about you?"

"Yeah."

If she was, it was just barely.

As we were being seated on the balcony, Else appeared in the doorway, uncertain whether she should intrude or not. Mom waved her up and she joined us.

"Did they get anything out of the guy I brought in?" I asked anxiously.

"Not yet, but he will talk," Else said with a confident smile as she leaned back in her chair.

"How do you know?" I asked.

"He's afraid. He doesn't want to die. He's not Muslim, so giving his life for Allah means nothing to him."

"How long before he breaks? We don't have that much time left." I was painfully aware that I had wasted four precious hours sleeping. There were only sixty hours left to find and rescue Bart and Dad.

"Probably between midnight and dawn, when he hasn't had anything to eat or drink, or any rest, and he's been interrogated constantly. By that time he'll be ready to give us what we want."

Else was the epitome of blonde beauty and cool, regal elegance. She could have been a duchess discussing the problems of her manor. It seemed contradictory for her to discuss interrogation methods as easily as servant problems.

"Have you heard any more from your father?" Mom asked.

"No. You know I'd have let you know immediately."

We studied our menus silently. What more was there to say? We had no news. No leads. And time was running out.

Else entertained us through dinner with tales of jet-setters she'd guarded, of princes and kings who courted her, of princesses and queens who hated her, and life in the fast lane in Europe. It was pleasant to be distracted. I even enjoyed my dinner and managed to keep my arm tucked against me the whole time. That didn't stop it from aching, but it did keep me from wincing with pain and revealing to my mother how bad it was.

"What are you doing tonight?" I asked Mom.

"More of the same. We've got the tribal police looking on the reservations, state police watching highways, sheriff and police departments 'rounding up the usual suspects,' and the FBI doing all they can. Sky has the gray cells working overtime trying to outguess them and figure out what they'll do. We're sort of in a holding pattern. And you?"

"I'm going to visit a turquoise mine, and there's my ride now." Jaqueez pulled up in the half-circle driveway and got out of the car.

"You said he was a Casanova." Mom clutched my arm. "Are you sure you want to do this?"

"He has an important clue, a piece to the puzzle. I have to follow it through."

"Please be careful." The universal admonition of the mother tongue.

Only as I met Jaqueez did I remember that Oz was going to come as backup. I looked around. No sign of him. He must have forgotten. Or he was busy interrogating the terrorist. I couldn't take him away from that.

I debated momentarily, fingering the turquoise pendant with uncertainty. Cancel, and lose what might be my only opportunity to glean the information I was sure Jaqueez could provide, or postpone and take a chance on getting it later?

There simply might not be a later. I felt impelled to go. I would do whatever was necessary to find my husband.

Jaqueez postured and posed, showing off his physique in a too-tight knit shirt and trying to impress every female we passed on our way through the lounge and lobby. No small feat, since it was the dinner hour and Rancho Encantado's dining room was a very popular place. In addition, some of the celebrities' advance personnel had begun arriving, so there were "pretty people" everywhere. Enough to keep an egotistical Don Juan like Jaqueez reeling.

"Where is this turquoise mine?" I asked as he opened the car door for me and bowed as I got in. When Bart did it, it was charming. With Jaqueez, it was nauseating.

"South of Santa Fe on the Turquoise Trail," he said, pulling away from the Ranch.

"Shouldn't we have gone in the daylight? It'll be dark when we get there."

"The mines are on private property now and closed to the public."

"Then how are we going to get in?" My heart skipped a beat. Breaking and entering wasn't something I'd planned tonight.

"Jaqueez always finds a way," he laughed, showing gleaming white teeth, a perfect ad for tooth whiteners. "I have been there many times. We arrive at dusk, when no one else would have business there. We reach the mine as darkness falls. A very romantic time." He reached for my hand. I didn't offer it. A frown creased his too-handsome face, then quickly disappeared.

"I have a problem, Jaqueez. I hurt my arm, and I haven't time to go to the doctor to have it looked at." I pushed up my sleeve to reveal the ugly, swollen arm.

"Mi amor!" he exclaimed. "I will be so very careful when I . . . explore . . . the . . . mine." He did a sickening impression of a seductive Valentino, with raised eyebrows and a lecherous leer. And it was only the first of a continual flow of innuendos that became increasingly blatant as we passed through Santa Fe, drove down Interstate 25, then turned south on the Turquoise Trail toward Los Cerrillos.

"Tell me about the mines," I said to distract him.

"These are the oldest turquoise mines on the North American continent. The Spanish mined them after the Indians, and the Anglos after that. Your Tiffany jewelers in New York said these had the best turquoise of any in the world. There are still veins showing in the rocks, where we will find our keepsake of this wonderful night."

Try as I might, I could not keep him on the subject of turquoise and off the subject of Jaqueez. He was obsessed with himself and his conquests. I learned more than I ever wanted to know about him. He had an associate degree in music and dramatic arts from a European college, and was working toward his bachelors degree before heading to Hollywood. He was determined to become the next heartthrob of the nation. Interspersed with all this less-than-fascinating information was a continual flow of suggestive remarks.

"Are you sure your major wasn't erotics?" I asked when I couldn't take any more of his sensual suggestions and innuendos.

"*Que?*"

"Erotics. The science and art of love. I'll bet you've read every bit of erotica ever written."

"*Que?*"

"Erotica is literature dealing with sexual love. In fact, I'll bet you could write a best-seller on the art of seduction."

"Oh, *mi amor*, I could do that."

Gag.

It was an idea that appealed enormously to him, excited him, I think, even more than the idea of seducing me. *Good.* The only thing that excited me was finding Bart. What key did Jaqueez have to Bart's location? What had ever possessed me to think that he had one?

Rolling hills gave place to higher, more defined peaks. The road twisted and turned and suddenly, without warning, Jaqueez swerved off the highway onto a secondary road, then left the pavement for a dirt road. Around a sharp curve, a padlocked gate barred the way. A large "NO TRESPASSING" sign declaring that violators would be prosecuted hung next to an equally large one that proclaimed this was private property.

Jaqueez turned off the car and opened the door.

"We can't go in there," I said. "It's private property."

"*Si, mi amor*. But we will not hurt anything. We leave the car here, climb over the fence, and walk in. What man would deny another a little *amor?*"

Probably the owner of this property.

"Are you sure this is a turquoise mine? You've really been here before?"

Jaqueez looked pained. "*Mi preciosa*, I showed you my turquoise. It all came from here, each piece a memento of a special night. See, the sun is gone. Our moment has come."

As he leaned across the console toward me, one hand reaching for my waist, eyes half closed, lips parting, I opened the door. "Then let's go. I've never been in a turquoise mine."

I hopped out of the car. "Can I carry something, or can you handle it by yourself? Of course, I probably wouldn't do much good with my arm."

Jaqueez stared in disbelief, his mouth open. If no one had passed up his kisses before, he was in for a shock tonight.

I squeezed between the gate and the fence post, tearing my blouse on a piece of barbed wire that scratched my shoulder and drew blood. Jaqueez reacted quickly. He was out of the car in a flash, offering a clean handkerchief and begging to attend it himself.

"It's only a scratch, Jaqueez. Let's go to the mine before it's completely dark."

His eyes lit up. "The basket." He returned to the car, retrieved a huge picnic basket and a quilt, and handed them over the fence to me, then vaulted effortlessly over the top. "I, too, am anxious to get to the mine. This will be a vacation neither of us shall forget, I think."

"Are you on vacation? I thought you were working at Rancho Encantado."

"I offered my services to help in the dining room when they were short-handed. I am a guest, too."

Something was askew. I couldn't see any guest at Rancho Encantado working the dining room.

I stayed one step ahead of him, just out of reach of his wandering hands, which would not have been possible if he hadn't been burdened by the heavy basket.

"What do you have in the basket? It can't all be food. We'd never be able to eat that much in a week."

"*Mi gatita*, I have pleasures you have never dreamed possible in this basket of delights."

Fortunately, we reached a small, rocky hill and no comment was necessary as I climbed ahead of him. Just at the top, surrounded by piñon and loose rock, loomed what appeared to be a huge rabbit hole. If it had been a straight-in entrance, like most mine shafts I'd seen pictures of with heavy wooden beams around the entrance, I could have almost stood upright in the portal. But the terrain sloped at about a forty-five degree angle, and the ground fell away and disappeared inside the black void. Standing outside the gaping cavity, I felt like Alice in Wonderland just before she fell into the White Rabbit's hole.

Jaqueez set the basket down in the rock chips left after the turquoise had been chipped away, reached up into a large juniper next to the hole, and pulled down a rope ladder.

"You are prepared, aren't you?" I said. "Is that the only way in?"

"It is the easiest. I do not wish to tire you before our . . . activities."

"How thoughtful. There's only one problem. I'll never be able to climb down that with my bad arm."

"Then I shall lower you on a rope, and you shall not hurt your arm one bit."

"What's in the mine?"

He sidled up to me, lowered his voice, and whispered, "A palace of pleasure, a den of desire."

Where did he get those corny lines? From watching old movies? "Then I guess we might as well spread our picnic up here. I may have given you the impression that I was here for the same thing you are. Actually, I really need your help."

"Ah, I can be very helpful. For instance, I can help you get comfortable. Clothes are very confining, don't you think? I will free you from confinement." He took off his shirt and moved toward me, his hands outstretched.

I stepped away. "That wasn't what I meant. I need your help to find my . . ."

"I can help you find passion, pleasure . . ."

I darted around the tree. "You didn't let me finish. I'm looking for my husband."

"I will be a husband, a lover, a companion. Anything you desire." Jaqueez grabbed my arm and pulled me to him.

"You didn't hear me," I said, pushing against him with both hands, regretting it as my sore arm met his bare chest. I nearly passed out from the pain. "I didn't say I wanted to find *a* husband. I said I wanted to find *my* husband."

"Tomorrow we will look for him. Tonight I teach you in the art of love. What did you call it, erotics? I like that word."

"I'm not much into that sort of thing myself, and I know my husband wouldn't approve," I said, dodging his kiss.

"Jaqueez will teach you, you can teach your husband. We all benefit."

"You mean my husband would be happy to have you make love to me, as it would make me a better wife?" His logic was astonishing.

He looked at me with surprise. "Of course. I teach you how to please a man. He would be happy to have you know how to . . ."

I interrupted him. "Jaqueez. Will you sit right there for just one minute and let me tell you something?"

"Tell me later, *mi amor*, after the passion, when we are speaking quietly of . . ."

"Jaqueez, let go and listen. Read my lips. There will be no passion. My husband has been kidnapped, and I felt you could help me find him."

"I bring you to my palace of pleasure, and you say there will be no passion? This I cannot believe. Many protestations I have heard, but this is the most inventive. I saw you were different. I knew you would be wonderful." He wrapped his arms around my waist again.

"No, Jaqueez. Listen to me. My husband was kidnapped. I only have a few hours left to find him before he'll be killed. I need your help."

"Then let us use these precious hours wisely. I shall first console you, then we shall plan how to find your husband."

He grabbed my hand and pulled me back to the basket and the quilt. "Here, we need a place to sit." He spread the quilt on the ground near a piñon tree, the only place in the area that was dirt instead of rocks.

Then he opened the basket, removed two wine glasses, a bottle of wine, a small camp light, and a little tape recorder, which he turned on. Soft, romantic music drifted across the dimly lit night.

"Now, sit beside me and tell me of your husband." He sat on the blanket and poured the wine, offering me a glass.

"No, thank you. I don't drink wine."

"Nonsense. Everyone drinks wine. It is medicinal. It will make your arm feel better, help you relax, so you can tell me how I can help you."

He patted the spot next to him. I sat on the edge of the quilt opposite so our feet were between us.

"Jaqueez, when you spoke of the turquoise at the Ranch, I felt impressed that you knew something that would help me find my husband. Do you have any idea what that could be?"

"*Mi amor*, I told you how I could help you." His eyes glistened with desire again and he started to move toward me.

"No. Stay there and listen. It must have something to do with the mine. What's down there?"

Jaqueez smiled. "Drink your wine, *mi bonita*. I will take you down."

He swallowed his drink, got to his feet and pulled me to mine, dropped the rope ladder into the hole, and tossed the quilt down after it. "I will go first, to catch you if you fall. You follow." He looped the picnic basket and the handle of the lamp over one arm and started down. "See. I can climb down with one hand. You can, too."

I watched him lower himself easily into the mine, then motion for me to follow. *Is this a good idea, Allison? Is the information you think he has worth the cost he might exact—or can you handle this Lothario?* Undecided, I stood at the edge of the mine, clutching the turquoise pendant. *You said you'd do whatever it takes to find Bart. This is your only clue. Go for it.*

I did, though the climb down was laborious and painful. Before I reached the bottom, Jaqueez lifted me by the waist off the ladder.

"Now, *mi amor*, I will show you wonderful things."

Chapter Twenty-Six

Jaqueez set me down, whirled me to face him, and wrapped me in his arms. "You tease," he growled lecherously. "You play hard to get. But you're only playing. You make it more desirable to have that which is denied. Now you will deny me no more. And I—I will deny you nothing."

"What part of no don't you understand?" I said, struggling to free myself from his smothering embrace.

"Ah, you make it sweeter still."

He grabbed both arms and twisted them behind me. A resounding crack told him what excruciating pain screamed at me. My arm was broken again.

I sagged against him as blinding, searing pain flashed through me, so intense I was afraid I'd lose consciousness. Jaqueez let go of my arms and held me against him, supporting me. My knees wouldn't hold me up. Waves of nausea washed over me. I fought the temptation to succumb to the dark void of oblivion that unconsciousness would produce.

"*Mi amor*, I am so sorry. I did not know that would hurt you so."

Jaqueez lifted me in his arms and carried me to the blanket, treating me ever so gently. But as he laid me down and knelt above me, his fervor overcame his compassion. "I have never made love to one who was injured, who was so helpless." His hand fingered my blouse where blood stained the white sleeve a deep crimson.

I touched my arm, felt the jagged bone protruding from my skin. Same place as last time. Same break all over again. Same pain—teeth-clenching, blazing hot-white pain that took my breath away. Cold crept through me, chilling my very bones. The first stages of shock.

"Please get me to a hospital, Jaqueez."

"Oh, I will. But first I will comfort you, caress you, and love you." He knelt over me, a knee on each side of my legs, and leaned forward to kiss me.

"I don't think so," I said. Mustering all the strength I could summon, I brought my knee up as hard as I could. Jaqueez gasped and doubled up, rolling off the quilt onto the cold, hard floor. "Pain and lovemaking should never be used in the same thought. Please take me to the hospital." I struggled to sit up, waited momentarily for the world to stop spinning, then got unsteadily to my knees, and finally to my feet.

Clinging to the rope ladder for a minute, I ignored the piteous moans and groans coming from the disgusting bit of humanity rolling on the floor in pain. He didn't know what pain was.

I tried to climb the ladder, but couldn't get past the first rung. I nudged the moaning male with my foot. "Jaqueez, I need to go to the hospital. Please get up and take me."

The look in his eye when he finally rolled over and sat up was murderous. "*Bruja*," he breathed. "You can fly there on your broomstick." He got slowly to his feet and staggered, bent over, to the rope, then slowly pulled himself to the top.

"You wouldn't leave me here alone," I said, hoping he really wouldn't. Knowing he would.

"I am being generous in leaving you the light and the blanket. You deserve neither," he said as he disappeared into the black night above.

"Will you at least send help?"

No answer.

"Where are you going?" I tried again to climb the rope ladder, tried to keep him talking in the darkness overhead till I could climb out of this cold prison.

"Back to Barcelona, where my obvious talents are appreciated. If I can use them again."

I was on the first rung, straining to pull myself up to the second, when he leaned over so the dim camplight illuminated his face. No longer handsome, it was twisted now into a hateful smirk. "If you are able to get out, take care not to pass out on the way to the road. The coyotes and cougars would not be so forgiving as I have been, *Bruja.*"

"If I'm a witch, beware of my evil spells. I cast one on you now." I grasped the necklace and prepared to chant some gibberish to scare Jaqueez into helping me up.

Suddenly the grandmother's words came back to me. "You must only use your power for good."

What power? If I had any power, I certainly wouldn't be so helpless now. But I decided to expend my waning energy on escape instead of revenge, even though my spell would have been nothing more than a sham to unnerve him.

"Hasta nunca, Bruja"

"Till never, yourself. I'm sure Maria, and every other girl you've tried to seduce, feels the same way. You're not a great lover, you're really just a *violador.*"

Jaqueez spat. He missed. His footsteps faded.

This was all my fault. I knew Jaqueez was a Casanova. I knew what he would try when we got here. What did I hope to accomplish by putting myself in this position?

You hoped to find Bart—hoped to learn something that would lead you to him.

I started shivering. Blood ran down my arm, dripped from my fingertips. First things first. *Take care of yourself before you go into shock and bleed to death.*

Which would be the better course, to continue going up and try to get out before I fainted from loss of blood, or to go back down into the mine, stop the bleeding, then try again?

You actually could die down here. There was a distinct possibility Jaqueez would not call and give my location. I could be dead a long time before someone stumbled across the mine and my corpse. It would serve me right for leaving without my purse. No gun, no radio, no way of contacting anyone. Stupid!

I tried to climb out, but each movement increased the bleeding and produced prodigious pain. There was no decision to be made. Take care of the arm.

Getting off the rope ladder was almost as hard as getting on it in the first place. Finally settled on the blanket again, I searched the picnic basket for something to use on my arm. I was stunned at its contents. The basket was full of erotic toys. Wine, song, and erotica—Jaqueez' idea of a picnic.

I tore the voluminous bottom ruffle from my skirt, fashioned a compress, secured it in place with more of the fabric, then used the rest of the ruffle to bind my arm against me so it wouldn't move as I climbed the writhing rope.

Resting for a minute, wrapped in the blanket to keep from going into shock, I leaned against the rough rock wall of the mine, mustering strength to face the dreaded climb out. The romantic music on the tape player rankled and irritated me. I hit the stop button, and the stillness of the mine crashed down with morose intensity. Shadows cast by the dim camp light loomed dark and desolate, forming images of Native Americans who first worked the mines, then had been forced into slave labor by the Spaniards who conquered them. Somewhere, far back in the deep bowels of the mine, in the darkness the small light couldn't penetrate, I heard the incessant dripping of water, like the ticking of a clock.

The only thing that got me on that rope again was the reminder that Bart and Dad only had a few hours to live. Their clocks were running out of time. I couldn't give up just because I hurt a little, just because climbing that flimsy ladder one-handed seemed the most daunting thing I had ever faced.

As I reached for the ladder, I heard a cheery "Hallo" from the darkness above.

"Hello!" I called as loud as I could. "I'm down here."

A friendly face surrounded by long, graying hair appeared above me in the entrance. "I saw lights. No one's supposed to be here, so I thought I'd better see what was going on."

"Thank heaven you came. My arm's broken—can you please get me to a hospital?" I clung to the rope while he pulled the ladder up and out of the mine. Quick and easy.

Trader Todd Brown lived just a mile from the mines, had crawled in and out of them for years. He'd been curious about night visitors to the private property and had come to investigate.

As we walked to his pickup, Todd half carrying me, half supporting me, I explained what had happened, and my reasons for being in such a predicament. He remained tactfully silent and non-judgmental.

The ride to the hospital seemed interminable. Every bump in the road was agonizing. Todd talked incessantly to take my mind off the pain. His attempt was only partially successful.

"My wife, Patricia, and I own a twenty-one room adobe which houses the Casa Grande Trading Post, the Cerrillos Turquoise Mining Museum, and the Cerrillos Turquoise and Jewelry Shop. We also run a petting zoo, which keeps the kids entertained while their folks shop." He looked at me, huddled in the corner, trying not to cry from the pain. "Want me to tell you about the animals?"

I nodded.

Todd described the goats, llama, exotic chickens, and various other inhabitants of the zoo. He described the glass telephone wire conductors that lined the roof of their historic adobe home. He told me about his turquoise mining, about his family. By the time we reached the emergency room, I felt he was one of my oldest and dearest friends.

As soon as we reached the hospital, Trader Todd called Mom at Rancho Encantado. Then he stayed with me until she arrived. At least, that's what they told me later. I don't remember a thing from the time I settled on the gurney until I woke between clean sheets at four o'clock Sunday morning. Mom was asking Pepper if she could take me home with her when they released me, as she needed to be back at the control room as soon as she could get there.

"Did you find Dad?" I asked, wishing the moment the words were out I hadn't spoken them. My head was splitting, and the effort in speaking intensified it.

"Alli! You're awake. The doctor said you might sleep the rest of the morning. How do you feel?"

"Don't ask. Did you find Dad?"

"Else and Sky are still questioning Jilani Hashemi, but they think he'll break any minute and tell us where they were moving Jack. I want to be there."

"Go. Find him, and Bart, too." I closed my eyes and gritted my teeth.

"Pepper, ask the nurse for the pain medication the doctor prescribed." Mom leaned over the bed and kissed my cheek. "Bye, hon. I'll be in touch."

"She'll be at my house until you need her," Pepper said, walking Mom to the door of the hospital room. She came back with the nurse, whose shot produced welcome oblivion for another couple of hours.

Six o'clock. Sun shining through slats in the venetian blinds created stripes on the wall and on Pepper, who was bent over a book.

"What are you reading?" I asked, waiting for the blinding pain that never came. My headache was gone.

"Good morning. How do you feel?"

"Better. Almost human, in fact. What's got you so interested?"

"The *Ensign*. I'm giving the lesson today in Relief Society. I hope you won't mind being alone for a couple of hours. I didn't want to get a replacement at the last minute, since I thought you'd probably still be sleeping anyway."

"Relief Society. I've heard of that." At the moment, I just couldn't remember where.

"The women's auxiliary of the Church."

"Right. What's your lesson?"

"The importance of studying the words of Christ."

"What time is church?"

"Ten o'clock. In fact, Dr. Evans will probably be here any minute. He's a member, and he likes to get to sacrament meeting on time, so he starts his Sunday rounds early."

The good Dr. Evans made his appearance at that moment, cracked a couple of passably funny jokes, declared me releasable anytime I felt like leaving, and cautioned me to take at least a month of R & R to let my arm heal. Nothing strenuous at all.

"See you in church, Pepper." Dr. Evans waved and whistled his way down the hall to his next patient.

"Cheerful fellow," I commented.

"Very nice man. What do you think? Want to sleep a while, and then go home with me? Or spend the day in bed here?"

"You're kidding. He said I could go anytime. I'm outa here. Give me my clothes, what's left of them, and let's go."

"Your mom threw your clothes away and brought your suitcase." Pepper gave me a loose, flowing caftan that was just the ticket for donning over the cumbersome cast.

They delivered me to the front door in a wheelchair, over my objections, as I thought I could handle walking just fine. I hadn't planned on the weakness that hit my knees as I traversed the short distance to the car. I was still pretty shaky.

Pepper handed me my purse as we drove away from the hospital. "Margaret said to please not forget to take your purse with you again. Your gun and radio are in there."

"I could have used them at the mine. Thank heaven for Trader Todd. Bart says God knows everything about us, but he usually sends someone to help instead of working miracles himself. The appearance of Todd was certainly an answer to prayer, and a miracle for me."

"I can't wait to meet your husband. He sounds like an interesting man."

"You believe he's still alive? That makes only about two of us. Why?"

"Maybe the same reason you do. Maybe from the whisperings of the Spirit. Have you any clues to where he's being held?" Pepper asked, glancing at me.

"No," I said slowly, trying to sort out my thoughts. "I never felt Jaqueez had anything to do with the kidnapping, but I thought he had some knowledge that would help me. I really felt Jaqueez could give me something." Then I laughed at the irony. "Well, he certainly tried hard enough to give me something. It just wasn't anything I wanted, and it had nothing to do with finding Bart."

I told Pepper the tale of the attempted seduction. She shook her head as she pulled into her driveway. "Allison, or Melanie, or whoever you are, you need more than just the protection of the turquoise necklace. You need a legion of guardian angels to protect you. Whatever were you thinking to go off with him alone?"

"Of how to get my husband back," I answered softly.

My radio buzzed in my lap.

"Yes?"

There was no one on the other end.

Chapter Twenty-Seven

"Hello? Anybody there?" I asked into the silent radio. "Hello?"

Mom's voice, quivering with emotion, finally answered. "I was so excited I couldn't speak. Sky wrested a location from Jilani Hashemi. We're on our way. Just had to let you know."

"Please tell me the minute you know anything."

"I promise."

Excitement roiled inside me. I suddenly knew what a volcano felt like just before it exploded. The damper on the exhilaration of the moment was that I didn't have matching information on Bart.

Pepper's apartment was decorated in subtle but authentic Santa Fe style. It was neat, simple, and homey. Her husband, Ramon, greeted us at the door. He was tall, six-foot plus, with the high cheekbones and aristocratic nose of the Native American, long, shining black hair tied at the neck, and dark, probing eyes. His white shirt was open at the neck, awaiting the tie that hung loose over his broad, muscular shoulders. He was the most ruggedly handsome man I had ever seen. Except for Bart, of course.

They settled me on the comfortable sofa, covered me with a soft, handwoven blanket, and took turns inquiring of my needs as they moved quietly around the apartment getting ready for church. There was an aura of peace and serenity in the room that normally would have had me relaxed and contented. Instead, all I could think of was Dad. Where was he? Where the terrorist informant thought he should be? Or had they moved him again, and would Mom arrive too late? And Bart? An aching question.

Ramon departed for a meeting, giving Pepper a long, warm kiss and embrace before he left. I closed my eyes, pretending not to see. Their display of affection only intensified my longing for Bart and emphasized my worry and fear for him. Where was my husband? How was he? Would we find him in time? I didn't even know where to start looking. Why had Jaqueez' clue never materialized, as I was so certain it would?

"You're not sleeping," Pepper noted from the dining room table where she had settled with books spread out before her.

"I'm too keyed up. I can't wait to hear from Mom. I'm only lying still and not walking the floor so I won't disturb you. Otherwise, I'd be climbing the walls by now."

Pepper laughed. "You won't bother me. However, if you aren't going to relax and get some sleep, would you like to soak in a hot tub?"

"Sounds wonderful."

The hot sudsy water worked miracles with my mental well-being. I soaked till I resembled a prune, then managed to shampoo my hair one-handed and rinse it without getting my cast wet, using the little pitcher Pepper left. Fortunately, this cast was only from just above my elbow to my fingertips, much like the small one Dr. Cooper had given me a couple of days ago, not like the first one that covered my shoulder, too. This was manageable.

I thought of the tense morning ahead, the strain of waiting for news from Mom. Digging into my suitcase, I found a two-piece ivory linen dress suitable for church that could accommodate the cast. Donning the turquoise necklace had now become a habit.

Thank heaven for naturally curly hair. Then, thinking of heaven, I remembered my deliverance from what could easily have been my tomb. It was time to do a little catch-up on gratitude. I got to my knees. Bart said ingratitude was one of the greatest sins. I certainly wasn't ungrateful. I added a fervent plea for Dad and Bart's safe deliverance, and asked to be shown how I could be their guardian angel, as Trader Todd Brown had been to me.

"Where do you think you're going?" Pepper asked as I came out of the bathroom.

"I might as well go to church with you as sit around here and go crazy. I'll take my radio. If Mom calls, I assume there's somewhere I can go to hear the message."

"Allison, are you sure you feel up to it?"

"Yes. What I'm *not* up to is the wait."

By the time we arrived at sacrament meeting, I knew I'd made a mistake in not staying horizontal. I swallowed another couple of pain pills and tried to concentrate, but the only thing I got was the concept that it's important to not only *believe in* Christ as our Savior and Redeemer, but to *believe* that Christ actually has the power to redeem us from our own personal sins as he says he can. I'd have to mull that over when my mind wasn't muddled with pain and drugs.

Sunday School was a blur. "You don't look so good. Do you need to leave?" Pepper asked when class was over.

"What happens next?" I said, trying to look interested and alert, and wishing it was time for another painkiller.

"Relief Society. It's an hour. Can you handle that, or should I take you home?"

"Of course not. I'm fine. I want to hear your lesson." It really wasn't a lie. I did want to hear her lesson. And other than being in incredible pain, I was fine.

I tried to be as friendly as those who introduced themselves to me, but I wasn't in a chatty mood at the moment. I was glad when the meeting started and I didn't have to smile at anyone. Just grit my teeth for an hour until I could take another pill.

Pepper distributed several three-by-five cards to the ends of the rows, and whoever wanted to participate in the lesson took one. The woman sitting next to me handed me the last one with a scriptural notation. Noting I had no scriptures, she whispered she'd loan me hers when it was time to read.

I think the gist of the lesson was the importance of studying the holy scriptures. I tried to concentrate on Pepper's teaching and ignore the intense, throbbing pain in my arm. The scriptures being read were about water, Jesus Christ being the fountain who offered living water, or life and the love of God, freely, to all who would drink.

Suddenly I had no trouble concentrating. Every fibre of my body focused on what Pepper was saying. Something buried in my subconscious scrambled to climb out of the foggy depths of my mind onto center stage. Something extremely important. What was it? I racked my brain trying to retrieve the elusive, vital clue.

Then the helpful soul next to me thrust her Book of Mormon, opened to Mosiah 18, into my hand and broke my concentration. It was my turn to read a scripture, which Pepper would then discuss.

"And behold, here are the waters of Mormon . . . and now, as ye are desirous to come into the fold of God, and to be called his people, and are willing to bear one another's burdens, that they may be light;

"Yea, and are willing to mourn with those that mourn; yea and comfort those that stand in need of comfort, and to stand as witnesses of God at all times and in all things, and in all places that ye may be in, even until death, that ye may be redeemed of God, and be numbered with those of the first resurrection, that ye may have eternal life—

"Now I say unto you, if this be the desire of your hearts, *what have you against being baptized in the name of the Lord,* as a witness before him that ye have entered into a covenant with him, that ye will serve him and keep his commandments, that he may pour out his spirit more abundantly upon you?"

Those words burned into my heart and mind. What *did* I have against being baptized? I'd had the six missionary discussions. I'd read the Book of Mormon twice. Had even received a witness that it was another testament of Christ. And, yes, I acknowledged, I had received a witness that this was Christ's church on the earth.

What did I have against being baptized?

The covenants I'd just read were certainly easy. I'd be covenanting to be a ministering angel to someone in need.

The promises he made if I accepted were incredible—redemption, eternal life, and his Spirit poured out abundantly.

I looked up. Pepper was watching me intensely. "Would you like to comment on the verses you just read, Melanie? I think you have an insight that might be interesting for you to share as we conclude our lesson."

Briefly, I explained that I'd been investigating the Church but had been hesitant to commit to baptism. For some reason, that hesitancy and doubt had disappeared as I read that scripture.

As I spoke, that thing, that nagging, obscure thought that had been trying to climb out of my subconscious popped up, crystal clear.

Water. Dripping water. My dream of Bart, waist-deep in water. Jaqueez and the turquoise mine. Bart was in the mine!

I leaped to my feet, almost fell over because I did it too fast. Grabbing the back of a chair, I waited until the blood got back to my head, then headed for the door. Pepper concluded her lesson in a one-sentence testimony and was at my side before I'd reached the hall. "What happened?" she demanded.

"I know where Bart is. We've got to go back to the mine."

"I'll get Ramon and Tomas," Pepper said, disappearing around the corner.

I radioed Mom. They were still searching. Nine hours had elapsed since she'd left me at the hospital, jubilant with hope that soon she'd have Dad safely out of Saladin's hands. She'd spent six of those hours driving over miles of dusty, bumpy back roads. Six fruitless hours of scouting abandoned cabins and ancient ruins. Jilani Hashemi had taken them on a wild-goose chase. Now they were back at the holding pen, and Hashemi was paying for his deceit. Sky and Else had resorted to the Islamis' own methods of wresting information from a reluctant subject, and they were not pleasant.

"Mom, I know where Bart is. At least, I think I do. We're heading there now. With any luck, we'll know something in the next two hours."

"I hope so. Alli, I told you Anastasia does not pay ransom to terrorists. Saladin knows that. I think he hopes because I'm a woman and he's holding my husband, there will be a change in policy. There won't be. That's why we've got to find them immediately. Have you heard anything from your father?"

I caught my breath and tried to sound natural. "No, but I haven't actually tried to reach him. I'll work on it on the way to the mines."

Mom had never planned on paying the ransom. That bit of news hit me like a rampaging buffalo. Morally, I had to agree that putting money in the hands of people to use for killing innocent people was wrong. But this was my own father and my husband. Wasn't that different? It was to me. Mom had more courage than I'd thought possible.

Pepper rounded the corner with her husband and brother in tow, moving as fast as they could through the throng of people pouring into the halls. "We'll make a quick stop on the way to change clothes," Pepper explained as we hurried to the car.

Ramon and Tomas left their cars in the parking lot and piled into Pepper's four-wheel drive van, Ramon at the wheel. "How did you figure out Bart is at the mines?" Pepper asked on the way to her house.

"I had a dream the other night that Bart was waist-deep in water in a cave. I've had this feeling that Jaqueez had some clue to Bart's whereabouts, even though I felt he didn't have anything to do with the kidnapping. It had to be the turquoise mine. That was where Jaqueez took all his victims to seduce them."

"Did you ever find your father?" Tomas asked.

"Not yet. The terrorist you stuffed in my trunk told Anastasia he'd take them where Dad was being held, but either they'd moved him, or Hashemi took them on a wild-goose chase."

I called Todd Brown on Pepper's cell phone and asked him to meet us at the turnoff to the mines in an hour. It would take us that long to get there.

At the house, Pepper helped me into my jeans and tied my shoes. I could have dressed myself, but there wasn't time for me to struggle on my own with the cast hindering every movement.

Ramon had grabbed a loaf of bread and a jar of peanut butter, and had thrown some cans of soda into a bag. As we sped out of the city and into the rolling hills below Santa Fe, Pepper spread the bread with a thick coating of chunky peanut butter and passed us each some. "Thanksgiving dinner it's not," she laughed, "but at least we won't starve. We're always famished by the time church is over."

I had to agree I was hungry, and this simple meal tasted as good to me as a juicy steak, or a heaping plate of pasta, or even a thick-crust pepperoni pizza. Washing down a couple of pain pills with the soda, I leaned my head back on the seat and closed my eyes. Hunger relieved, I waited for the medication to work its magic and provide relief from the acute pain throbbing through my entire left side.

Concentrating, I tried to reach Dad. I couldn't. He'd been drugged for so long I was getting worried. Didn't they let him come out of the sedation even long enough to eat? A horrible thought flitted across my mind, but I blocked it before it became a full-blown idea. I didn't want to even think of the possibility that he was dead. But if Saladin planned on killing them anyway, why waste time feeding them?

The pain-riddled ride to the mine seemed never-ending. I would have no good memories of this stretch of highway. I hoped I'd have good memories of Santa Fe—but that would depend entirely upon our abilities to outwit the nefarious Saladin.

Aware the car was slowing, I opened my eyes. Trader Todd Brown was leaning against his car at the side of the road to the mines. I must have slept, but I was wide awake now.

Pepper rolled down her window and I did introductions. Todd gave instructions. "Follow me in. Pull the gate closed behind you, but don't lock it. We'll have to walk partway. Sure you can handle that, Melanie? You don't look too good."

"I'll handle it. Thanks for coming." I flashed him a smile that I hoped would be convincing, though I'm sure it fell far short of what I'd hoped to accomplish. He looked dubious.

"I already carried you out once. I'm not anxious to do it again." A friendly grin accompanied the jibe.

"I'm not anxious for you to do it again, either. Let's get this in gear. There aren't many daylight hours left."

Todd led in, unlocked the gate I'd torn my blouse on last night squeezing through, and Tomas shut it behind us when we drove through. It took only minutes to get to the foot of the hill where the mine was located.

Todd unrolled the rope ladder again, but this time I didn't have to climb down. I clung to the rope as they lowered me over the edge. Ramon was waiting at the bottom to catch me.

"There is a possibility there could be someone guarding Bart," I warned, "but since Saladin is short-handed right now, I'm guessing that Bart will be alone." To be on the safe side, I slid my gun out of my purse and into my pocket.

Todd passed out flashlights, and we silently turned to the dark interior of the ancient turquoise mine.

Chapter Twenty-Eight

My heartbeat quickened as we filed quietly into the depths of the mine, the crunching of pebbles underfoot the only sound I could hear.

I wanted to call out to Bart, to let him know we were near, but on the chance that Saladin had left someone watching him, I didn't.

Todd led us past a couple of arteries that branched off from the main tunnel. "Those are dry," he pointed out. "The water is up ahead."

But when we reached the area of the mine that was supposedly under water from seepage, the water was very shallow, and there was no sign anyone had been there for a long time.

"I was so sure he was here," I said, looking with acute disappointment at each pitying face that stared at me. "Could there be water in one of the shafts we passed? Maybe he's there."

Todd shook his head. "We'll check, but they're dry."

They were dry. And not very long. It only took a minute to determine that Bart wasn't in the mine.

"Now what?" Ramon asked as we climbed out of the cool, dark mine into the bright, warm sunshine.

"Are there more mines here?" I asked Todd.

"Yes. But it will takes hours to check them all." He pulled a geographical survey map from his pocket and pointed to dozens of little marks. "We'll start on the close ones and work our way through. I can pretty well tell you the ones with water. Want to check those first?"

"Melanie has the necklace. Let it tell her where to look," Tomas said.

"Tomas, I don't know how to use the power of the necklace," I objected.

"What did Grandmother tell you when she gave it to you?"

"To tune myself to Mother Earth and Father Sky. She said to listen, and the wind would tell me, and to watch, and the creatures would teach me."

"And have you done that?" Tomas asked.

"I don't have the first idea how to go about it."

"Tomas, take her to the top of the hill and teach her what you know," Pepper said. "We'll see if we can come up with a plan in the meantime."

I followed Tomas to the top of the little hill and settled down next to him on a smooth rock. Down below, Todd, Pepper, and Ramon pored over the map.

"It is not easy to go deep within yourself, to put aside the thoughts that crowd and clutter your mind, but you can do it if you train yourself. Picture a beautiful, quiet place, a safe place. A peaceful place, of harmony, serenity. Go there in your mind. Watch yourself walk into it."

I closed my eyes and pictured a stand of tall, majestic pine trees on the edge of a meadow filled with wildflowers. White and yellow daisies bowed in the wind that cooled my face. Blue lupine and pink primroses nodded on the banks of a sparkling, gurgling creek that wound through the meadow. The clean, pungent smell of pine permeated the air.

Tomas began to gently prompt me. "People walk toward you. They are very important people. You are happy to see them."

Along a footpath by the creek, two personages dressed in white approached me. I was hesitant at first to go to them, until I felt the love that radiated from them.

"Ask them to help you," Tomas instructed, as if he saw what I was seeing. "Tell them what you need. Listen to their answers."

I walked through the flowers to the path by the creek and met the two beings who were surrounded by a wonderful warm light. I didn't need to tell them anything. They knew my question before I asked. One pointed to a beautiful white bird soaring above. I understood I was to follow it.

"Did you ask? Did you get an answer?" Tomas' questions brought me back to the sun-warmed rock we were sitting on.

"How did you know what I saw?" I stared at the young man next to me, feeling he had been privy to my innermost being.

"It is always the same. Your god will come to you if you are receptive and know how to approach him, and if you are a worthy vessel."

"There were two. Did you see them?"

"I have seen them many times. They used to come to me as the gods of my fathers, in the clothing of my fathers. Now they come in pure white robes."

"What made the difference?"

"I'll tell you later. Now we must find your husband. What are we looking for?"

"Didn't you see it? I thought you saw everything."

"It was your quest, not mine. What do we look for?"

"A white bird?"

"That's a question. Was that your answer?"

"I think so."

"Let's go."

Tomas descended the little hill in front of me. I could still see him as a young brave, bare-backed, buckskin clad, long hair blowing in the wind. The aura of mysticism in the southwestern desert played strange tricks on the mind.

"We look for a white bird that will guide us," Tomas announced as if this were an everyday occurrence. As if he had just received a telephone call or telegram with instructions.

We searched the deep blue, cloudless skies for the white bird. But none appeared.

"I think while we're waiting, we should take a look in the next mine. There's only one other right here that I know has water, especially at this time of year," Todd said, pointing at another little hill.

The whole area was nothing more than a series of rocky hilltops dotted with piñon and scrub pine. Todd led the way while I stumbled along behind, trying to watch the treacherous, rocky footing and at the same time look for the elusive white bird.

High above, a hawk circled—the only movement I could see in the bright azure sky. Suddenly it dove silently toward the ground, and I watched in fascination as it swooped up a tiny creature about halfway up the hill. With a flash of white wing, it soared again into the sky and disappeared in the blinding brightness of the sun.

The white bird!

But it didn't point to anything. I looked at Tomas. He hadn't seen it. Pepper was still walking with Ramon behind Todd. They hadn't seen it. Had I imagined it?

"Todd, is there anything up here on the side of this hill?" I asked.

"Don't think so. Why?"

I bit my lip. It sounded so . . . ridiculous. "I saw a white bird up there."

"Let's go look," Tomas said, heading up the hill while Todd consulted his map. This was steeper, climbing from this angle, and my arm was throbbing by the time we reached the rock. It would have been easier to go around the foot of the hill and approach it from the slope.

"Where did it land?" Tomas said.

"It didn't. It just swooped up a little mouse or something and flew off. But the big rock, by that juniper, is where the mouse was."

"The map shows there is a mine up there," Todd called, "but I'd forgotten about it."

Tomas stopped just short of the rock. "Todd, Ramon. Come here."

There were footprints in the dust, many fairly recent footprints, leading to the man-high rock, and away from it again. The men examined the footprints that led around the rock to the tree.

Tomas squeezed between the tree and the rock and disappeared. Todd followed. Ramon and Pepper looked at each other, then at me.

"There must be something there, or they'd have been right back out," I said. "Let's go."

There was, indeed, something there. A narrow opening, barely tall and wide enough for the muscular Ramon to fit through, led to a wider passage. Todd and Tomas were descending into a gently sloping tunnel, their flashlights dancing over the walls as they went.

I hurried to catch up. "Is this another turquoise mine?" I asked Todd breathlessly.

"Yeah. I completely forgot about this old shaft. I was only here once, years ago, with a friend of mine who knew about it. There was a bad story about this place—lots of Indians were supposed to have been killed when a tunnel collapsed. The restless spirits of the dead supposedly keep watch over the place, to make sure nobody gets any more turquoise out of it."

"They can have all the turquoise. I just want my husband."

We walked in silence for a few minutes. The hair on the back of my neck was standing on end. I didn't like this tunnel. I didn't like the feeling down here; it was oppressive, smothering.

Suddenly the tunnel ended abruptly. A rock slide blocked the passage from floor to ceiling.

"Looks like this is as far as we can go," Todd said, shining his light over the tumble of rocks.

"It can't be. Bart has to be here." I bent, clutched a rock with my good hand, and started moving the rock pile.

Pepper grabbed me. "He's not there."

"Then where is he? This is where the white bird pointed."

"Are you sure you saw a white bird?" she asked softly. Her arm was around me, gently leading me back toward the entrance.

"No. It was a hawk. But underneath it was white. I thought . . ." What did I think? That Tomas was well-meaning, but may have been smoking peyote? That their grandmother was having grand delusions about the supposed powers of a turquoise necklace? "Pepper, I could brush this off as a lot of hokum, but I don't think your grandmother was deluded, and I don't think Tomas was high on rabbit weed or anything else. I think Bart is here. I can't give you any proof, or even any valid reasons. I just think this is the place."

"Then let's look," Ramon said. "Tomas and I will tackle the slide. Pepper, you and Melanie go with Todd and see if we missed any tributaries on the way in." They turned to the rock slide and began moving stones. We headed back to the entrance, examining the rough-chipped walls of the tunnel as we went.

"What else do you remember about the mine?" I asked, playing my light over walls that had probably been carved by Indians long before the Spaniards came to this country.

"I think this was the mine where they found so many artifacts," Todd recalled. Several hundred turquoise beads, some pieces of inlay, half a dozen pendants, pottery shards. If I remember right, that was why we came down here. We were just kids, and wanted to see if we could find something to sell to the museum."

"Did you?" I asked.

"No. We got the bejeebers scared out of us and hightailed it before we had a chance to look. Thought the ghosts of those Indians were after us. We heard this moan . . ."

We all froze. A long, low, moan flowed out of the ground under our feet.

"That's it. That's the same sound we heard forty years ago," Todd exclaimed.

"What was it?" I whispered, chills shivering down my arms.

"Ramon! Tomas! Come here," Pepper called.

They came running.

"Listen."

The sound came again, haunting and plaintive. I shuddered at the mournful, melancholy sound that was surely long-dead souls bewailing their fate.

"I think we'd better leave," Pepper said, clinging to Ramon's arm.

"Good idea," Todd said, turning toward the entrance.

"Wait. Listen." I grabbed Pepper's hand. The sound came again, more intense, as though the spirits were agitated that we were still here. Or that we were leaving?

"Hello!" I shouted. "Anybody there?"

The wail that answered was more human than anything we'd heard. My heart pounded.

"Hello! Where are you?"

There was no answer this time. We stood motionless. Waiting. Waiting for a sound, a response, a resolution to the mysterious noise.

I shined the light at my feet where the sound seemed to originate. There was a small crack in the rock that ran the width of the tunnel. It widened as it reached the wall. Every light played on the crack, following it up the wall, where it formed a narrow crevice, unnoticed as we came in.

Tomas was the first through, then Todd, and I was right behind them, squeezing through a V-shaped opening that was so narrow on the bottom we had to step over it, and only wide enough on top to go through sideways. Whoever mined this artery had to have been small and agile, unless the rock had shifted closer together over the centuries. The crack under our feet widened, leaving a small ledge on each side just the width of a shoe, making walking treacherous. I was feeling decidedly claustrophobic in the confines of the narrow space, but there was no way to turn around and go back.

Gradually the shaft opened into a long, narrow room. Water dripped from rocks overhead into a black pool at the far end. Some kind of equipment ran into the water on one side; I could see rusting cables, and an old ladder fashioned from a tree.

My heart stopped.

A human head with white-blond hair stuck out of the water next to the cables. But only the very top was visible above the dark, murky water.

Chapter Twenty-Nine

"Bart!"

I rushed to the edge of the water, but Tomas was there first, stretching to grasp the rusting cable.

Suddenly the head reared up. Bart took several deep breaths, then started to slide back under the water.

"Bart, can you hear me?"

The head jerked back up. Bart sputtered and coughed. "Princess?" He slid under water again.

Tomas struggled with the cable. It wouldn't give. He plunged into the water beside Bart.

Bart's head came up again. He gasped for breath. "Tied to chair." He submerged again.

Ramon jumped in with Tomas, and between the two of them, they raised the chair so Bart's head was out of the water and he could breathe. Tomas dove underwater and cut the ropes while Ramon supported the chair.

Todd dragged Bart out of the water and onto my waiting lap. Bart couldn't even raise his arms to put them around me, and I only had one good one to hug him with. We were a sorry pair.

Bart coughed, then pressed his head back down into my lap. He was shaking all over from the cold, and his swollen fingers had no grip as I wound mine through his.

"We've got to get him out of here and get him warm," I said.

"That'll be kind of tough through that little crevice, unless he can walk," Todd said thoughtfully, playing his light around the small chamber.

"Bart, can you talk?" I asked, bending to lay my face on his. "How did they get you in here?"

"Walked in. Only way." His teeth were chattering so violently he could hardly get the words out.

"Then we'll have to take you out the same way. Tomas, if you take one side and Todd takes the other, it may work."

Ramon and Tomas lifted Bart to his feet, then the smaller Todd replaced broad-shouldered Ramon and they started for the breach in the rock.

"I've got a couple of blankets under the seat in my pickup, Ramon. He'll need them," Todd said. Ramon hurried back through the narrow opening to retrieve the blankets. Pepper followed, and I was right behind Todd and Tomas as they half carried, half dragged Bart to the small entry.

Straddling the crack in the floor of the cave was the difficult part. Twice Bart's feet got wedged down in the narrow fissure and I had to free them by reaching around Todd's legs and jerking Bart's pant leg. There was no room for maneuvering in the constricted passage.

Once through, they got in position to continue the half-drag, half-carry tactic. But before we'd taken a step, the low, haunting moan flowed through the old turquoise mine, sending chills up my spine.

"We're outa here, man," Todd said, and they hurried toward the narrow entrance of the mine. Tomas went through while Todd held Bart up against the rock, then Tomas pulled Bart through while Todd steadied him.

Ramon reached the foot of the hill carrying the blankets as we emerged from the mine. Long shadows stretched down the hillside as Todd and Tomas struggled to get Bart to the bottom. He could not stand up on his own. "Get his wet clothes off," Ramon directed, "and wrap him in a blanket. I think it'll be easier if we use the other blanket as a stretcher and carry him out."

As they stripped Bart's dripping clothes from him, no one spoke. His skin was white and shriveled from being submerged so long. His extremities were swollen grotesquely. The skin between his toes had begun to split.

"Allison?"

I knelt at Bart's side. "I'm here."

"Is that you?" He was still shaking violently. "What happened?"

He attempted to touch my hair, but he was too weak to get his arm more than a few inches off the ground. I'd forgotten I was now a blonde instead of a brunette.

"They say blondes have more fun, and when you disappeared, I wasn't having any fun, so I decided to test the theory."

"And?" Bart's attempt to speak through blue, quivering lips exhausted him.

"And I'll tell you all about it after we get you to the hospital."

Bart was a big man, six feet four inches of solid muscle. The three men were having no picnic carrying him over the rough, rocky terrain. I clung to him with my good hand every inch of the way back to the car. Now that I had him back again, I wasn't about to let go for any reason. The joy and relief at finding him alive almost overrode the pain in my other arm. Almost. It certainly made it less significant.

Ramon folded down the backseat in Pepper's van and they laid Bart on it kitty-corner to accommodate his long legs, which still hung over the edge. I curled up beside him and tucked the folded blanket around his shoulders. When Todd had extracted a promise to tell him the end of the story, we said good-bye and sped for the hospital in Santa Fe.

I radioed Mom the good news. She had some of her own: they thought they'd finally located Dad. Thought he was being held at Saladin's headquarters, but the place was heavily guarded. They were formulating a plan to get in.

Pepper handed me a bottle of sun-warmed water that had been left sitting in the van. I squirted a few drops at a time into Bart's eager, open mouth.

"Have you had anything to eat or drink since you were kidnapped?" I asked.

"No. Afraid to drink the water."

The effort to speak was too much. Bart closed his eyes and lay shivering under the blankets. I lay as much of my body over his as I could to add warmth without adding too much weight, not knowing if he had injuries, or what other effects all that time in the water might have had.

He stirred in a few minutes, opened his eyes, and murmured, "Update."

I introduced Pepper, Ramon and Tomas, and told Bart about the necklace and Pepper's grandmother.

"So now you're up to date. Oh, not all." I had to break the news about Xavier and his brother, the evil twin. I left out the part about Jaqueez and my newly repaired arm. That could wait. I snuggled down, my head on Bart's shoulder, and we quietly reveled in the fact that we were alive, and together, the rest of the way into Santa Fe.

At the emergency room, they took Bart's core temperature, which was dangerously low. They started him on heated fluids intravenously, both to rehydrate him and to warm him up from the inside; then they wrapped him in a special "body blanket" with pouches of water in which the temperature was gradually raised to warm him from the outside.

Diagnosis: dehydration, hypothermia, sensory deprivation, swelling and loss of feeling in limbs. Prognosis: A couple of days in the hospital and he'd be almost as good as new, only because he was in top physical condition to begin with. The rope burns on his wrists would heal in a few days, and feeling would probably return in a few hours when his circulation was back to normal. Apparently there had been no chemicals in the water, as he had no caustic burns. But the splits between his toes would make walking painful for a few days until they healed.

Bart was admitted to the hospital without any objections on his part, which only proved how bad he felt. Pepper convinced Dr. Evans I needed to be admitted in the same room, as that was the only way he'd be able to keep me down and let my arm heal. I thought of objecting, but since I couldn't think of anywhere I needed to be, besides near Bart, I acquiesced. Pepper, Ramon, and Tomas, their parts accomplished, quietly retreated down the hall as we were taken to our room.

We bribed the physician's assistant to push the beds together, citing the obvious need for rest, which we wouldn't get if I had to keep walking over to the other bed.

Bart slept fitfully, waking frequently to make sure I was still there. I was. Right beside him. I even relaxed and dozed a bit myself; but exhausted as I was, in case Bart needed me, I wouldn't let myself escape into a deep, restorative sleep.

About midnight he woke, finally able to think and speak coherently. We snuggled together in his bed in the half-light of the quiet hospital room and talked. His story was frightening.

"Saladin planned to kidnap the four of us, collect the ransom, then kill us. He was furious his plan failed because of a bunch of kids at the museum. Two men had been assigned to hide and guard each of us, in separate locations, and given free rein to do whatever they wanted, including their choice of termination when the time came."

"Everyone believed you and Dad were on the helicopter that crashed. They all thought you were dead," I said, stroking Bart's hand, which had almost returned to normal in both temperature and texture. "And I thought my life had ended when they told me they'd found your watch and wedding ring on one of the bodies. But I still couldn't believe it."

"They took my watch and ring just before they separated me and Jack," Bart explained. "I heard them say something about sending them to you as some sort of scare tactic. Later, the guards talked about the helicopter flying into a mountain. Between the crash and all the men Anastasia captured, Saladin's organization was hurt big time. His second contingent wasn't due in until just before all the celebrities arrived, so he called the guards back in." Bart paused, resting from the exertion of the narration, then continued.

"They tied me to the chair, rigged the cable on a timer so it dropped slowly into the water, and left. They didn't plan to come back. The only thing that saved me was the fact that they didn't tie my legs. At the end, I managed to get a foot on the rung so I could rear up out of the water and gasp a lungful of air, then I'd relax and hold my breath until I needed to do it again. Another couple of hours, and the chair would have been too low. I'd have drowned if you hadn't come."

Just thinking about how close I'd come to losing him gave me chills.

"I have a question for you," I said, breaking the comfortable silence. "What was that unearthly noise in the mine? It scared the wits out of me."

"Just the wind whistling through a slit in the rock. It unsettled me at first, too, but when it was the only sound in my watery prison, I didn't mind it after a while. It sort of . . . kept me company."

"Listen and the wind will tell you. Watch, and the creatures will teach you."

Would we have ever found the tiny entrance to the shaft where Bart was hidden if we hadn't heard the haunting wail of the wind? Did the hawk and the mouse point the way to the mine Todd had forgotten about and hadn't noticed on his map? Or had any of that made any difference? Would we have found the mine and Bart anyway? We'd probably never know for sure.

"Isn't that a different cast?" Bart asked as we lay side by side on the sterile white sheets.

"Observant, aren't you? Yes. When Mom and I changed our looks so we could stay at Rancho Encantado, I took off the other cast so it wouldn't be an obvious giveaway to my identity. I just wasn't careful enough, and ended up breaking it again."

"How?"

"In the first turquoise mine. Trader Todd Brown found me and brought me here to the hospital. That's when I met Dr. Evans."

I had to change the subject quickly. I didn't want Bart to find out about Jaqueez or any of the other narrow escapes I'd had until this was all over and we could laugh about them together. If he asked pointed questions, I'd have to tell him. I couldn't lie. Maybe get by with half-truths for now, but not lie.

"Bart, what are we going to do about Dad? Mom said if we didn't get him back by midnight tomorrow, it would probably be too late. Is that right?"

"What did Saladin tell Margaret?"

"At first he gave us seven days to collect the ransom, then after he'd lost so many men, he cut it to seventy-two hours. That's six o'clock Tuesday morning."

"What time is it now?" Bart asked.

"After midnight."

"Where's your radio?"

"In my purse."

"Let's see what's happening."

I retrieved my purse from the little nightstand drawer and gave the radio to Bart.

"Oz, can you hear me? What's going on?"

"Bart, is that you?" The reply came instantly.

"In the flesh, which isn't in great condition at the present, but it could be worse. I'm alive, and that was questionable for a while."

"It's good to hear your voice."

The emotion in Oswald Barlow's voice was sincere. He really meant it. That was a great relief, in view of his recent declaration of feeling for me. I knew that would never be mentioned again by either of us.

"News of Jack?" Bart pressed.

"There's a possibility he's being held in Saladin's headquarters. We captured Jilani Hashemi, or rather, your clever wife did, and he led us through the back roads for several hours trying to locate the place where he thought they were transferring Jack. At first we figured he was stalling, then we decided they'd changed plans and hadn't taken Jack there at all."

"You found Saladin's headquarters?" Bart asked, leaning back on the pillow and cradling me against him.

"Hashemi finally told us where it was. He decided there was no real reason to die for Allah, like most terrorists are prepared to do, when he didn't even believe in him. For all Margaret's goodness and compassion, and her history of leaving the messy stuff to others, I think if he hadn't eventually broken and told her, she might have resorted to a little arm-twisting herself. The woman's amazing."

Bart kissed my cheek. "They both are. What's the plan?"

"David's checking now to see if that's actually the headquarters, and if Jack is there. Margaret finally went to bed for a couple of hours, and everyone else is getting a little shut-eye till he gets back and we can make a plan."

"Call me when you learn anything."

Bart turned off the radio and lay very still for a long time. I thought he must have gone back to sleep. I should have known better. When I tried to pull the blanket up over his shoulder, he spoke softly. "I'm fine. Better get some sleep for the next couple of hours. Then we'll take a rain check on the bed rest and escape from this institution."

He checked the IV in his arm and turned the drip up slightly.

Chapter Thirty

I slept. I dreamed—a terrifying dream of Bart floating face down in the water, and Dad tied in a burning house, drugged, unable to get out.

I sat straight up in bed. Bart was beside me, watching me, very much alive. "Bad dreams?"

I shuddered. "Awful. How do you feel this morning?" I looked at the window. "It is morning, isn't it?"

"It's getting there. And we'd better get out of here before the place wakes up."

Bart sat up on the edge of the bed and turned the IV off. He pulled the needle from his arm, secured the tape, and stood, tentatively, holding the edge of the bed.

"Sure you're ready for that, Hercules?"

"Ready or not, here we come. Do we have a car?"

"No. Pepper's friend left her car for us when they flew to Santa Barbara to make Saladin think we were leaving, but Mom's using that."

"Call a cab. Do I have any clothes?"

I checked the closet. "Just the ones you came with." They were hanging there, dry but very smelly. I tossed them to Bart and pulled out my own.

"What's in the area?" Bart asked as I called the cab company. "I can't stand these very long."

"Nothing that would be open at five a.m." I pulled on my clothes, dirty and almost as rank as Bart's. They'd been soaked when I'd held him, dripping wet from the water. We were a sorry sight—wrinkled, dirty, no toothbrushes, hairbrushes or toiletries of any kind. Pepper had been going to bring us those first thing this morning. We didn't look too robust, either. Bart really needed another twelve hours in bed on the IV. He couldn't get his shoes on—his feet were still swollen—so he hobbled to the door in his dirty socks.

I peeked out the door. The nurses' station was busy, but no one was in our end of the hall and there was an exit sign two doors down. We went for it. Walking nonchalantly to the end of the hall, Bart held the door open for me and turned to see if anyone had seen us.

Apparently not. We hurried as fast as Bart's sore feet would take him when no one was looking and strolled leisurely when a nurse rounded a corner, trying not to laugh at the look of disgust and disdain on her face as she passed us.

The taxi was waiting, but the driver seemed none too happy about his prospective passengers. "Do you have any money?" Bart whispered as the cab pulled away from the hospital.

I checked my purse, grateful Mom had sent it with Pepper. "We're in luck," I said with relief, holding my wallet open to show Bart a handful of twenty-dollar bills.

"Good." Bart flashed a couple at the cab driver. "We need to go to Rancho Encantado."

The taxi driver glanced in his rearview mirror, saw the money, and nodded.

"I had a dream last night, too," Bart confided, touching my hair. "I dreamed a seductive blonde kept trying to get in my bed, telling me my wife wouldn't mind her being there at all."

"Was that a dream or a memory?" I laughed, remembering Else's forthright confession to having tried to seduce Bart. He looked puzzled.

"Else?" I said simply. He winced at the memory.

"Should we tell Mom we're coming," I asked, mercifully changing the subject, "or just drop in and surprise her?"

"Where is she?"

"Now that you ask, I'm not sure. I just figured they'd all be at the control center, but they might not be." I pulled the little radio out of my purse.

"Mom, where are you? What's going on?"

"At the control center. What are you doing awake so early? How's Bart? And how are you feeling?"

"Bart's off the IV already," I said, trying to keep from laughing, "and we're both feeling great. So good, in fact, that we're out of the hospital and on our way to the Ranch."

"You're *what?*"

Bart took the radio. "Thought you could use another couple of hands, Margaret. They might not be completely up to snuff just yet, but it's better than nothing."

"Who released you two?" Mom fumed. "You were supposed to spend the night, and . . ."

David Chen's soft voice urgently interrupted Mom's tirade. "Mrs. Alexander, I'm in place, but things aren't good here."

The taxi driver strained to hear the conversation. Bart turned the volume down and we put our heads together with the radio between so only he and I could hear.

"What's the matter?" Mom asked.

"Looks like they're planning to leave," David reported.

"Where are you?"

"On the mountain behind the house. There's lots of activity in the rooms with windows facing the mountain. I can't get close enough, even with the glasses, to see the front of the house. It's built into the mountain, and the deck in front overhangs a steep cliff."

"Have you located Jack?" Mom asked, a new urgency in her voice.

"I haven't seen him, but there's a storage room between the house and the attached garage they occasionally go in and out of."

"Is there any way you can get in there and check?"

"Too much activity right now, but it's time to move. If you have the chopper set Dominic and Lionel down just on the other side of the hill, they can come from the top through the trees without being seen. There'll be a lookout watching the road, but somebody needs to come up that way. Maybe you and Sky. If the chopper could get close enough to drop Oz and Else around the side of the hill, they could come up east of the house and you'd have it covered. Like I said, the front is inaccessible because of the cliffs."

"Keep trying to check out that room in the garage. We've got to know if that's where they're keeping Jack. Back to you in a minute."

The radio was silent for only a second before Mom came on again, her voice still crisp and businesslike. "Bart and Alli, where are you?"

"Ten minutes from Rancho Encantado," Bart answered.

"We'll be gone by the time you get here. Come to the control center. You two can man it, and that will free up an able-bodied person."

"Where's the house?" Bart asked.

"If you need to know, I'll tell you. In the meantime, get your buns here and take over the monitors. No heroics. You're sidelined for the time being." Then she added softly, her mother-voice returning, "You should have stayed in the hospital, both of you, but I'm glad you didn't. We need you."

"Mom, where are Bart's clothes?"

"His suitcase, and Jack's, are in the control center. Hurry. We're leaving the monitors unattended till you get here, and that's a worry." The radio fell silent.

"How fast can you get us to Rancho Encantado?" Bart asked the driver.

"How fast you wanna be there?" he answered.

"Yesterday."

"You paying the tickets?"

"Sure."

The driver tromped on the accelerator and the cab leaped ahead. At this speed, if we did get a ticket, it would be very expensive.

But we didn't. We even stayed on the road all the time, which didn't seem likely on a couple of the turns he made. I directed him to the corrals, the closest driveway to the control center, just above the pool and Cantina. He turned around with a grin. "Fast enough?"

"Just right," Bart said, tossing an extra twenty over the seat.

I was out of the taxi in a flash, but Bart was not moving any too good. "I'm a little stiff, and my feet don't seem to be working very well," he said. "Run to the control center. I'll be there as fast as I can. Then you can go change clothes. That way the monitors won't be unmanned so long."

I hurried down the path behind the pool. What if they'd locked the control center when they left? How would we get in? What if they hadn't locked it, and someone else had already gotten in?

But it wasn't locked, and no one was there. Only the eery, quiet hum of computers and machines. I watched on the monitor as the taxi left, and saw vehicle activity going northeast on State Route 592, up and over the hills behind the Ranch. I'd bet that was Anastasia. We hadn't passed anyone coming out, and that was the only other way out of here. I extended the field and watched their progress on the winding road into the Sangre de Cristo Mountains above us. Probably somebody's ski cabin. I noted the location, then switched the monitor back to its original area of focus, the Ranch and its environs.

I turned as Bart came in the door, obviously in pain. "Okay?" I asked, hurrying to his side.

"Maybe they had a reason for wanting us to stay a little longer in the hospital," he said, grimacing as he settled into the chair in front of the monitor.

"What can I get you besides a couple of aspirin and a bed?"

"Some clean clothes for starters, and then that salve they gave me for my feet. Did we bring that from the hospital?"

I produced it from my purse, then found his suitcase and pulled out a blue polo shirt, pair of lightweight khakis, and some clean underwear and socks. "Will these do?" I asked, holding them up.

"Just fine. Want to undress me?" He tried to smile suggestively, but his expression came out pained instead. His fingers couldn't undo the buttons on his shirt or his pants, so I did have to undress him. He was too miserable to even make a pass at me. Bad sign. He really wasn't well at all.

We managed to get clean clothes on him, and I massaged some of the antibiotic salve into the painful slits between his toes. He collapsed into the chair in front of the monitor and stared at it, as if trying to focus, or make sense of what was there.

"Will you be okay if I go change clothes?"

"What?" He seemed not to hear me at first. "Yes, of course I'll be okay. Just hurry back."

He wasn't okay.

I hurried to the Ranch house, slipped in unnoticed through the patio, picked up the phone the minute I got to my room, and called the hospital.

"May I speak to Dr. Evans, please? Thank you, I'll hold." While I waited for him to answer, I stripped off my smelly clothes and stretched the phone to the closet to see what I had left to wear.

To say the good doctor wasn't pleased with either of us was an understatement; but since he'd had his share of macho types who wouldn't obey doctor's orders, he at least understood. I was to literally pour fluids down Bart and keep him off his feet as much as possible. Bed rest was best, but since that didn't seem likely to happen, at least resting whenever possible. And make sure he got a little nourishment. He'd have Pepper run by some pain pills for me and some sedatives for both of us—just on the off chance we ever got near enough a bed to use them. I couldn't tell if he was being funny, facetious, or downright flippant.

As I donned clean jeans and a Henley tee, I looked longingly at the shower, but I didn't dare take the time, not knowing exactly in what shape I'd left Bart. A quick stop by the kitchen was the only detour I made, ordering some breakfast to be sent to the control center as soon as they were geared up for cooking. I confiscated a pitcher of ice water on my way out.

Bart was sitting, elbows on the desk, head supported by both hands, staring into the monitors. "Any activity?" I asked, handing him a glass of water, then rubbing his shoulders and neck.

"Very little. Staff coming to work. Someone feeding the horses. Do you mind watching a while? I need to stretch out for a few minutes. Thought I could use a bunk over there."

I helped him to one of the bunks lining the far wall in the end of the portable building. He sank, exhausted, to the bed and closed his eyes. No invitation to join him, no innuendos, no jokes, not even a smile and thank-you. My husband was not a well man.

"Alli, are you there?" Mom called on the radio.

I hurried to my radio. "Yes, we're in the control center. Where are you?"

"Getting into place. Alli, I have a bad feeling about this. Have you been able to contact your father?"

"Actually, I haven't tried lately."

"See what you can do. David found Saladin's headquarters in an old ski chalet. Hashemi thinks that's where they have Jack, but David hasn't been able to determine if he's there or not, or if Saladin is. I hate to try to take the place, putting our people in jeopardy, at the expense of losing Jack or Saladin."

"I'll see what I can do."

I didn't have a good feeling this morning, either. Maybe it was caused by Bart's condition. I was used to seeing my normally robust husband on his feet and ready to go. Maybe it was my lack of sleep and the constant pain in my arm.

I tried to make contact with my father. And failed. Maybe it was the feeling that time was running out. The sands of my father's life were sifting through the hourglass too swiftly, and I didn't know how to slow them down.

Concentrating, I tried again. It was as if he simply wasn't there. Or as if there was no longer any connection between us. Chills shivered down my arms. I dropped my head and said a fervent prayer for his protection, afraid it was out of our hands now. We needed more than our puny, mortal efforts could accomplish.

Turning up the sound on the monitors, I went back to check on Bart, who was out of sight behind all the equipment. He was sleeping soundly. I covered him with a blanket and went quietly back to the desk.

I tried again to reach Dad, concentrating until my head ached. Then I saw him, dimly, slumped in a corner of a windowless room. He didn't respond to my calls, didn't move, didn't even seem to be breathing.

Suddenly I had the impression of gasoline fumes—acrimonious, caustic, overpowering.

Chapter Thirty-One

I grabbed the radio. "Mom, if Dad's in that building, you'd better get him out quick. I think they're getting ready to torch it."

Margaret Alexander wasted no time. "Report positions."

Dominic and Lionel had just joined David in the trees on the hill behind the house. Oz and Else were approaching from the side. Over the radio, I could hear the car engine gearing down as Mom and Rip Schyler climbed the hill to the house.

Mom's voice was all business. "Approaching the cabin. We'll go straight into the garage, hit the storage room, and hope Jack is there. Take the place! Now!"

I switched one of the monitors to the location I'd noted previously and watched the tiny blue blips surround the rectangle perched on the side of a mountain. The car approaching was a steady green line that slowed, then merged into the rectangle.

Suddenly little blue blips spread out from the house, like cockroaches fleeing from a light. The rectangle exploded into a bright red smear on the screen. The blue blips from the house abruptly stopped moving, and the blue blips from the woods merged on them and the bright red smear.

The green line had disappeared.

Suddenly another monitor came to life. An unidentified car approached Rancho Encantado from the Los Caminitos subdivision just above the Ranch. All local vehicular traffic had been identified and coded so it appeared on the big monitor as a steady line of movement. Any unidentified vehicles flashed bright red. Automatically, a third monitor zoomed in to present a closeup of the encroacher.

A big, dark sedan with heavily tinted windows slowly curved around the twists and turns on the state road, then entered the gate to Rancho Encantado. I watched as I pressed the radio.

"Mom, what's happening? Are you okay?"

No answer.

She could be too busy to answer her radio. Or . . . she could have been caught in the blast.

"Oz, Sky and Mom drove into the garage. What happened to them?"

No answer.

"David, Dominic, anyone. What happened to Margaret and Sky?"

The little blue blips converged on the garage where the green line had disappeared.

Glancing at the other monitor, I watched the dark sedan pass the Ranch house, the parking lots, tennis courts, and stop across from the stables, right at the spot where the taxi had dropped Bart and me off less than an hour ago.

"Mom, can you hear me? Are you okay? Oz, Else, Lionel—please. Anyone, tell me what's going on."

"As soon as we know, we'll tell you," Else breathed heavily into her radio. "We can't get close enough yet to see."

Two men dressed in dark suits emerged from the car and followed the path along the pool, turning toward the portable control center. I couldn't see their faces clearly. The sun had barely cleared the mountains, and the trees cast deep early-morning shadows along the path. I ran to the door and locked it, took my gun from my purse, set it in the drawer in front of me, leaving it slightly open—just in case—then turned to the radio again. It was probably FBI, but I didn't want to be bothered until I knew what was going on up on that mountain. And if they weren't FBI . . .

"Mom, please answer me."

There was no answer, from her or any of the others.

Suddenly the door burst open, literally torn from its hinges.

"And who have we here?" The pockmarked face was familiar.

"Saladin!"

"You know me? Do I know you?"

He stepped closer. The second man remained at the door, his gun drawn.

"Allison? I should have known that treacherous woman would

double-cross me. She's here, too, isn't she? You never left." It was a revelation that further enraged an already angry man.

Saladin's eyes scanned the equipment that surrounded me. "Ah, you're watching your father burn. I rather hoped I'd have the ransom in hand before you found out he was dead. No matter; I have you. Margaret will give anything for her only daughter, her only remaining family member."

The radio interrupted Saladin's gloating. "Allison, I have bad news." It was Else, too quiet, almost a whisper. Then an interminable silence.

I grabbed the radio. "What? What did you find?"

She started, stopped, then started again. No need to finish. She was crying. I knew what she was trying to tell me.

"The house went up like fireworks. It was too hot to get to them. There's nothing left but the shell, and it won't be here much longer."

"The car?"

"Exploded. Burned. But I don't think either of them were in it. The doors were open. I think they'd had time to get into the storage room." Her voice shook with emotion. She took a deep breath. "If it's any consolation, I think they died together. One of Saladin's men confirmed that Jack was being held in the storage room off the garage."

Tears burned my eyes. I turned to Saladin, the radio still clutched in my hand. "Guess what, Saladin? With my mother and father dead, the estate is tied up until probate is finished. You can't get your hands on a penny of that twenty million. What are you going to do now? Kill me?"

Saladin folded one arm across his chest and stroked his ugly chin with the other. "Of course. I would be doing you a favor. It would be cruel to leave you a widow and an orphan, all alone in the world, without anyone to love you."

"What on earth could you possibly know of love? You profane the word even speaking it. Go away. You've already taken my life by taking those I loved. Isn't that enough?"

"And leave those extraordinary genes in existence? You have too much of your father's tenacity and your mother's fire, not to mention their perceptive minds, to be allowed to live. Somewhere down the road our paths would cross again, when you were older and wiser. You are a threat to me. Mousa, kill her."

Saladin stepped aside to give his gunman a clear shot at me. I spun in the chair, scooped my gun from the partially open drawer behind me, and was spinning back when something hit me in the chest as I turned, slamming the turquoise necklace against me. It ricocheted into a monitor screen, shattering it into a thousand pieces.

I got off one shot before the man slumped to the floor, three bright red bullet holes in his forehead. As he went down, his finger still on the trigger of his automatic weapon, bullets sprayed the room.

Saladin arched and spread his arms, a look of horrified surprise on his face, then pitched forward onto the desk beside me.

Bart hobbled from behind the stacks of equipment, grabbed Saladin by the collar and shoved him to the floor, pressing the gun to his throat.

"Are you okay, Princess?"

Before I could answer, a familiar voice shouted through the radio. "Allison! What happened?"

I scrambled to my feet and hit the conference button on the big radio. "Mom! They said you were dead."

Saladin made a sound, wrought indistinguishable by the gun shoved in his throat.

"We thought we were. Did I hear Saladin?"

"He's down. How did you know he was here?"

"You kept your radio on. I was just coming on to tell you Else was wrong and we were alive, when we heard what I thought was Saladin. So I kept quiet."

"How did you get out?"

"When the explosion and fireball ripped the house apart, we hit the floor, and found a trap door leading to a stone staircase and path down the mountain. Other than being singed a little here and there, we're fine. All three of us."

"You found Dad?"

"Still foggy from the drugs, but alive. And you?"

"Bart's got everything under control. He'd been resting back on the bunks where he couldn't be seen, and Saladin thought I was alone. Of course, Saladin thought Bart was dead already, figured Dad would be momentarily, and was overjoyed when he heard Else report your death."

Another sound from Saladin—this time there was no doubt what he was saying. A dying oath. A cursing of all infidels, especially us. Then silence. Blessed silence.

I went to Bart and buried myself in his arms. When I could finally speak without bursting into tears of relief, I looked up into his deep blue eyes. "Nice bit of shooting, Dead-eye. Thanks."

"Any time. Any time at all," he said softly, running a finger down the side of my cheek. "Just protecting my major investment."

"Investment?"

"I've invested more effort, time, money, and passion in you than any other thing in my life. You also have my heart. I couldn't live without that, any more than I could live without you."

As Bart's arms tightened around me and he bent to kiss me, I cried out in pain.

"What's the matter?" He let go and stepped back.

I unbuttoned the Henley and looked at my breast, where an ugly purple welt the size of a silver dollar had formed. I examined the necklace. One of the large chunks of turquoise was shattered, its silver setting twisted and misshapen.

"The necklace will save your life. You must not take it off until the danger is over."

"She said it would save my life," I whispered, looking up at Bart, who had paled considerably in the last ten seconds. "It literally did."

"Your guardian angels were certainly busy today, Princess."

"Yes." They certainly were. *Thank you, Father, for my life, and for giving me back Bart and my parents.*

I took a deep breath. "Okay. Let's get you back on that bunk before you end up on the floor with Saladin." I glanced at the body on the floor and shuddered.

Blood seeped onto several sheets of paper Saladin had pulled onto the floor as he fell. An intriguing photo caught my eye. I helped Bart to the bunk, then ran back to the papers, lifted them carefully by the corners, and let the sticky red liquid drip off. They were faxed photocopies of old newspaper articles reporting an automobile accident after an opera performance several years earlier. Pictures of a formally dressed man and woman taken before the opera proclaimed, "Tragedy Strikes Family."

"What are you looking at?" Bart asked, raising himself up on one elbow.

"Ghosts," I answered, scanning the article. Paper towels removed the top layer of blood, leaving a dark pink stain, but the printing was still legible. Perching on the edge of the bunk, I read the article to Bart, then told him about the couple who had been seen, together and separately, but didn't register on the monitor.

In a separate follow-up article, a tragic story unfolded about a small boy who had been left with friends while the couple, his parents, attended the ill-fated opera. Arrangements had been made to return the boy to their rooms at Rancho Encantado at midnight when the parents expected to return.

The couple, not realizing their friends had just died, returned the boy as planned. He jumped out of the car, waved them off, and was never seen again.

I shuddered as I turned the page where the article continued. Icy fingers of disbelief crawled up my skin. It was the little boy in my bedroom.

The article reported the boy had apparently gone back to his room and waited for his parents. When they didn't come, he went looking for them, and got lost in the brush behind the Ranch. Searchers found his tracks, along with blood on some rocks where he had apparently fallen into the arroyo, but no body.

I stared at Bart in horror. "That's the same boy. I've seen him. I've touched him. I wiped his tears away. He was in our room."

Bart pulled me down on the bunk beside him and wrapped his arms around me. "Some believe spirits can't go on to the next life until they've straightened out things in this life. I can't explain these apparitions, but . . ."

Oz burst through the open door. "Alli! Bart! Where are you?"

"Back here," Bart called.

Oz rounded the corner of the equipment and stopped in mid-stride, embarrassed at finding us embracing on the bunk. "Hope I'm interrupting something," he said, recovering.

"Unfortunately, no," Bart said. "The spirit is willing, but today the flesh is very weak."

"Not too weak to take on Saladin," Oz observed wryly.

Mom came in, followed by Dominic and Lionel carrying Dad. They laid him on the bunk across from Bart. He smiled weakly and reached for my hand. I took it. He closed his eyes and relaxed back on the pillow without speaking, still clutching my fingers.

"Is he okay?" I asked.

"He's in and out," Mom said. "I'll have him checked out at the hospital, but we had to see what was going on here first."

"Everything's under control," I said. "Except the main monitor. It's sort of out of commission."

"Guess it doesn't matter, now that we've taken out all of Saladin's men," Sky observed.

"Only the first contingent. But without Saladin to direct them, the second wave should be manageable," Bart said.

"Who solved the mystery of the ghosts?" I asked.

"Else got into the newspaper files when it was her turn at the monitors," Dominic said, looking pleased with himself, "and I solved your ghost horse mystery."

"Oh?"

"It was Maria's brother, Juan. He spent his college savings on a horse. Since he couldn't keep it at home, he and Jake built a corral out in the brush and were training it at night . . ."

"Out where I found you hog-tied," Oz broke in.

Dominic ignored the interruption and continued. "They figured they could get back his money winning races before he had to break the news to his folks. In case the horse was seen, they bleached his mane and tail so people would think it was the legendary ghost horse."

"All the loose ends, neatly tied," Else smiled.

"Not quite," Bart said, sitting up and swinging his legs over the side of the bunk. "What about you being hog-tied?"

"Allison has a lot to catch you up on, old boy," Oz laughed. "Tales that may curl even your straight blond hair."

Dad squeezed my hand and winked a sleepy eye. "Guess it's time Allison joined Anastasia as a full-fledged agent. If she's going to keep plunging into the thick of things, she'd better be prepared."

Bart opened his mouth to object. I pounced on top of him and pushed him back onto the bed, smothering his objection with a kiss.

Mom laughed. "You're outnumbered, Bart. A good man knows when he's beaten."

"Oh, to be beaten thus." Oz feigned removing a hat in a sweeping gesture. Then, taking a deep bow, he backed away to take care of the bodies littering the control room floor.

Not one to gloat over winning, I said contritely, "If the head of Anastasia ordains it, I'll have to follow orders. When do I start?"

Bart groaned.

Chapter Thirty-Two

Dad was admitted to the hospital for observation and blood tests to see what Saladin's men had been injecting him with. Bart didn't need to be admitted; he'd never been released. Dr. Evans threatened restraints if either of them even thought about leaving before he signed their official releases.

Mom and Oz turned the terrorists, the living and the dead, over to the local police and got everything squared away with them and the FBI, then joined us at the hospital.

Dad occupied my former bed, Bart was tucked in his same bed under a couple of blankets, and I snuggled comfortably on top of the covers next to him. We spent the afternoon filling in our personal pieces of the puzzle, until it had all come out. Almost. Then Oz opened his big mouth.

"You didn't forget to tell him about Jaqueez, did you, Allison?" The gleam in his eye was not lost on Bart.

"Jaqueez?" Bart said, turning to me.

"Didn't I tell you about Casanova, the one who first gave me the idea you might be in a turquoise mine?"

"Casanova? No. I'm all ears."

Oz was enjoying this. I wasn't. I knew immediately what Bart's reaction would be—and my parents'. Dad might possibly revoke his offer of Interpol training when he heard how I'd gone with Jaqueez without any backup, or without leaving a precise destination. Hindsight was wonderful.

Though I glossed over the incident, downplaying my own foolishness, my folly was apparent to everyone. Fortunately, Pepper and

Ramon dropped by to see us at that very minute, and I was saved the scolding I knew I'd get from Dad, and whatever Bart was about to bestow on me. Bart needed another introduction. He didn't remember them from the mine. He'd been in even worse shape than I thought.

After their questions had been answered, Pepper leaned forward and asked if I'd told Bart about my insight during Relief Society.

"There's more you haven't told me?" he asked, wrinkling his forehead in a disbelieving frown.

"So much has happened so fast, how can I possibly remember everything? I'll probably be recalling bits and pieces and snippets for the next year—how I came upon a certain fact, what triggered a particular insight, someone's reaction to something I did or said."

That last had been directed pointedly at Oz, and he fielded the remark deftly with a zinging reply. "Did you know your wife has a temper? I'm earnestly watching out for her in your absence, trying to protect her from leering Lotharios, and what thanks do I get? A finger in my chest and a lecture to mind my own business."

My retort was cut off by Mom's radio. "Sky here. Thought you may want to know," he said slowly, "Xavier had two more brothers working for Saladin. We located them in San Diego, recruiting terrorists for Hamas. Just a little item of interest to keep you from getting too complacent in there. How's everyone doing?"

"A lot better before you broke that nasty bit of news," Mom said. "Anything else?"

"Nope. Nice and quiet here, except for hourly arrivals of advance people for the celebrities. This place will be bursting at the seams by tomorrow morning. Guess I should have brought my autograph book."

"Somehow I don't see you asking anybody for an autograph," Mom laughed. "A date maybe, not an autograph."

Sky came on again, all levity absent from his voice. "We can't expect to keep the lid on this much longer. Some enterprising reporter is going to blow the story sky high, and it'll hit every newsstand in the world. When it does, we've got to be ready for whatever worms come out of the woodwork. Xavier's family was close. I expect to see those two worms soon."

"Thanks, Sky. Did Dominic and Lionel get the monitors up and running again?"

"Yes. Perimeters are secured, Madame X. We'll see you in a couple of hours?"

"I'll be there."

"How could Xavier's brothers find out so quickly their sibling was dead?" I asked. "You just turned his body over to the sheriff a couple of hours ago. And can I ask what happened to Xavier?"

"You can ask, but I can't tell you," Mom said. "I didn't ask. And word has a way of spreading faster than the measles. Someone involved with the bodies does a 'Gee whiz. Guess what I just did!' to a family member or friend, who turns to another family member or friend, who repeats it to someone who just happens to be a reporter, who digs up the whole story—all in the space of a few hours."

"In this case, though, there's been some pretty high-profile stuff going on for four days, and the press can't stand to keep the lid on a good story like this forever," Pepper said. "The DA's office has been crawling with reporters, some who smell a huge story in the making, some just routinely sniffing."

"But nothing's been in the paper yet?" Dad asked.

"Not yet. But I hold my breath every issue that hits the stands," Pepper said. She stopped as someone opened the door. "Whoops. I spoke too soon."

Tomas appeared, holding the newspaper in front of him so we could read the huge headline: "Terrorists Hit Santa Fe!"

"Looks like some reporter hit pay dirt," Bart said. "That means the grapevine's had the word for a couple of hours at least, a couple of days at most. Guess we'd better check out of this fancy hotel and get back to the Ranch."

The door opened again and Tomas stepped aside as Else entered, absolutely elegant in a simple, plain black sweater and slacks. She carried an oversized straw bag and wore a matching wide-brimmed straw hat and big dark sunglasses. Tomas stared open-mouthed at the regal beauty next to him.

Else glided to the bed, kissed my cheek, then leaned across me and kissed Bart's. "You two look too good to be in a hospital. Isn't there a law about using hospital beds under false pretenses?" She moved to Dad's side and took his hand. "On the other hand, you and Margaret could probably use a lot more down time. I don't think your wife has slept more than three or four hours since you disappeared." She kissed his cheek. "Welcome back."

After introductions, she looked at the roomful of people, as if suddenly realizing how many were there. "But how can you possibly get any rest with all these people here, well-meaning as they are?" She made shooing motions with her hands as if to scoot all the visitors out the door.

In mid-motion she stopped, pulled her radio out of her bag, put it to her ear so we couldn't hear the transmission, then dropped it quickly back into the voluminous straw bag. "Pepper, get your people into the bathroom. Allison, unplug Bart's IV. Margaret, get Jack on the floor . . ."

The door suddenly flew open and two men burst into the room, automatic weapons drawn. Xavier's brothers. They couldn't have looked more like Xavier and his dead twin if they'd actually been quadruplets.

Tomas froze against the wall. Pepper and Ramon were in the act of standing. I'd reached for Bart's IV. Mom hadn't had time to react. No one stirred. Even time stood still, that moment of terror frozen in an eternity of horrible anticipation.

Else was the first to move. In one swift motion, she raised the straw bag and fired through the end of it. The thunderous explosion of gunfire, the powerful ack-ack-ack of the automatic weapon, filled the room with deafening noise. The two terrorists were flung backward, out the door and into the hall by the force of the bullets.

No one spoke, stunned by the sudden appearance of the gunmen, astonished at Else's immediate reaction. Oz was on his feet and out the door, gun in hand, before any of us regained our wits. There was no need for his gun, or a doctor. Only the coroner.

Else spoke quietly into her radio. Dominic and Lionel converged on the room from opposite ends of the hall and poked their heads in the door long enough to determine that everyone was okay. "That wasn't much of a heads-up, guys," Else chided the two.

"Since when did you need a warning?" Dominic grinned, performing his pantomime of the bullfighter gracefully dodging the charging bull. "Your reflexes are like those of a matador."

"We got a little hung up clearing the halls," Lionel explained. "Couldn't convince some of these nurses their patients could wait a few minutes while we rid their hospital of some vermin."

"Good job, people," Dad said, as though they'd done nothing more than smuggle him in a Big Mac and a Coke. "Who's minding the store?"

"David Chen's at the monitors. He drew the short straw."

"The short straw?" Tomas finally spoke for the first time.

"Someone had to remain behind and man the monitors," Dominic explained, "the most boring job to be done. When Sky got word Xavier had brothers who were two or three hours' flight from here, we figured we'd better have a plan. There was no question who was to be in the room. That's Else's forte. Nobody's faster."

I watched Tomas' expression as he gazed in awe at Else, who at the moment was trying to figure how to keep things from falling through the hole in the bottom of her bag. "I should buy these by the gross. I'll never find another I like as well," she pouted prettily, causing the desired effects: everyone laughed, the tension was relieved, and she could gracefully exit. Tomas followed her from the room and I wondered if his sudden interest was in a new vocation or the elegant Else herself.

Dominic and Lionel disappeared to help Oz with the bodies, and it was suddenly quiet in the room. There was an almost audible exhale of held breath, a collective sigh of relief, the exhausted calm descending after the storm.

Bart spoke first. "Back to the insight during Relief Society."

"What?" It took a minute for me to even remember what he was talking about, to bridge the short gap in conversation that had seemed hours ago instead of just minutes.

"Before we were interrupted, you were telling me about an insight you had during Pepper's lesson," he reminded me.

"I'd planned to tell you when we were alone—break the news gently sort of thing."

"Now will do just fine," he said, trying not to look apprehensive.

Chapter Thirty-Three

"I had to read Mosiah 18:8-10 in Pepper's lesson on Sunday."

Bart nodded. "The baptismal covenant."

"As I read the words 'what have ye against being baptized?', they sort of burned into my heart and mind. I kept asking myself what *did* I have against it? Nothing. It finally seemed so very right. And immediately after that I connected you, the water, and the turquoise mine, and knew where to find you. Something else I hadn't told you yet."

The calm expression of pleasure on Bart's face belied the excitement and joy in his eyes. His arm tightened around my shoulder and he kissed my cheek.

"This is one of the happiest days of my life—the life I thought was over in that mine. Know what I regretted most as the hours ticked away and I slid deeper and deeper into that cold, watery grave?"

I shook my head.

"That I hadn't put everything on hold, let the terrorists have the diamonds in San Francisco, the Tenors in Santa Fe, and anything else they wanted, and taken the time to teach you the gospel myself. I figured I was a dead man, you didn't have a testimony yet, and probably wouldn't look into it any more after I was gone. And we'd be alone, separated, for the rest of eternity."

"We have a font right here," Ramon said, "if you don't want to wait until you get back to your own ward."

"Think Bishop O'Hare would mind if we jumped the gun on him?" I asked. "He's our bishop in Santa Barbara—or will be, if we're ever there long enough to make it to church," I explained to the others.

Then I remembered one more thing. I turned to Bart. "Did I tell you I'd completed the discussions in New York?"

"Another little item you forgot to mention. What did you have in mind?" Bart asked, trying to be nonchalant, but hardly containing his absolute joy.

"I thought I'd lost both my parents and my husband in Santa Fe. In fact, I supposedly lost Dad twice—once in a helicopter crash and once in the fire that killed Mom, too. But I got you all back again, alive. A resurrection, of sorts. This might be a good place to continue the metaphor."

Bart nodded. "And?"

"How about washing away the old life in the Rio Grande, down by the San Ildefonso Pueblo, and leaving here with a fresh new start? Anastasia gets a new agent, you get a new partner, we get to choose a new place to live, and begin a new life as ministering angels."

"Ministering angels?" Bart said, puzzled.

"Another insight," I laughed.

"Do you plan to do all that before or after we make sure this benefit concert comes off?" Dad asked.

"Before," Bart said.

"After," I said simultaneously.

"Well, while you two discuss it, remember that we have some serious shopping to do. The concert is less than a week away. When the Tenors and their famous guests arrive tomorrow, we'll be busy protecting them from hangers-on as well as ne'er-do-wells, right up to the minute of the concert. Did you bring a dress?"

I shook my head.

"We have most of tomorrow to find something elegantly suitable to mingle with the 'beautiful people' and not stand out like the security we'll be."

Bart turned to Ramon. "Sounds like tomorrow is all scheduled up. What would it entail to get us baptized tonight?"

"An interview with the bishop or the missionaries, white clothing, a phone call to your bishop, and an authorized priesthood holder to do the job."

"How soon can you get that together?" Bart asked.

Ramon glanced at his watch. "Five o'clock on a Sunday evening? Maybe two hours, since we don't have to fill the font."

"Let's do it," Bart exclaimed, reaching for the IV.

"Wait a minute," I interrupted. "You can leave that right there until Bishop O'Hare is contacted, and all the arrangements are made. Ramon, you're an elder, aren't you?"

"Yes."

"Would you mind baptizing us?"

Pepper and Ramon exchanged amused glances. "I don't think he'd mind," Pepper said. "I'll run by the church and pick up the baptismal clothing while Ramon takes care of the rest. I think Dr. Evans might be convinced to let you out of the hospital long enough to get the job done—if you invite him to come along. Plan on coming right back here for the night, though, or you'll have a fight on your hands, and even a baptism won't be enough leverage to pry you loose from those beds. You'll also have to ask him about your cast; I'm sure he'll be able to find some plastic wrapping to protect it."

Pepper and Ramon left to make the arrangements. Bart relaxed on the bank of pillows behind him and closed his eyes, a look of peaceful satisfaction on his wan face.

"Sure you feel up to this today? We really don't have to rush it, you know," I said. "I'm not going to change my mind."

"I'm not worried about you changing your mind. I'm just worried about you actually living long enough to take the plunge, what with your disposition for finding trouble."

"Don't even start on that. Dad, do you feel well enough to come? Or are you interested?"

"Bunny, I've missed too many of your special occasions. I wouldn't miss this for the world. Although, I'm not sure it will register that it's really you I'm watching. I can't get used to my two favorite women being blue-eyed blondes."

At sundown we converged on the banks of the Rio Grande at a spot Tomas had chosen, three of us clothed in purest white. The backdrop was spectacular. Black Mesa loomed above us, silhouetted against a sky of deep aquamarine streaked with pink, purple, and blue clouds from one horizon to the other. Huge cottonwood trees soaked their roots deep into the muddy banks, and green pasture flowed down to the water's edge. A bird sang joyously overhead, hidden somewhere in the green branches, and his mate answered from high above him.

Ramon led Bart waist-deep into the gently flowing river that shimmered golden in the setting sun. Raising his right arm, he bowed his head and said a baptismal prayer. Then he lowered Bart into the water, immersing him completely, and brought him quickly up again. A quiet thrill went through me. Just like John the Baptist, and with that same priesthood authority.

They came up out of the water, and Ramon and Dr. Evans laid their hands on Bart's head, confirming him a member of The Church of Jesus Christ of Latter-day Saints, and bestowed upon him the gift of the Holy Ghost. Then they ordained him to the office of a priest in the Aaronic Priesthood.

It was my turn. I took the turquoise necklace off and gave it to Pepper. "This belongs in your family. Maybe your daughter will be the next one to wear it, or Tomas' daughter, when he has one. I wish I could thank your grandmother for letting me wear it."

"Did you ever discover the last gift she promised would help you find Bart?" she asked, slipping the turquoise necklace around her neck.

"I think it was the gift of faith—faith in myself, faith in my own intuition, faith in God to hear and answer prayers."

Bart took my hand and led me silently to the water's edge. "What are you doing?" I asked as he stepped into the river.

"I'm going to baptize you. It was Bishop O'Hare's idea. I've just received the priesthood, Princess—the proper authority to baptize."

His eyes never left my face as he backed into the water, leading me by the hand. I scarely felt the water swirling gently around my legs, was barely aware of it tugging softly at the dress about my knees. I was lost in the wonder of the moment, lost in the depths of Bart's blue eyes and the love I saw there.

Ramon followed us into the water to make sure Bart performed the sacred ordinance properly. Bart held up his right arm, repeated the words Ramon had used, and lowered me under the water. As I came up, Bart enfolded me in his arms and held me for a long moment. Neither of us could speak.

I waited for something to happen, some wonderful, miraculous change, but I didn't really feel different. No, that wasn't true. A quiet peace filled my heart that had not been there before. An assurance that I had just done something very important. Something very right.

"One year from today, Princess," Bart whispered, his voice husky with emotion, "I promise to take you to the temple of your choice, so we can be sealed as a family for all eternity."

"It's a date," I answered, wondering if anyone in the world had ever been so filled with joy as I was at that moment.

About the Author

Lynn Gardner is an avid storyteller who does careful research to back up the high-adventure romantic thrillers that have made her a popular writer in the LDS market. For her first novel, *Emeralds and Espionage,* she relied on her husband's expertise as a career officer in the Air Force, interviewed a friend in the FBI, and gathered extensive information on the countries in which her adventure took place. A writer's workshop at BYU-Hawaii provided the opportunity for research on the setting for her second novel, *Pearls and Peril,* and intensive research in San Francisco, one of her favorite cities, furnished her with material for *Diamonds and Danger. Turquoise and Terrorists* was carefully researched during Lynn's recent stay in the high desert of New Mexico.

Lynn and her husband, Glenn, make their home in Quartz Hill, California, where Lynn is director of the stake family history center. They are the parents of four children.

Among her many interests, Lynn lists reading, golfing with her husband, traveling, beachcombing, writing, family history, and spoiling her four granddaughters and two grandsons.